ASHES OF UNION

Dallas Totilo

Published by IronWell Press.

Printed in thc United States of America.

ISBN: 979-8-9937841-1-3 (Printed)

ISBN: 979-8-9872464-7-4 (Electronic)

To my parents, Mark and Rebecca, known to me as Daddy and Mama. I could not have done it without the knowledge of writing from my beautiful mother, author of over fifty books. And my father, whose vast knowledge of history propelled me to understand the world around me.

Contents

I.

A More Perfect War

April 2, 2044 – Year 1 – Los Angeles, California

"What the fuck do you mean he's enlisted?!" Jessica Parker cried out, gripping the steering wheel. The faint orange color of the morning sun stretched out over the seemingly endless span of Interstate 5, the road ripping under the bald tires of her sedan. This was the start of a bad morning for her, having only arrived in Los Angeles just a few hours earlier. The air was tense, the sweet scent of jasmine boba tea filling her nostrils as she fought to make sense of what she'd just heard.

"Jessica, your son Mitch is eighteen. Try as you might, it is his legal right. Daniel told you because he believed you might reconsider—maybe even change your mind about the separation."

She laughed bitterly, sounding ragged and uneven, like a house crumbling slowly. "Change my mind? So my kid signs up for a war no one admits is coming, and my husband wants back in on our marriage after me leaving him because he accused me of being first in work and not at home?!" She pauses to sip her boba tea. "You don't get it, Miles. This isn't just a story anymore, it's everything—our country is heading into the shitter, and my family is bleeding in it."

Her fingers tormented a lock of auburn hair, curling and uncurling with nervous cadence. The cup of boba tea, resting precariously in the cup holder, sloshed gently with each bump in the road. Its comforting, warm sweetness was fragile solace amid the chaos swirling inside her. The demands of being a reporter were something Jessica prided herself on, and conviction in chasing a story was a priority for her, whether she lived or died. Being in the midst of the riots in Houston in the summer of 2033 was just one milestone Jessica achieved in her storied career.

Miles sighed softly. "Jessica, Daniel is scared. He's watching you disappear into your work, chasing a story that's tearing us all apart, and it's killing your family. He wants stability—he needs it."

Jessica swallowed hard. Her eyes stung with tears, blurring her vision with memories rushing in: Daniel's pale face under the dim yellow kitchen lamp, voice barely above a whisper: *"I don't know you anymore, Jess. You're slipping away, just like our sons."*

Blinking fiercely, Jessica forces the tears back, returning focus to the road. "I don't know how else to be," whispering softly. "If I'm not chasing this story, what am I? Who am I?"

Outside of her collapsing world, the rest of civilization woke to a troubling reality. In the years that passed from the pandemics and crippling wars within Europe and the Middle East, the United States found itself with a decaying infrastructure. Mental instability among average Americans heavily increased with each passing year, causing unstable radicals to rise within many states. The government's inability to adapt and being years behind trends caught up to them as the methods proved ineffective in quelling the rebellions. Although the prospect of another war was welcome, as many in Congress prided themselves on being war hawks within many circles.

The distant roar of freeway traffic mixed with the faint faraway crackle of a news report: protests erupting in urban centers, governors threatening secession, military units placed on high alert. The fractures in the nation were no longer speculation—they were deafening.

Jessica's mind raced. Years ago, she found herself on the front lines as America was overseas attempting to secure a foothold in the shifting global order. Like the British Empire fighting Napoleon and the Seven

Years' War before the American Revolution, the overreach sapped military strength, drained public trust, and collapsed the very institutions meant to hold the country together. What was once an undisputed world power was now a nation divided, as it was in 1861.

"Miles..." she said softly. "If the country falls, if it truly collapses... what happens to us? To my family?"

The lawyer hesitated. "It's why Daniel filed. He can't stand the chaos and is afraid it will swallow you whole."

Exhaling slowly, her breath trembled in her chest. "I don't want to lose him. Or Mitch. But this—" she gestured at the cracked windshield, an image of the divided nation she chased, "this story is all I have left."

Silence fell over the car. The call disconnected. All that was heard was the sound of the road, and rattles over the bumps. A new message lit the screen.

From Daniel: "*He ships out in two weeks. I tried to talk him out of it. I failed. I'm sorry.*"

The words struck her in the stomach, her chest tightening painfully, and her breath came shallow and rapid. The steady hum of the engine was the only sound she could focus on, the miles flying by under her tires.

She drank slowly of the now lukewarm boba tea, the tapioca pearls sweet and chewy but failing to reach the bitter knot in her stomach. Thoughts tumbled—cities burning, families torn apart, soldiers on both sides lost to a war no one wanted but everyone feared. Her son was going to be somewhere in the middle of it all..

Jessica blinked hard, gripping the wheel ever so tightly. The road ahead was long, the horizon uncertain. The country was in what many considered hell, and there was no turning back.

* * *

Jessica pulled off the highway onto a cracked street corner just a few blocks away from the Federal Building. The morning sun had climbed higher, casting long, jagged shadows that stretched like dark fingers across the cracked pavement. She stepped out of her car, the crunch of gravel and broken glass underfoot sharp in the quiet moment before the storm. Her boots pressed into the scattered debris—discarded flyers, plastic bottles, a smashed protest sign faded by the morning light. The faint, bitter scent of smoke and dust hung heavy in the air, mixed with the sharper smells of gasoline and moisture.

Voices swelled, a tangled chorus rising in pitch and volume with every passing second. The crowd, once scattered, had swollen into a dense, restless sea of bodies flooding the neighboring streets. Jessica grabbed her camera bag and adjusted the strap, the familiar weight settling against her hip. The low drone of a police siren echoed distantly as the National Guard moved into position, their armored vehicles rattling ominously like thunder approaching the horizon.

"Simon!" Jessica called out, spotting the tall, lean figure of Simon Alexander weaving through the crowd. His scruffy beard was flecked with gray, and his eyes, sharp and calculating, scanned every face and movement. The heavy NBC vest stretched over his worn jacket, the bulky camera hanging from his shoulder as if it were an extension of his arm. He gave her a curt nod and a half-smile. "Ready?"

Jessica forced a tight smile back. "As ready as I'll ever be." Her voice was calm, but inside her chest, a storm was building—an electric tension that prickled the skin.

They began threading their way through the swelling mass. The air vibrated with shouts and chants, words tangled in a fevered mix of hope and rage. Signs rose like jagged teeth: "*End the war!*" "*Give me freedom or give me death!" "Justice for thee, but not for me."* The sharp colors of spray paint and marker strokes blurred together as the crowd surged forward, thick in smelly odors and determination.

By now the National Guard had formed a line, a living wall of steel and helmets. Faces were hidden behind dark visors, rifles locked and ready. Jessica caught the flicker of unease in some eyes—hands twitching near triggers, quick glances exchanged in silent warning. It was a *perfect moment*, Jessica thought, snapping a photo as she walked.

Her pulse hammered louder, the distant thunder of boots striking pavement sending vibrations up her spine. The tension was a living thing, pressing down like the heat of a summer afternoon. Suddenly, laughter cut through the din—a sharp, defiant burst that made Jessica's head snap toward the sound.

A figure pushed forward, parting the crowd like a knife through fog: a young woman, barely twenty by the looks of it, with a shock of electric purple hair that caught the sunlight and threw shards of color across the faces near her. Her eyes blazed with fierce conviction, a wild grin stretching across her face. Her faded denim jacket, adorned with pins—rainbows, peace symbols, a worn patch stitched with the word "*Resist.*"

Jessica moved closer, her reporter instincts kicking in. "Hey," she called, voice steady despite the chaos. "I'm Jessica. I'm covering this for the *Tribune*. What's your name?"

The girl stopped, eyes locking onto Jessica with fierce intensity. "Jesse," she said, voice clear and ringing. "I'm here to make a stand. I'm here to change the world—setting my friends free—queer, hippie, all of us who've been silenced and shoved down this dying system."

Jessica nodded, craving more, needing to understand the drive of this mysterious person, but before she could speak again, Jesse was swept up by the chaotic chant, disappearing back into the crowd like smoke.

"Who the hell was that?"

"I don't know, Simon. But there's something... I don't know what it is." Jessica stopped, attempting to gather her thoughts into words. The crowd pressed inward, squeezing the air from Jessica's chest. The space between bodies shrank, flesh brushing flesh, the heat thickening like fog. The sharp tang of dampness mingled with the sour bite of fear. Her breaths came shorter, shallower—each inhale felt like a fight against the tightening coil in her ribs.

She clutched the camera strap, her knuckles blanched from the strain. To her left, a man clutched a cardboard sign with trembling hands, eyes wide and searching. To her right, a mother shielding a young child, voice barely above a whisper but fierce with determination. *What sort of mother brings their child to such a protest?*

The crush of bodies pressed harder, blurring the edges of her vision. Panic prickled the back of her neck. The air felt thick, and the sounds around her warped into an overwhelming cacophony.

Then, through the surging crowd, she saw Jesse again. This time, the young woman accepted a heavy, olive-green metal box from a hooded figure shrouded in black. Jesse's smile was unsettling—calm and chilling in its certainty. Soon she melted back into the sea of faces, vanishing again. Jessica's body became cold, as a shiver went up her spine. *This is not good.*

In the distance near the National Guard's defensive line, the commander barked rapid-fire orders, his voice strained but resolute. His troops shifted uneasily, some faces grim, others pale—the rattle of gear marking their tension, eyes flickering nervously. It wasn't more than a second before the tense calm became shattered.

Jessica's eyes bolted to an opening where Jesse was standing. Her shoulders were squared, hefting an RPG. *God no!* Jessica thought, realizing what was about to unfold. Jesse aimed with a grin and squeezed the trigger with a look of determination. The rocket swooshed through the crowd, smashing right into the defensive line.

The explosion tore through the street, hurling bodies, glass, and debris into the air like rag dolls caught in a storm. Jessica's camera swung up, the lens locking onto the blast. Flames licked at the shattered concrete, screams tore through the charged air, and panic erupted like wildfire. *Click! Click! Click!*

Her horror heightened at the sound of a blood-curdling order by the commander. "Shots fired on my command! Open fire! Open fire!" Jessica's worst fear has now become a reality.

Gunfire erupted—sharp cracks and rattles, screams and shouts flooding the streets. The crowd scattered, tripping over each other in desperate flight, some grabbing rifles and pistols from fallen comrades, returning fire with raw desperation.

With her heart pounding in her ears, Jessica kept her hand steady, capturing the harrowing chaos—the blood, the fire, the violent splintering of a nation breaking apart.

The air filled with acrid smoke and the sharp stench of burning rubber as the explosion echoed through the streets. Jessica's breath caught, eyes wide behind her camera lens as bodies tumbled and chaos exploded all around her. People screamed—some in pain, others in shock—and the crack of gunfire shattered the fragile silence that followed.

Her boots pounded against the cracked concrete, weaving through the fallen signs and broken glass. A crowd of united people waving in protest, fractured instantly into desperate clusters, many scrambling to safety while others froze, wide-eyed and scared for their lives.

* * *

Jessica's camera swung between frantic shots of injured civilians and guardsmen seeking cover behind overturned vehicles. The sickening thud of bodies hitting the pavement mixed with blood-curdling cries for help.

A figure caught her eye—a young woman with the same purple hair, the same denim jacket, but torn and smudged, eyes blazing with murder instead of fear. It was Jesse. She stumbled over debris, hands grasping at something heavy: a fallen guard's rifle. Her hands trembled, but she raised the weapon, opening fire on the chaotic scene in front of her, each shot with a raw scream of rebellion.

Jessica's pulse thundered in her ears. *Click! Click! Click!* Capturing Jesse's desperate stand—the hatred in her eyes, the wild anger—and then the crack of gunfire echoed sharply. Jesse staggered, clutching her side as blood blossomed through her jacket. She collapsed hard, the rifle slipping from her grasp. Her fierce eyes dimmed slowly, but a faint, bitter smile lingered on her lips.

Around her, the National Guard regrouped swiftly, barking orders through clenched teeth. "Hold the line! Push them back! Don't let them break through!" Their rifles cracked in disciplined bursts, targeting those who pressed forward with stolen weapons or desperate fury.

Jessica took a shaky breath, her hands still steady on the camera. She moved among the wounded, kneeling to snap photos of a young man clutching a bleeding arm, whispering reassurances no one could hear. Nearby, a mother cradled her sobbing child, eyes wide with terror.

The street was a tableau of broken dreams and shattered hopes, a mirror reflecting the nation tearing itself apart. The protestors who had once chanted for freedom were now caught in a brutal fight for survival.

Jessica's gaze hardened. She had come here to capture a story, but it was no longer about ideals—it was about blood, loss, and the unbearable cost of a country on the brink of collapse. She swallowed the lump in her throat and raised her camera once more. This was the truth she had to confront, no matter how dark.

* * *

Minutes After the Explosion – National Guard Defense Line

The thick smoke curled lazily upward, a choking haze hanging low over the shattered street like a dense fog of despair. Captain Marcus Hale crouched behind the twisted wreckage of an overturned patrol vehicle, sweat stinging his eyes and streaking down his dirt-smeared face. Once crisp and sharp, his uniform was now stained with grime and dust, the insignia on his chest dulled under the weight of what he carried—a responsibility heavier than any combat load.

Around him, the air pulsed with tension. His soldiers—young men and women barely old enough to drink or vote—were scattered, some trying to aid the wounded, others gripping rifles with hands trembling like leaves in a storm. Their faces were weary, eyes wide with a mixture of adrenaline and dawning horror. The lines between duty and conscience blurred with each passing second. It had been centuries since a war had broken out within the borders of the United States, with many confused as to how a second war would look.

The radio on his belt hissed and crackled, voices overlapping like the turbulent waves of a stormy sea. Orders flew in broken fragments, some calling for restraint, others screaming for escalation. His ears rang with the echoes of the chaos—screams, gunfire, the dull thud of bodies hitting pavement.

Marcus's heart pounded in rhythm with the mounting panic around him. His hands shook as he lifted the secure handset of the military landline, the cold plastic slippery against his clammy skin. His voice, usually steady and commanding, came out strained. "Command, this is Captain Hale. The situation has rapidly deteriorated. Armed protesters have fired on the perimeter. We've taken casualties. Firing seems to have stopped. Requesting immediate guidance."

Static filled the brief silence, then a voice—calm, deliberate, and without a hint of hesitation—cut through. "Captain Hale, until all enemy combatants are confirmed, you have your standing orders."

Marcus blinked, a cold knot forming in his gut. "Sir?"

"Shoot them," the voice repeated, flat and unyielding.

"Sir, with all due respect, American citizens are in the line of fire. There's chaos, but..."

"No exceptions, Captain Hale." The voice interrupted, clipped like a cold command from a distant, detached authority. The line went dead.

This can't be happening. Marcus stared at the receiver as though wanting it to speak again, to explain, to retract the words that twisted his insides like a knife. His mind raced, cycling through the countless briefings, training exercises, and ethics seminars drilled into him over a decade of service. The rules of engagement, the use-of-force continuum—all dissolved in reality's harsh glare. Now, there was only one order.

Nearby, Corporal Jennings approached, his face fatigued and drawn, sweat glistening on his brow. "Captain, what are the orders?" His voice trembled as much as his hands.

Marcus choked on his spit. He glanced at his unit, their youth striking in the stark light of terror. Some clutched rifles like lifelines; others had their heads down, eyes darting between the commander and the chaos beyond. Many were just men and women, wrestling with the heavy cost of the duty thrust upon them. Only the following words they heard next went beyond duty, to something darker.

“Open fire,” Marcus whispered, voice thick with dread.

The reaction was immediate and raw. Murmurs of disbelief, whispered protests, some nearly silent sobs. “Captain... Sir...” One soldier whispered, voice barely audible over the gunfire and screams. “This is murder.”

Marcus’s jaw clenched. “We’re soldiers. Follow orders. That is all we have left.”

The first shots cracked through the thick air like thunderclaps—sharp, cold, and final. Protesters fell beneath the disciplined bursts, cries of pain and rage rising in an agonized chorus. The street became a battlefield of shattered ideals, torn loyalties, and fractured futures.

Marcus closed his eyes briefly, memories flashing like lightning—the broad smile of his wife on their wedding day, the faces of his parents who raised him on the stories and sacrifices of those before him. He observed Jesse’s wild purple hair in the distance, the fierce light of her eyes as she sprayed bullets. She was no longer a symbol of protest but a casualty of a nation unravelling at the seams.

The commander’s breath came heavy as the weight of his command crushed him. This wasn’t war; it was a massacre disguised in the language of orders and protocol. The orders were clear, but the morality was muddled in blood and smoke. Was there a way out? Could the outcome have been any different than what it became?

Behind him, a soldier let out a choked sob. Marcus forced himself to look away and focus on the immediate—keeping what remained of his unit alive, holding the line against a breaking world.

Salty liquid soon reached Marcus's mouth. *Tears... am I... crying?* Marcus thought. His mind had not caught up to what his eyes were showing him. Reality wasn't registering in his soul. But what he was seeing was unmistakable.

Marcus's gaze could not be broken as he stared, for ahead of him was a mother holding a son. Lifeless. Curled up on the ground in each other's arms.

* * *

Bitter smells filled the air even as people ran. The crowd was no longer just a mass of bodies—it was a living, breathing beast, pressing from every side. Jessica's breaths came shorter, her chest constricting with each inhale like a fist squeezing her lungs. The sounds around her swelled to a deafening roar: shouts, chants, the rattling of helmets, the clatter of boots, and the sharp bark of orders from the Guard pushing down the street. It was a brutal symphony—chaotic, relentless, and suffocating.

She gripped her camera strap with desperate force, her fingers quivering as sweat trickled down the back of her neck and dripped onto her collar. The scent of dust, salt, burning rubber, and something darker—horror—filled her nostrils, thick and choking. Every inhale was a battle against the growing claustrophobia clawing at her lungs.

Faces blurred into a swirling mosaic—some young and fiery with conviction fading into the chaos; others older, marked by horror and fatigue, their eyes hollow and resigned. Some pushed forward with courage, fists raised, while others trembled, eyes darting for escape routes. She felt trapped in a narrowing corridor of flesh and fury, the walls closing in with every surge of movement.

Her chest pounded like a frantic drumbeat, echoing in her ears louder than the cries around her. Her hands gripped her camera tightly, knuckles white. The heavy lens dragged at her side, a reminder that she was here to record it all—no matter how close the danger was.

Suddenly, a sharp shove from behind sent her staggering sideways. The jolt knocked the breath from her lungs. She caught herself against a hot metal street lamp, the rough pole biting into her palm as the crowd surged past like a wave crashing over a rocky shore.

The pressure of bodies was overwhelming; each step forward was a fight against the tide. Her vision tunneled, the world shrinking to the narrowest silver of focus: faces pressed close, voices rising into a cacophony, and the unmistakable tension vibrating in the air like static electricity.

She tried to steady herself, willing to panic to retreat, but it lingered beneath the surface like a snake coiled to strike. The crowd's desperate energy and heaviness in the air whispered of, something breaking beyond repair.

Jessica's eyes searched for Jesse's shock of purple hair, a beacon amid the chaos. A fleeting flash caught her eye—a hint of color—only for it to vanish again, swallowed by the restless sea of bodies. *Wait, she's dead. What am I thinking?*

Her mind raced: her awareness was crumbling. This wasn't just a protest anymore. It was the first violent attack in a country already splintering, a spark setting tinder to dry wood. The question burned hotter than the sun overhead: How far would this fracture spread? How many more would die before the fighting stopped? How far would the nation fall before it reverses course and heals—or shatters completely?

* * *

The sirens blared around the streets. The smoke still hung in the air like a suffocating shroud, curling through the cracked streets of downtown like a specter of destruction. Jessica sat alone on the sidewalk, her boots on top of broken glass and twisted metal, her stomach still tied in knots: no thoughts, no words, just heavy breaths attempting to process the situation. The air was thick—not just with dust and smoke, but with a heavy, suffocating sense of loss. It pressed down on her like a physical weight, a silent indictment of everything that had happened.

Around her, the crowd had calmed, but chaos and panic still ran rampant. The crowd that had surged so violently just moments before had splintered into fragmented pockets of stunned survivors. Faces streaked with dirt and tears, eyes glassy with shock and disbelief. Some sat motionless, dazed and numbed by the violence they had witnessed. Others rocked back and forth, hands clutching at bleeding wounds or comforting trembling loved ones.

Jessica lifted her camera, which she placed on the sidewalk by her side. Its once-polished lens was now smudged with dirt and sweat. She barely noticed the grime. Her eyes burned with a desperate need to see everything—every shattered window, every anguished face, every broken body. She was a witness to history's cruel turning point, and the enormity of it threatened to swallow her whole. Scrolling through every picture was a needle to the heart, yet she persisted in seeing the photos.

"Jessica!" A voice cut through the haze. It was sharp, familiar, grounding.

Simon Alexander pushed his way toward her, dodging debris with the ease of a seasoned cameraman. His face was drawn and grim, the day's exhaustion etched into the lines around his eyes. His hands trembled slightly, stained with soot and smudged with dirt.

"You okay?" he asked, voice low but steady.

Jessica gave a tight nod, clearing the knot in her throat. "As much as anyone can be, Simon."

She stood up and followed Simon through the crowd. They fell into step together, weaving through the wreckage toward the makeshift press staging behind the barricades. Reporters huddled in clusters, exchanging fragmented updates, their faces taut with exhaustion and the raw edges of disbelief. The weight of what they had just witnessed clung to them like a second skin.

Simon shook his head slowly. "This was a goddamn massacre, Jess. What happened out there... I don't even know how to put it into words."

Jessica's eyes drifted back toward the smoking ruins of the armored vehicle, now a twisted wreckage that looked more like a tomb than a piece of military hardware. "That girl, Jesse, she fired that RPG," she said softly, voice thick with sorrow. "I saw her. She was so young... Yet so determined."

Simon's gaze darkened, a flick of anger and helplessness crossing his features. "She was a kid. Most of them were. And they just launched a full-scale war."

Jessica's fingers absently twisted a strand of her hair—a nervous habit she hadn't managed to shake. The memory of Jesse's fierce smile in those final moments haunted her. "This isn't just a story about protests or politics anymore. This is now something deeper... something sinister. A country tearing itself apart from the inside."

Her voice dropped, almost to herself. "And now it's placed us right in the middle."

Simon placed a steady hand on her shoulder. "We must show the world what happened here today, Jess. No matter how dark, how horrifying."

She looked up, meeting his gaze. "I intend to. But it's more than just telling a story now. It will be about holding people accountable, all people."

A distant rumble vibrated through the street—the grim soundtrack of unrest flaring somewhere else in the city. The violence was spreading, metastasizing.

Jessica's phone buzzed in her pocket. She pulled it out, her hand quivering slightly as she read the message—a cryptic text from her White House contact. *"Things are worse than you think. Stay safe."*

Her eyes narrowed. She pocketed the phone without replying.

Around her, the city was unravelling. The fragile veneer of order had cracked, revealing the raw, jagged edges beneath. A war was beginning—not just of guns and explosions, but of ideology, fear, and desperation.

Jessica stared off into the distance. The road ahead was now long and dark, but she was ready to walk it—because the world needed to see what was coming.

* * *

Jessica collapsed onto a stiff hotel bed, the weight of the day pressing down on her like a lead blanket. Her hands shook as she peeled off her jacket, still damp with sweat and dust from the protest. The dull ache in her head throbbed in time with the pounding of distant sirens outside. Her camera lay abandoned on her bedside table, lens smeared, a silent witness to the carnage she had just filmed.

The room was quiet except for the air conditioner's hum, struggling to keep the stale air at bay. Jessica's mind spun, replaying the moments she'd seen: Jesse's defiant smile before she fired the RPG, the shouts, the gunfire, the chaos swallowing the streets. The faces—so many faces—etched into her memory forever. She couldn't even turn on the TV for updates on the unfolding chaos. All the sound in the world, thoughts running harder than the air conditioner.

Her phone buzzed sharply on the nightstand, jolting her from the spiral of images. The screen read: Daniel.

She hesitated for a moment, then swiped to answer. "Hey," she said softly.

"Mom! Hi!" Sebastian's bright voice burst through, followed by Mitch's quieter but insistent, "Are you okay?"

Jessica's throat tightened. "I'm... hanging in there, boys. It's been a long day."

"We saw the news. The shooting. Mom, are you safe?" Sebastian asked, worry bleeding through his words.

Jessica cleared her throat. "Yeah, I'm okay. Just shaken." She could hear her boys' breath, their chatter quiet in the background. "How are you two holding up?"

Daniel's voice came in next, calm but with an edge Jessica recognized all too well. "They're fine. We're all fine. But Jessica, you need to come home. Think about what you're doing—"

"Doing? Reporting? You know, doing my job?" She interrupted sharply. "You think I will sit quietly on the sidelines while everything falls apart? The country is being split down the middle, and my son enlists to fight a coming war I'm documenting?"

There was an unnerving silence. A whispered voice from Daniel was heard. "Boys, can you give me and your mother a minute?"

Jessica swallowed hard, readying herself to hear what she considered more bullshit on an already shitty day.

Daniel's sigh was heavy. "Jessica, it's not that simple. You're putting yourself—and all of us—at risk. You're obsessed, and it's pulling us down with you."

Jessica bit back at the sting. "You left. You walked away because you couldn't handle my job, my life. Don't pretend you care now."

"Jessica, I'm here when you're not right now. I'm keeping this family safe!" Daniel's voice cracked with frustration.

"We're already broken," she shot back, voice rising. "I'm doing what I have to do. Maybe you should try doing the same."

There was a pause, and tension was thick enough to suffocate the room, although the air conditioner was doing a good job at that, with Jessica breathing heavily.

Suddenly, her phone buzzed again—this time with a message notification from Eli – WHA flashing urgently across the screen.

Jessica's breath hitched. Daniel had begun to speak again, but she cut him off mid-sentence. "I have to go. Something's come up. We'll finish this discussion later."

She ended the call, not giving Daniel another chance to speak or protest. Her hands shook as she stared at the screen. Then, without hesitation, she dialed Eli's number.

"Jessica," Eli's voice was low, urgent, tinged with exhaustion and something colder—fear. "It's worse than we thought."

Jessica sat up straighter, wiping a tear she hadn't realized had fallen. "What do you mean?"

"There's an emergency meeting brewing in the Situation Room. The president and other advisors are terrified—California's on the brink of secession. The governor calling an emergency session? They see it as a declaration of war waiting to happen."

Jessica's fingers clenched around the phone as if it were the only thing keeping her tethered. "Are they certain California will break away? Does the president believe the Union will fall apart?"

Eli's voice dropped to a whisper. "It's not just talk anymore. Some in the administration want to act—hard and fast. Military mobilization, martial law, and clampdowns on potential militias. They believe this is the only way to stop the rebellion before it spreads like wildfire."

Jessica's breath caught. "This is horseshit. This madness will tear the whole country apart."

"Exactly," Eli said grimly. "There's no consensus. The president's top men are split—hawks pushing for decisive action, others begging for caution. But the president... he's feeling the pressure. His patience is wearing thin."

A heavy silence hung between them.

Jessica's voice was barely above a whisper. "I don't know if I can report this. Nothing concrete has happened, and this will only stoke flames."

"You have to," Eli insisted. "They deserve to know what's coming. And so do you."

The line went dead.

Jessica stared at the phone, her heart hammering against her ribs. The room suddenly felt colder, darker. The distant city lights outside flickered uncertainly through the blinds, casting long shadows across the walls.

She pulled a hand through her tangled curls, twisting them anxiously. Outside, the wind shifted, carrying a faint, metallic tang that made her skin prickle. She swallowed hard, sensing that whatever was coming next would change everything—not just the country but her life and the world she thought she knew.

April 4, 2044 – California State Capitol – Sacramento, California

Jessica's car pulled up along 10th Street near Capitol Park just after 7:00 a.m. The sun had barely cracked the horizon, casting long golden fingers across the California State Capitol's white neoclassical dome. The light seemed at odds with the dread in her chest. Sacramento was quiet—too quiet. As she stepped out of the car, the only sounds were the distant bark of a police dog and the low mechanical thrum of news vans setting up across the plaza.

She zipped her press vest over her long black coat, slung her camera around her neck, and scanned the area. Police had already barricaded the front lawn. Riot officers stood shoulder-to-shoulder behind the iron gates. Their faces were blank primarily, save for the occasional downward flick of the eyes to check gloves or baton straps. The National Guard trucks flanked the rear parking lot. A heavy belt-fed machine gun sat perched on the roof of a Humvee, unmanned—for now.

Jessica exhaled through her nose and popped off the lid of her boba tea. Still half-melted. Still full of caffeine. She took a sip, then tapped her recorder to test its red light.

"Jess Parker, Sacramento, April 4, 2044. No official comment from the governor's office yet, but multiple sources say she'll address the legislature today. And... yeah. That's where this all starts."

She ended the note and pocketed the mic. Behind her, the air swelled with the murmurs of a growing crowd. People were gathering in small groups on the edges of the cordoned lawn: activists, militias, families waving California flags. Some carried homemade signs:

ENOUGH IS ENOUGH

SOVEREIGNTY NOW

RECALL D.C., NOT OUR RIGHTS

The split was stark. The older crowd wore faded denim, desert camo hats, and American flag patches pinned to their vests—the younger ones dressed in mismatched tactical gear and bright scarves, some with full-face masks. Jessica noted the lack of unity between them. This wasn't one movement—it was five to six movements with a common enemy and no consensus on what came next.

"Morning, Jessica." A familiar voice.

She turned. It was Simon Alexander; his NBC vest dusted with crumbs from a breakfast bar. He handed her a coffee.

"Extra shot. You looked like hell last night on your feed."

Jessica took it and offered a tired smirk. "I still feel like I'm breathing tear gas."

"You probably are." He nodded toward a patrol officer in the distance, tossing canisters into a duffel. "You think they're going to let us inside?"

"They have to. This is a government proceeding. It's still public, technically."

Simon shrugged. "These days, the word 'public' doesn't mean what it used to."

Jessica's phone buzzed again. It was a message from her contact in the governor's office, a young legislative assistant named Emilia Torres. It was short.

"Get inside. She's going to do it today."

She looked up at the Capitol steps. The large bronze doors were just now being unlocked. Staffers in suits shuffled through, accompanied by state troopers and a few aides whispering frantically into earpieces.

Well, I'll be damned. Jessica finished her drinks in one long pull, wiped her camera lens, and squared her shoulders. "Let's go watch history unfold."

* * *

The rotunda was humming when Jessica stepped inside. Marble floors echoed with the tapping of boots, the clipped voices of aides, and the rustle of reporters jockeying for prime positions on the chamber floor. The air smelled of varnish, sweat, and cold coffee. Tension settled like dust in the sunlight filtering through the dome's oculus.

At the far end of the assembly hall, the Speaker's podium stood ready beneath the seal of the State of California. The Governor had not yet arrived, but the room was packed—journalists, lawmakers, press aides, military advisors, and a handful of lobbyists who hadn't fled Sacramento. Jessica pushed forward, her press badge worn like armor.

Simon whispered beside her, "She'd better make it count. They won't forgive her for what's about to happen."

Jessica didn't answer. Her fingers curled around her camera. A dull ringing buzzed in her ears, like the static before a power surge.

Then the chamber doors opened.

Governor Elena Ortega strode in with a calm resolve that belied the storm outside. Her dark pantsuit was crisply tailored, her gray-streaked hair pulled into a bun. She walked without hesitation, flanked by two

National Guard officers and her Chief of Staff. Her eyes scanned the crowd—not cold, but focused, steady.

She climbed the steps to the podium and took the microphone without preamble.

"My fellow Californians," she began, her voice firm and clear, amplified across the rotunda and piped outside for the crowds.

"I stand before you today not as a partisan. Not as a politician. Not as a progressive. But as a citizen of this state and of this nation... and as a mother, a daughter, and a patriot."

A ripple moved through the room. Lawmakers leaned forward. Phones lifted into the air to record. Reporters' fingers flew across touchscreens.

"For years," she continued, "we have tried—tried to work within a system that no longer hears us. We have pleaded with Washington to fund our crumbling infrastructure. We have begged for wildfire aid, water rights, fair taxation, and dignity in the face of a climate catastrophe. And we have been ignored."

A pause.

Jessica zoomed in through her viewfinder. Governor Ortega's expression was not angry—but it carried the weight of a decision long considered and finally made.

"And now, after the massacre in Los Angeles—after the federal government authorized the execution of unarmed citizens—we are left with no choice."

Gasps. A few voices muttered. But no one moved to stop her.

"This morning, I am calling an emergency joint session of the California Assembly and Senate. In that session, I will introduce legislation to secede from the United States of America, and to form an independent government capable of protecting our people, our values, and our future."

Chaos. Some lawmakers shot to their feet. Others pounded the desk. A few shouted objections while others clapped—scattered at first, then building into a roar among the gallery above.

The governor raised her hand, and the room slowly settled.

"I do not make this choice lightly," she said, her voice nearly a whisper now. "This is not a rebellion. This is an act of preservation. Survival within a crumbling nation."

She glanced upward, where a small group of National Guard officers stood watching. Jessica saw one of them nod subtly.

"I will not pretend this will be simple. War may come. Some believe it has already arrived. But if we do not act, our children will inherit a nation too broken to fix. And if I must be branded a traitor for choosing California over murder, then so be it."

She stepped back from the podium, stone-faced. For a long, pregnant moment, the chamber was frozen in silence.

Then a wave of noise surged—shouts, applause, screams, weeping. The Speaker struggled to bring order, banging his gavel over and over. But the chaos couldn't be tamed. It had already begun.

Jessica snapped a photo of Ortega as she turned away from the mic, backlit by the soft golden dome above her. In that moment, she didn't look like a politician.

She looked like the first President of something new.

Jessica leaned against the wall just outside the rotunda, her throat dry and stomach knotted. She'd watch riots. She'd seen bodies in the streets. But the words *secede from the United States* still hit her like an electric jolt straight to the chest. Hours felt like weeks, yet minutes found their way to feeling like eternity.

"Five minutes," she muttered to herself, slipping past two Capitol guards and down the hallway toward the side exit.

Outside, the crowd had doubled. Thousands of people were gathered now behind the barriers, pressed against metal fencing and chain-link perimeters. The National Guard had reinforced its presence. Trucks with mounted weapons flanked each intersection near the Capitol steps.

Jessica wove through the chaos and ducked into a café two blocks down—a local hole-in-the-wall called Newton's Press. Its sign was half-lit, and the display case inside was half-empty. Still, it smelled like bacon, eggs, and burnt espresso. A local news anchor blared quietly from a wall-mounted TV, replaying clips of the Governor's address.

A man behind the counter looked up with bloodshot eyes. "Holy shit, that was you photographing that speech?"

Jessica raised an eyebrow. "You saw it already?"

"It's been trending for over an hour now. The whole internet's on fire." He rubbed his eyes. "What the hell happens now?"

Jessica didn't answer. She instead asked for a bacon-egg sandwich and a black coffee. As the barista turned away, she pulled out her phone. Five missed calls from Anthony. Two from her editor. One from Daniel.

And a text from Mitch.

"Mom... Did California really just do that? They've called in all of us early. We're about to report and be locked down."

She stared at the message until her eyes blurred. When the coffee hits her hand, she almost flinched.

"On the house," the barista said. "Seriously... thanks for what you all do."

Jessica offered a weak smile, took her paper bag and coffee, and stepped back into the morning light. It was brighter now, but somehow colder. The wind had shifted, carrying the scent of exhaust, tear gas, and something sharper.

From her spot on the corner, she could see the giant TV screens that lined the edges of the plaza flashing a live update:

BREAKING: CALIFORNIA LEGISLATURE TO CONVENE EMERGENCY SESSION ON SECESSION.

Across the lawn, she saw a scuffle break out near the edge of the east gate—someone threw a smoke bomb, and riot cops surged forward. Screams cut through like sirens. Jessica didn't even have time to sip her coffee.

She stuffed the half-eaten sandwich into her bag, threw the coffee away, and began jogging back toward the Capitol steps. She reached the side entrance just as the press queue was being reshuffled.

A Capitol staffer stopped her at the door. "Ma'am, the Assembly's already seated."

"Press," she snapped, flashing her badge. "I have to be in that room."

"Then you'd better hurry. They just started the roll call."

* * *

Jessica slipped back into the press gallery, breathless, the Capitol rotunda buzzing louder than before. The Assembly Chamber looked like a pressure cooker about to blow. Rows of lawmakers were seated at their desks, each framed by the polished wood and gold trim of California's legislative chamber. A massive state flag loomed behind the Speaker's podium.

She found Simon already there, camera raised, his mouth tight.

"They started the roll," he muttered without looking at her. "It's bad."

Jessica lifted her camera just as the Speaker of the Assembly, an older Latino man named Fernando Chavez, repeatedly slammed his gavel.

"The chamber will come to order! The chamber will come to order!"

The crowd ignored him. Across the aisle, two assemblymen were screaming at each other, one in a worn suit and a California lapel pin, the other red-faced and pounding his desk with an open hand.

"This is insanity! You think we can start a full-scale war with the goddamn United States and win?!"

"You'd rather lie down and let them shoot our children like they did in Los Angeles?"

Shouts rang out from both sides. A few lawmakers openly panicked—one woman near the back was crying silently, her face buried in her hands. Another man had his head down on his desk, whispering into a rosary.

Jessica whispered to Simon, "Get audio on everything. Don't stop recording."

The Speaker's voice cracked the chamber again. "This chamber will come to order! We are convened under Article XII, Section Three, granting emergency powers to the Governor. Today, we vote to ratify or reject the proposed Declaration of Secession from the United States."

Murmurs of "*traitor,*" "*hero,*" "*madness,*" and "*finally*" circled through the benches.

One Assemblyman—Robert Klein, known in many political circles as a centrist—stood to speak.

"Mr. Speaker."

"The chair recognizes the Assemblyman from San Diego."

"Thank you. Listen when I say these words; this is not a decision," he said, voice low but unwavering. "It's a descent. Once we do this, there is no undoing it. We will not just be Californians—we will be enemies of the Republic. Think about that before you raise your hand."

Applause came from his side of the chamber, and boos came from the opposite side. As he sat down, another representative stood. Young, Black, and in her early 30s, Maya Onwuachi was a rising star from Oakland.

"Mr. Speaker. I stand before you with tragedy ingrained in my hands. I was at Market Street," she said, her voice cracking. "I held the hand of a protester as he died. Shot in the neck. I saw a mother searching for her daughter in the smoke, and a guardsman screamed that they had orders to 'clean it all up.' If that's what the Republic looks like now, then maybe we're better off enemies."

A shocked silence fell. Then loud applause. Then another burst of yelling.

The Speaker shouted again. "This is not a debate session. The motion is on the floor. All members, prepare for a recorded vote."

Aides scurried around with ballots. Digital screens flickered to life at each desk. Jessica watched as hands trembled as representatives awaited the moment to vote.

"We will now proceed to the vote. Begin the roll call."

Silence fell over the chamber, for the most critical vote of the politician's lifetime began. All those observing could do was hold their breaths and pray that mercy be shown on the innocent. *Click! Click! Click!* Jessica tapped.

The voting was underway. Beep. Beep. Beep. Votes lit up on the master screen in real time. YEA... YEA... NAY... NAY... YEA... YEA... YEA... NAY... The split was razor-thin. Jessica felt her pulse hammer in her throat. Sweat beaded down her spine.

Then—

A gasp. Two final "YEA" votes appeared. The board froze.

46 YEA / 34 NAY

The gallery erupted. Some legislators jumped to their feet, cheering. Others were openly weeping. A small group stormed out, throwing their voting tablets across the floor. One woman collapsed into her chair, sobbing uncontrollably. Jessica saw a man in uniform whisper something into his earpiece and exit the chamber with urgency.

The Speaker banged the gavel. "On the vote of the motion laid upon the table; The YEAs are 46, the NAYs are 34. The motion is agreed to. The California State Assembly hereby ratifies the Declaration of Secession."

Jessica's hands were shaking too much to film. She caught only fragments of faces—joy, horror, disbelief.

Simon looked over, his voice hoarse. "Jesus Christ on a motorbike... They really did it."

Jessica just whispered. "It's happening."

The Next Day – California Senate Chambers

If the Assembly chamber had felt like a powder keg, the Senate was a boiling cauldron—quieter, but tenser. The senators carried themselves with more weight, as if they knew the decision they were about to make would be etched into history books—or indictments—forever.

Jessica followed the camera crew into the upper press gallery, flanked by two Capitol guards now visibly armed with sidearms and body armor. Even here, the rules had changed among the marble and mahogany of the state's most sacred political floor. Safety was no longer a guarantee. Tensions were at an all-time high. It's not every day that a state would pick a fight with a government armed with more nuclear warheads than there were states.

The chamber floor below was hushed. Forty senators sat in carved oak chairs, some flipping through folders, others staring ahead with deadened eyes. A few were on their phones, thumbs shaking as they scrolled. One senator, an elderly right-leaning party member from the Inland Empire, sat slouched, his face ghost-white.

Jessica leaned toward Simon, whispering. "Any idea how close the whip count is?"

He glanced down at his notes. "Twenty-one needed to pass. Rumor is it's locked at twenty. The whole state's watching for one name—Collins."

Jessica blinked. "Darren Collins? The one who ran on 'moderate strength' in San Diego?"

"Yeah. Marine vet. Centrist. No one knows where he stands."

California politics is a mystery as old as the pyramids. But one thing was always sure: former military veterans who had served always held a knack for war. On this day though, no one knew where the veteran's mind was. The horrors of what was seen in war, perhaps glorifying it, holding a burning desire to either fight the government for what they did, or stand with them because of witnessing their sheer power.

A sharp rap of the gavel brought silence. The President pro Tempore, a tall woman with silver hair named Carla Carrasco, stood behind the dais.

"Members of the Senate," she said, her voice firm but not cold, "you have heard the motion. The Assembly has passed a Declaration of Secession. As President of this chamber, I remind you: should we ratify it, the Governor will sign it within the hour. At that moment, the State of California will officially consider itself no longer bound by the authority of the United States government."

A few senators shifted uncomfortably. One made the sign of the cross.

In simpler times, a move like secession would have triggered a long, rigid constitutional process. But devastation rampaged across America in the 2020s. The wars and political crises of the 2030s shattered the court system, leaving only fragments of federal authority. The 2040s were anything but simple in America, as nothing was ever normal.

"This is not a decision made lightly," she continued. "Nor should it be made out of fear. But history will not care for your comfort. It will care for your conviction."

She looked over the room. "Now—any final comments before the vote?"

Silence. The room grew cold, silent as the grave.

Then... movement. Senator Darren Collins stood. The chamber held its collective breath. He was square-jawed, with a face made for campaign ads. But now he looked like a man carrying fifty pounds of guilt.

"As many of you know, I was a Marine, serving in the Middle East, fighting in Europe, and serving in intelligence," he said, voice low. "I swore an oath to defend the Constitution of the United States. And I still believe in the America that oath represents."

He paused. Some nodded in agreement.

"But I also watched the live footage of American citizens being mowed down by our own troops on Market Street. I've gotten over a hundred calls from constituents, mostly veterans like me, asking why our kids are dying while D.C. plays emperor."

His voice cracked. "My daughter is twelve. I question if her school is going to be bombed by American jets next."

More eerie silence filled the chamber. *This is not good*.

"I don't want this vote. I don't want an already coming war. But the America I swore to defend doesn't exist right now. It's been ravaged by its thirst for power, decimated to the point where it's reaching the Soviet Union of '91. And if the only way to fix it is to break away... then I vote with my conscience."

It was a damning statement. The nation that once helped push the Soviet Union to collapse was now standing where Moscow had stood in 1991—at a crossroads, teetering at the edge of uncertainty.

Collins sat, cold in his anger. Jessica could only stand and watch as the Senate proceeded with impending destruction.

The President pro Tempore nodded, then stood. "Very well. If there are no more comments, then we will proceed. The clerk will call the roll."

And just like that, the voting was underway. Names began being read off, and votes slowly rolled in. Jessica watched in silence.

One by one, names were called aloud.

"SENATOR CHANG?"

"Yea."

"SENATOR REED?"

"Nay."

"SENATOR CASTRO?"

"Yea."

Each vote echoed in the chamber like a gunshot. Jessica counted them in her head, silently mouthing each response. *17...18...19... 20...*

Then a pause. As if time was frozen. Collins had delayed his vote as the roll call went around him. And now the moment of truth had arrived, his name was called again to receive his vote. *My son, think of my son.*

"SENATOR COLLINS?"

It was as if a pin drop could be heard.

He stood slowly. "Yea."

21.

Gasps. A few cheers. Some sobs. One senator ripped off her microphone and stormed out. Another slammed his fists onto his desk and screamed, "You just declared war on us all! You bastard!"

The clerk continued. The final count:

YEAS: 21

NAYS: 19

MOTION PASSES.

The chamber erupted; shouting, applauding, and crying. Jessica caught it all on her camera, as hands rose in defiance, despair, and disbelief.

Simon turned to her, eyes wide. "They really fucking did it."

She didn't answer. She was already reaching for her phone, typing the lead to her next article:

"*With a vote of 21 to 19, the California State Senate has joined the Assembly in passing the Declaration of Secession. For the first time since 1861, a U.S. state has formally broken from the Union. This is no longer speculation. This is now history.*"

She hit *Send*. And now the world has changed.

* * *

The rotunda echoed with footsteps, heels, and boots against marble, voices hushed under the grandeur of painted ceilings and golden inlays. The ornate doors to the Governor's ceremonial office were guarded by six armed members of the California State Defense Guard—formerly the National Guard, now sworn to serve Sacramento. The gold bear of the state seal gleamed on each soldier's shoulder patch, a stark contrast to the faded American flags still hanging in the lobby.

Jessica stood with Simon in the media pen just outside the double doors, which had been thrown open to reveal the Governor's desk inside. Every news outlet still operating west of the Rockies had sent someone. Most of the national press were locked out—Jessica's Star Tribune badge had been enough to slip through, but barely.

The cameras were rolling. Mics were hot. The story of the century was unfolding.

In the room, Governor Elena Ortega, flanked by Lieutenant Governor Joseph Hightower, stood at a podium with the Declaration of Secession. She was very calm. She wore a black pant suit with no lapel pin, and her clothes were slightly wrinkled. Her face was ashen, but her eyes burned.

Jessica could feel the heat through the lens.

"My fellow Californians," Ortega began, voice low and controlled. "What happened in Los Angeles was not a tragedy—but a betrayal."

Gasps rippled through the crowd. Cameras clicked furiously. The last time an action of this stature took place, no type of technology existed, no world wars had been fought, and refrigerators had not been invented. Americans found themselves completing a circle of human nature.

"When our citizens took to the streets to protest peacefully, the federal government responded not with dialogue, not with restraint—but with bullets."

She raised the document in her hand. "This declaration is not written lightly. It is not motivated by ideology, politics, or pride. It is born out of the oldest American principle: that a government becomes destructive to human life and liberty. It has forfeited its legitimacy."

Ortega looked into the cameras. "As of this moment, the State of California formally secedes from the United States of America."

The room held its collective breath. Awaiting the firing gun to be fired. In seconds, she sat, and she signed. One stroke. Then another. Then a final flourish.

* * *

The California Declaration of Secession

We, the elected representatives of the sovereign state of California, do hereby declare our separation from the government of the United States, effective immediately. This act was undertaken to defend life, liberty, and the rights of all Californians.

We do not seek war. But we will no longer tolerate or stand with a nation of tyrants in the name of unity.

* * *

A hush gave way to a roar. Cheering erupted outside, and crowds gathered at Civic Center Plaza broke into spontaneous celebration and song. Others sobbed or collapsed in the streets, overwhelmed by what it meant and what it cost. Many desired to live in peace after so much tragedy and loss, but now it had become a distant dream.

Jessica didn't cheer. She didn't speak. Her pen trembled as she wrote. She lowered her notepad, collecting herself, and looked at Simon.

"We are fucked." she said, her voice hollow.

Simon nodded slowly. "And now?"

Jessica looked past the Capitol dome to the horizon. Sirens were already wailing in the distance.

"Now we wait for Washington to answer."

* * *

TEXAS STAR TRIBUNE

"Signed in Ink, Sealed in Blood"

By Jessica Parker – April 5, 2044

At precisely 5:46 PM Pacific Time, Governor Elena Ortega signed the Declaration of Secession into law. It took under 10 seconds, but it will echo for decades to come.

I stood in the room. I watched her hand shake only once. She didn't smile. She didn't pose. She just signed. We're not America anymore. We're something new. Or maybe something doomed.

Either way, this is real.

Just like that, it was off to the races.

April 12, 2044 – Los Angeles, California

Strange times had settled over the country—a declaration issued, yet eerily quiet. Perhaps peace and a solution would prevail. It has been over a week since California seceded, yet neither side has fired a shot. Washington was frantic, yet the military made no efforts to mobilize.

California found itself on a war footing, with chaos in processing a chain of command. Despite mobilizing the National Guard, this was just one of several problems California would have to deal with should a war be fought. Cutting itself off from the rest of the country caused the need to create a border and set up trade and commerce laws outside U.S. jurisdiction. California relied heavily on the government for many of its problems, but now they were on their own. Or so they thought.

The sound that woke Jessica wasn't her alarm or a phone call. *What the hell? It's not time to go to the airport yet.* The daze of awakening, mixed with severe exhaustion, clouded her ability to realize it wasn't something from her room.

It was the deep, distant boom—low and slow, like thunder without lightning. At first, her half-awake brain theorized that it was construction or a minor quake—perhaps just California occurrences.

Then came the sirens.

They started faint, a mournful cry down the hills of Los Angeles, but quickly multiplied. Soon, they howled through the motel's thin walls from every direction—emergency vehicles, military, police.

Jessica sat up with a gasp, heart thudding. The motel's neon sign flickered through the blinds. Her phone was already buzzing, skittering across the cheap nightstand like it had something to say before she could process what was happening.

She reached for the remote, flipping on the news. The channel had already cut to breaking coverage:

"Explosions reported at Naval Base San Diego—details scarce but developing—"

A live aerial feed wobbled across the screen. Smoke—black, thick, and curling—rose in thick plumes from the coastline. Flames licking out of a long administrative structure near the waterline. A siren wailed in the footage's background, overlaid with a shaken reporter's frantic voice.

"We've just confirmed that several vessels, including the USS *Harmon*, are no longer responding to port control. Reports suggest that—oh my God—yes, we can see smoke now rising from the northern fuel storage tanks—"

Jessica's stomach turned to stone. *War has begun*. She reached for her phone. Six missed calls. Two voicemails. And a single new text.

Eli: "*Turn on the news. Call me now.*"

She hit dial. He answered on the first ring.

"Jess."

"What the hell am I watching?"

His voice was shaky but composed—barely. "San Diego is gone. Not officially, but functionally. The *Harmon* and *Saratoga* shelled its radar station, Jessica. They blinded the base in a sneak attack."

She blinked, feeling the world tilt under her.

"Wait—what?"

"We received some reports that some of the crew were turned months ago. We're just figuring it out now. Communications out of the Southern Command Center went dark at 4:52. We think... We think it was pre-planned. This wasn't a chain-of-command collapse. It was a coordinated strike. Someone opened the gates from the inside."

Jessica pressed her hand to her forehead. Her hair stuck to her temples with sweat.

"But they just voted a week ago—a week."

Eli sighed. "No. They didn't start planning this in a week. This was years in motion from what I discovered with my CIA and NSA contacts. They waited for the vote. Then they pulled the trigger."

He paused. "Listen—word is, loyalist marines were executed in their bunks. We have signals intel showing encrypted comms out of the base all week. D.C. didn't catch it. They were focused on Sacramento."

She stood and opened her window. The air outside felt... different. Tighter. Expectant. The kind of stillness that comes before a storm finishes forming.

"What about the other ships?" She asked.

"The *Toledo* and *Richmond* never even got out of the dock. Crew turnover. Sabotaged engines. We think civilians—California Sympathizers—were embedded in maintenance crews."

"And the *Harmon* and *Saratoga*?"

"Both are flying the California state flag now. Full mutiny. CO of the *Harmon* is dead. Shot. The XO flipped and took command. It is unclear precisely what happened on the *Saratoga*. Word is that the captain was a friend of Collins, and he seemed to work him over to turn, and had enough sympathizers among the crew to flip it."

Jessica's fingers trembled as she reached for her laptop.

"Jesus..."

"Don't say that yet," Eli said quietly. "I've been in meetings all night. Joint Chiefs are furious. The President is flying to Colorado Springs under emergency protocol. They're talking full naval mobilization. Total blockade of California. We're one step away from DEFCON 2."

DEFCON 2. A situation many assumed would be used if a nation across the ocean stirred trouble. Not because a state turned against the United States.

"There's something else. Unconfirmed right now, but we've received intelligence that Travis has fallen."

"Travis Air Force Base?? You've got to be shitting me."

This was reaching a dire state. Travis Air Force Base was one of the U.S. military's biggest bases in California, handling more cargo and passengers than any other military air terminal within the United States. If both Travis and San Diego have fallen, America now finds itself in a world of shit.

Jessica felt bile rise in her throat.

"Eli... do they know about the other bases? Pendleton? Lemoore?"

"They're checking now. Everyone's scrambling. No one expected California to move this fast."

She turned toward the television. The image zoomed in. The *Harmon* had pulled away from the smoldering harbor and was drifting calmly into open waters, its deck cannons now idle. A strange, eerie stillness. Then a flash—another missile—arcing inland. An explosion lit up the eastern edge of the base.

Jessica whispered, "So it's war. It has found us."

"Yeah," Eli said. "And we're already behind."

* * *

TEXAS STAR TRIBUNE

"Dawnfire: California's First Strike"

By Jessica Parker – April 12, 2044 – Los Angeles Bureau

The war began not with a declaration, but with betrayal.

At 4:48 a.m. local time, the USS Harmon and USS Saratoga, guided missile destroyers still officially part of the United States Navy, turned their guns on Naval Base San Diego. The ships, now flying the California Republic flag, crippled radar and communications nodes in a coordinated assault.

Minutes later, California State Defense Forces—once the National Guard—moved on the base's outer perimeter. Reinforced by unknown armored elements from inland and a localized no-fly zone enforced by drone activity, the defenders were outmaneuvered before they understood what was happening.

This wasn't chaos. This was calculation. Executed with chilling precision.

In less than a few short hours, California had its first major victory—and the United States lost control of the largest naval installation west of the Mississippi. With unconfirmed reports that Travis Air Force Base is also among the fallen, we are witnessing the beginning of a long, drawn-out, bloody conflict.

A civil war, unspoken and unthinkable for so long, is now a reality. The enemy isn't foreign. It's us.

And it's only just begun.

Hours Earlier – USS Harmon

Lieutenant Commander Nathan Briggs's boots echoed on the steel deck as he strode between consoles in the cramped command center of the USS *Harmon*. The hum of generators filled the air, a constant reminder of the mechanical beast they controlled—a warship at the edge of mutiny. A Glock pistol dug into his side, now a required accessory because of the state of affairs.

Tension was alive around him. The usually tight-knit crew had fractured under the weight of a civil war. Since California's secession, many had found themselves opposing ideologies. Expanding beyond the boundaries of the *Harmon* and *Saratoga*, reaching every corner of the country. At the same time, some scoffed because... it's California.

Half remained fiercely loyal to the federal government, believing it could do no wrong with the right people in charge. The other half were worn down by years of perceived betrayal and isolation, now openly sympathizing with the rebels. The prevailing theory? Many had reached their breaking point with how society had turned so nasty; something had to change. A civil war? A catalyst to bring about change that would twist the fabric of everything within the confines of America.

Briggs stopped beside Captain Steve Landry, who stood rigid, staring at the radar screens flickering with blips—friendly and hostile alike.

"Sir," Briggs said in a low voice, taut with urgency, "the situation below deck is deteriorating. The crew is divided. If we don't act, the *Harmon* could become a floating powder keg."

Landry's jaw tightened, "I swore an oath to my country, Briggs. Mutiny on my ship is treason."

"Sir, the country you swore an oath to is already dead," Briggs countered, voice rough with fatigue. "We're pawns in a game that's already lost."

No more was spoken. Suddenly, Petty Officer Ramirez burst in, breathless, face flushed.

"Captain—it's worse than we thought. The loyalists are regrouping, but most have armed themselves and taken key stations. They're preparing to lock down the ship."

Briggs' pulse quickened. "How long before they reach the bridge?"

"Minutes. Maybe less."

Landry slammed a fist against the console. "We'll put down the mutiny with force."

Briggs shook his head. "Captain—"

The communication crackled, a harsh voice breaking through.

"*Captain Landry, this is Admiral Simmons. Your orders are unchanged: maintain the blockade. Engage hostile forces.*"

Landry's hand hovered over the comms switch. "Admiral, with respect, the crew has fractured. If we don't act, the *Harmon* will be lost like the *Saratoga*."

Silence on the line. Then, "*Maintain your orders. Reinforcements are en route.*"

Briggs' blood began to boil. If potential reinforcements reach the hull of either the *Harmon* or the *Saratoga*, the battle will be over before it ever began.

The line went dead. Briggs exchanged a grim look with Landry. "No reinforcements are coming. We are on our own."

"The hell we are. We are putting a stop to this right now!"

Briggs brought out his Glock, pointing it at his captain. "No sir, we aren't."

"What the hell do you think you are doing?"

"I am relieving you of command, sir. This ship is now a warship of rebellion."

Landry scoffed, as if what he just heard was from a comic book. All the crew on the bridge were stiff and motionless, scared to the point that all of them were shitting enough bricks to build the pyramids.

"We are moving to strike first. Disable the San Diego radar station. Open a path for the rebels. We can no longer hold the line for a broken government."

Landry's eyes burned. "This is mutiny."

"Or salvation."

The weight of command began pressing down on both of the ships' leaders. One was burning to be a savior of his state, while the other remained a loyal soldier.

"They will hang you by your balls."

"Maybe. I don't care anymore."

"What is your malfunction, you little worm?"

"Sir?"

"I'm the commander of this fucking ship!! You will obey my order—"

A gunshot rang out. Briggs, a trusted hand of Captain Landry and his XO, was now his murderer. Landry plowed into the deck, lifeless. Brigg's heavy breathing was the only thing heard on the bridge.

"God forgive me."

Briggs holstered. All he could do was stare. The body of his captain, his friend, lay on the deck motionless.

Briggs looked up, barked, "All hands: This is the XO. I have... Permanently relieved Captain Landry of his duties. Man battle stations! This ship is now a warship of rebellion!"

Chaos exploded. The ship's crew scrambled—a symphony of shouted commands, boots pounding, metal clanging. The loyalists rushed to man weapons, while mutineers secured key points, locked hatches, and disabled communications.

Briggs took the fire control station. His hands danced over controls, locking targeting systems onto the glowing dome of the radar installation nestled in the harbor.

"Missiles locked, sir. Awaiting fire authorization."

"Fire," Briggs commanded.

The launch tubes erupted, hurling a salvo of Tomahawk missiles into the morning sky.

Briggs watched through the targeting scope as the missiles arced, streaking like comets before detonating in fiery blossoms against the radar dome.

Explosions shredded the night, sending showers of molten metal and sparks raining down. The base erupted in alarms and chaos. Searchlights swirled, spotlighting the dark silhouette of the mutinous warship retreating into the waves.

Gunfire erupted from the government vessels responding to the attack. USS *Harmon*'s deck shook under incoming fire.

"Brace for impact!" Briggs shouted.

Explosions rocked the ship as laser cannons slammed into the hull. Crew screamed, some thrown off balance by the concussive blasts.

Briggs gritted his teeth, issuing orders. "Damage control teams to sectors three and seven. Fire teams to repel boarders. Keep weapons hot!"

Below deck, enlisted sailors struggled to contain fires. Their goal was to seal ruptured bulkheads, which they did efficiently. The U.S. Navy trains for these scenarios every waking moment, and the first real test showed that it could be passed with flying colors. Tending to the wounded was another priority once repairs were complete, as many found themselves bloodied from the damage.

A young gunner's mate, Petty Officer Jenkins, shouted over the din, "Sir! They're trying to board the starboard side!"

Briggs grabbed his Glock and joined the firefight. The smoke thickened, burning his eyes and lungs. Explosions tore through the hull, buckling steel plates. Amid the inferno, Briggs locked eyes with a mutineer squad leader, both knowing this battle was as much about ideology as survival.

Soon, minutes bled into hours. Attacks were repelled, but how many more would there be?

"*Saratoga* to *Harmon*!"

Briggs made his way to the Communication Station. "*Harmon* here."

"*Retreat from the base with haste! We will cover your retreat!*"

"I don't understand."

"*We are blowing the base sky high. There is little chance of our escape. Leave and make way north!*"

Briggs hesitated. Blowing the base with everything they had meant that this was now a suicide charge, leaving as much damage as possible. But with *Harmon* in dire shape and many crew members dead, he had little choice.

"Understood. Godspeed *Saratoga*."

And so, the USS *Harmon* slipped into the dark of the Pacific, bearing scars of fire and betrayal. Briggs rushed to get binoculars and made his way to a glass to watch. All he could see was the *Saratoga* firing a barrage of missiles.

Explosions lit up the dawn. The *Saratoga*, true to its word, leveled Naval Base San Diego. Soon, nothing was left standing.

Briggs watched with horror as the *Saratoga* was hit with several missiles, causing it to become a fireball in the water. Soon, nothing was left of her, at least nothing Briggs could observe.

Briggs exhaled, voice raw. "We've changed the game. Now, we fight for our future—and our freedom."

* * *

TEXAS STAR TRIBUNE

"From the Front Lines: Inside the Rebel Struggle Against the West Coast Blockade."

By Jessica Parker – October 26, 2045

The desert sun hangs low over the cracked earth just south of Tucson. I sit beside Corporal Maya Torres, her face streaked with dirt and sweat, eyes scanning the horizon through a pair of battered binoculars. Around us, the ragtag division moves urgently, digging in, watching, waiting.

The President's blockade has tightened the noose. The U.S. Navy's warships encircle the western coastline, cutting off ports and choking supply lines. It's a military siege born from fear: a federal attempt to strangle the breakaway West Coast Alliance.

But the rebellion has survived by adapting. Despite losing the USS Harmon just a month ago, supplies have reached the rebels. They flow south to north, slipping through the porous Mexican border. Here, foreign powers quietly tip the scales—Chinese freighters, laden with weapons and medical supplies, dock in secret bays along the Baja Peninsula. From there, trucks and convoys traverse deserts and mountains, evading patrols and drones to feed the insurgent fighters.

The local cartel, tangled in this new war economy, plays both sides but mostly with survival. They provide safe passage for weapons shipments in exchange for currency and resources.

I asked Maya how the fighters feel about this foreign involvement.

"It's complicated," she said, voice low and steady. "Some of us hate it—we don't want our fight to be someone else's proxy war. But right now, it's life or death. We take what we can get. We're not proud, just desperate."

Nearby, Sergeant Connor Mendoza, a former paramedic turned insurgent, adds, "We're all caught in a chess game bigger than us. Foreign powers, cartels, the government... but we're the ones paying with blood."

The men and women around me embody exhaustion and resolve. Their faces are young, hardened by months of skirmishes, ration shortages, and the constant hum of drones overhead. They trade jokes in moments between patrols, but their eyes never lose that wary edge.

"This is not a war of heroes," Maya says. "It's a war of survivors."

At night, the skies light up with tracer rounds and distant explosions—the fight never fully sleeps. Communications buzz with updates on federal patrols intercepted or supply runs successful.

The blockade's effect is brutal: hospitals run short of antibiotics, food scarcity hits cities under rebel control, and morale wavers. But the alliance's leadership remains firm, betting on prolonged attrition and international pressure.

Behind me, a platoon prepares to move out on a supply run under the cover of darkness. I pack my gear, knowing that tomorrow I will follow—bearing witness to a conflict reshaping the nation.

Blockade Impact – Quick Facts

Naval Assets: *Over 40 U.S. Navy vessels, including Arleigh Burke-class destroyers, cruisers, and support ships, form a ring along the West Coast to enforce the blockade. Rebel mutinies have occurred on several ships, but have had minimal impact.*

Supply Interdictions: *Federal forces report intercepting an estimated 65% of unauthorized cargo shipments into California, Oregon, and Washington since early February of 2045.*

Humanitarian Toll: *Rebel-controlled cities report food and medicine shortages affecting over 3 million civilians. Local clinics operate on rationed supplies, with mortality rates increasing.*

Foreign Aid: *Unconfirmed intelligence suggests Chinese freighters deliver military-grade supplies to covert ports in Baja California, bypassing official sanctions.*

Government Statement

A spokesperson for the Department of Defense issued the following statement:

"The United States government denies all allegations of foreign assistance to the so-called West Coast Alliance. Our naval blockade is strictly enforced to prevent illegal smuggling and protect national security. Any claims of foreign involvement are unfounded and politically motivated."

November 22, 2045 – Rebel camp near Lake Tahoe, California

The camp was a sprawl of makeshift tents, tarps, and battered vehicles, nestled in a ragged valley surrounded by parched hills that shimmered in the afternoon heat. Dust curled up in the footsteps of soldiers moving between ration trucks, med tents, tanks, AH-64 helicopters, and radios barking static-filled orders.

Jessica Parker treaded carefully along the uneven dirt paths, her boots kicking up little clouds of sand. She pulled her jacket tighter against a dry wind that smelled faintly of gunpowder and burnt brush. Around her, men and women in worn fatigues carried scars—both visible and hidden—reminders of battles fought and lost. The hum of conversation was low but constant; some voices cracked with exhaustion, others with hope.

She paused near a group gathered around a small fire, watching as a young medic gently dressed a soldier's bleeding arm. The air was tense but alive with a raw sense of purpose. Cameras and notepads in her bag felt heavy—reminders that she was both observer and part of this war. As she passed, chatter and rumors buzzed in her ears.

"It seems we have captured Seattle."

"Not that it means anything. The government has retaken many of the bases we took in the initial assaults."

"Not Travis. The government launched a commando air raid yesterday. Word is it failed."

"Oh shit."

Jessica's phone buzzed sharply in her pocket. She pulled it out with a sinking feeling. The screen flashed a message from an unknown number.

"*Operation Phoenix has failed. Mitch Parker MIA, presumed KIA.*"

Her breath caught. She stared at the words, as if a tunnel had formed around them. Her heart pounded out of her chest. Then her phone rang—Daniel's name flashing urgently.

She answered, voice trembling, "Daniel?"

His voice was strained, low. "Jess... I'm sorry. Mitch... he was killed during a commando raid on Travis Air Force Base. The assault failed... many didn't make it back."

Jessica's world narrowed. Sounds from the camp dimmed to a distant murmur. Her hands gripped the phone tighter as tears burned behind her eyes.

"No," she whispered. "My baby boy... he can't be..."

Daniel's voice cracked. "I'm so sorry, Jess."

She stumbled backward, nearly dropping the phone. The dry earth felt like it was shifting beneath her feet. Jessica's knees became so numb that she didn't realize she had fallen to the ground. Her voice let out a blood-curdling scream of agony, yet was silent in the world.

Around her, life went on. Soldiers marched past. Orders barked through radios. But for Jessica Parker, everything had changed in an instant.

* * *

Jessica lowered herself onto the rough wooden crate, the grain pressing uncomfortably against her skin, but she didn't care. The camp's noise faded to a dull roar behind her heart pounding. The late afternoon sun cast a bruised orange glow over the valley, the shadows lengthening like fingers clawing at the earth.

Her fingers trembled as she opened the devastating message on her phone again, tracing the words with disbelief: *Mitch Parker MIA, presumed KIA*.

She swallowed hard, holding back the tightness in her throat that threatened to choke her. Years spent chasing stories of death and destruction had forged a shield around her, but now, facing the loss of her own blood, that shield shattered like glass.

None of the warnings, the grim reports from the frontlines, prepared her for this. She could almost hear Mitch's stubborn and fiery voice telling her he'd be fine and that he was fighting for something worth dying for. But the cruel silence that followed was deafening.

The wind tugged at her jacket, scattering loose strands of auburn hair across her face. She brushed them away absently, eyes fixed on a patch of cracked dirt at her feet. The dust swirled in lazy spirals, indifferent to the storm inside her. For a long moment, she let herself break—a silent surrender to the grief that pressed down like a stone on her chest. Then, a soft voice cut through the quiet.

"Ma'am?"

Jessica blinked, her tear-blurred eyes lifting to meet the gaze of a young soldier standing nearby. His uniform was caked with dust and sweat, his face drawn but steady.

"I'm sorry about your son," he said quietly, his voice carrying the hard edge of experience tempered with genuine sympathy.

She blinked back the sting, swallowing the lump that rose in her throat. "Thank you," she whispered, voice barely audible.

He took a slow breath, sitting beside her on the crate, careful not to crowd her space. Around them, the camp carried on—the distant clatter of vehicles, murmured orders, and the low drone of generators powering radios.

"War doesn't care who it takes," he said, voice low but certain. "You lose people. You keep moving because if you don't, it takes you, too."

Jessica's gaze dropped to her shaking hands, clasped tightly together. "It's... so goddamn unfair," she confessed, the rawness in her voice breaking through the professional armor she always wore.

He nodded slowly. "It seems like life is unfair, just because. Ain't war hell? It doesn't wait, doesn't pity. But it also shows who's still standing when the smoke clears."

She inhaled deeply, the words sinking into her like a bitter truth she needed to accept. The boy she loved was gone. The war was far from over. And she had a truth to uncover—the unvarnished, brutal truth.

"Thanks," she said again, voice steadier now.

He stood, giving her a respectful nod before disappearing back into the shadows of the camp. Jessica stayed seated a moment longer, watching the sun bleed over the hills. Whatever came next, she'd face it head-on because someone had to.

I didn't even get his name. Was he... an angel?

* * *

"A Rising Tide: China's Shadow Over the Western Rebellion"

By Jessica Parker, Global Affairs Correspondent – May 7, 2046

Two years have passed since the first shots rang out on Market Street in Los Angeles. What began as a fractured protest has spiraled into a fractured nation. The West Coast Alliance, spearheaded by California, Oregon, and Washington, has not only declared independence but secured foreign backing that has alarmed Washington and reshaped this conflict into an international powder keg.

Sources confirm the Chinese People's Liberation Navy has established clandestine supply routes through Mexico and the Pacific, delivering arms, medical supplies, and strategic advisors to the rebel forces. Satellite imagery and intercepted communications reveal a network of offshore vessels and underground convoys, facilitating a near-complete blockade run of the West Coast ports.

This alliance has turned a domestic civil war into a proxy battleground, with China keen to weaken American federal power while securing influence over the resource-rich Pacific states. The strategic calculus is brutal: support the rebels, erode U.S. control, and gain a foothold in the Western hemisphere.

The consequences are profound. The U.S. federal government's efforts to maintain control have become increasingly desperate and militarized, sparking fears of escalation. Already, the blockade chokes off vital supplies to the rest of the country, while Washington's rhetoric grows harsher by the day.

Rumors circulating in D.C. circles include an even more terrifying reality in the complexity of this war... Chinese troops on American soil. Time will tell if this fear becomes a reality.

June 10, 2046 – Rebel Camp Near Fresno, California

I want a hot shower... I want a fresh-baked apple pie, even if it's out of a damn can. Jessica's boots crunched against the rocky California soil as she moved cautiously through the rebel encampment, having returned to California after spending the last month entrenched with the 22nd Airborne Division of the *West Coast Alliance*. She found herself in harm's way several times over several days, encountering heavy aerial attacks while wandering the streets of an abandoned Seattle.

Stalemate. That is where the war has found itself.

The late afternoon sun cast long, distorted shadows across the dusty tents and makeshift barricades. The air, usually dry and sharp with sagebrush, now tasted of smoke and something metallic—like blood and fire had seeped into the earth.

Her camera hung heavy around her neck, but it felt like a lifeline. She'd traveled up and down the three states to tell a story about rebellion, fractured lives, and hope in the chaos. But this—this was beyond any story she'd imagined.

I want... home. My boys...

The weight of the war began to feel heavy on Jessica's shoulders. She had not seen Texas since she left for Los Angeles on that fateful day. Constant changes in the situation on the ground kept her on the move. Death and destruction had not slowed down as the government had hoped, with casualties reaching over hundreds of thousands. But in the thick fog of war, no one truly was sure how many had been lost.

Her phone buzzed as she walked. A text from Eli, her White House source and reluctant confidant.

"*Take cover, Jessica. It's happening now.*"

Odd.. What does that mea... She had no time to reply.

The unthinkable. It happened.

A distant flash, a burst of light brighter than the desert sun. the ground beneath her trembled—a slow, rolling pulse that grew into a deep rumble like the roar of a waking beast. Her breath caught.

She turned just in time to see it—the terrifying bloom of a mushroom cloud, rising like a monstrous, poisonous flower over the western horizon. The sky above the Pacific Coast was swallowed in an angry swirl of orange and gray.

Jessica's fingers scrambled for her camera. She captured the plume, her lens zooming in on the apocalyptic bloom that no photograph could ever truly capture.

Around her, the camp froze. Soldiers and civilians alike stared skyward, their faces pale and stunned. A man with a lined face and shaking hands whispered, "They did it. Those sons of bitches actually did it."

Jessica felt a wave of nausea; the heat from the blast enveloped the city, yet her skin burned. She looked down at her hands, suddenly realizing they trembled—not from cold, but from a primal, shaking fear. Around her, soldiers and civilians cry out.

"Where did that land??"

"That looks like... It's Sacramento!"

"A nuclear warhead on the Capitol??"

"God help us."

A young rebel approached her quietly; his eyes were shadowed with exhaustion and resolve. "You're that reporter, aren't you? The one recently with the 22nd Airborne? You need to tell the world exactly just what the fuck happened."

She nodded, swallowing hard, voice thick. "I will tell it. All of it."

Behind her, a child cried softly beneath a threadbare tarp. Jessica's heart clenched. This was no longer a distant war. This was their lives—burning, shattered, lost. A nuclear warhead. Used by Americans, against America. A chain reaction that could destroy the entire world.

As evening fell, the camp buzzed with tense energy. Radios crackled with fragmented news: fallout spreading, emergency shelters opening, curfews enforced, troops mobilizing.

Jessica sat near a dying fire, the darkening sky streaked with ash and stars—each one a fragile beacon in a night drenched with despair. Her laptop rested on her knees. Her fingers flew over the keys, pouring out words she struggled to say aloud:

"The Day the Union Burned: Nuclear Fire and the Fracturing of a Nation"

By Jessica Parker, Global Affairs Correspondent – June 11, 2046

Today, the sky shattered. A flash of blinding light, a roar that shook the very soul of this fractured country, and a mushroom cloud that marks the end of one America—and the terrifying birth of another.

The President's order was meant to stop a war already tearing us apart. But it has ignited a fury that will burn for generations.

This is not a battle of armies. It is a war on our very existence, oh our humanity. We stand on the precipice of a new dark age—where no one is safe, where trust is a relic, and where the question remains: what is left to fight for?

Ain't war hell?

She stopped typing and stared into the flickering flames, the bitter weight of those words settling in her chest.

Nearby, a weary soldier sat beside her, pulling his jacket tighter around his thin frame. He looked at her with tired eyes. "Pardon me, ma'am."

"No, it's okay."

"How are you holding up?"

"Like everyone else, just existing and moving."

"Can't say I blame you. No one was ready for what came. But we keep moving. Because if we don't, it's the end of everything. The war won't end here, trust me, you'll see."

Jessica nodded, swallowing back tears she refused to let fall. Her camera lay beside her, the lifeline that had also become weary. A silent witness to the darkness settling over a country on fire.

March 31, 2054 – Arlington Cemetery – Washington, D.C.

The morning air was sharp, biting into Jessica Parker's skin as she stood among the crowd gathered beneath the gray, oppressive sky. The wind clawed at her long, silver-streaked hair, whipping loose strands across her face. She brushed them away with a stiff hand, her fingers trembling slightly despite her efforts to remain composed.

The cemetery on the outskirts of Washington, D.C., was filled with soldiers in pristine uniforms, their faces a mix of solemn respect and shared grief. Family members clung to one another, some weeping openly, others staring blankly at the flag-draped casket resting on the platform before them. Arlington has carried many generations of soldiers. And now on this day, it held the next.

Jessica's lips pressed into a hard line. No tears came. Years of witnessing death—her loved ones and others—had forged a coldness around her heart, a brittle shell of survival. She felt detached, like a ghost wandering through a nightmare she couldn't wake from.

The bugle's mournful call—"Taps"—cut through the stillness, its notes hovering in the chill air like the sigh of a dying breath. Jessica closed her eyes momentarily, recalling the countless funerals she had covered as a reporter. But this one was different. This one was personal.

The sergeant stepped forward with deliberate reverence, folding the flag with practiced hands. He approached Jessica slowly, his eyes kind but burdened.

"On behalf of a grateful nation," he intoned, voice low yet steady, "we present this flag to the family of Lieutenant Daniel Parker, Continental Defense Force, killed in action. I'm sorry for your loss."

Jessica's fingers brushed the fabric as it was placed in her hands. The weight was heavier than she expected. The rough weave of the cloth bit into her palms—a physical reminder of the loss she carried. Around her, the world seemed to slow: the muted rustle of uniforms, the distant sobs of strangers, the faint scent of damp earth and pine. Her breathing became shallow, the sound of her heartbeat thudding in her ears like war drums.

She glanced down at the flag. Red, white, and blue now stained with dirt and the pain of sacrifice. The flag that had once wrapped around her husband's shoulders in life was now shroud marking his absence.

Memories crashed over her: Daniel's laugh, the warmth of his hands in hers; the night the phone call came, shattering her world; the endless nights of waiting and fearing. The war had taken him—like it had taken so many others—leaving a void that swallowed light.

She gripped the flag tighter, her knuckles whitening. Her legs felt weak, but she forced herself to stand taller, face the crowd, and bear witness to the final honor.

The ceremony concluded. Soldiers saluted, the band played a dirge, and the crowd slowly dispersed. Jessica remained rooted, clutching the flag as if it were the last piece of Daniel left in the world. Minutes passed like hours. The wind grew colder. Her eyes scanned the emptying field, catching glimpses of grieving families retreating to the warmth of their cars, of uniforms melting into the distance.

At last, the heaviness became unbearable. The flag slipped from her fingers, unfurling gently onto the damp grass. The stars and stripes lay still, a silent testament to love, loss, and the cost of war. Jessica turned away without looking back. Each step was heavy, dragging the weight of grief behind her like a shadow.

Her mind was a tangle of numbness and rage. *Ain't war hell?* she thought bitterly, the phrase echoing hollowly inside her. She hated everyone who'd cause this—her son who had fought and died at the beginning, her husband who had also died, the generals who'd let it come to this. She swallowed hard, pushing the storm of emotions deep down where no one could see. The world demanded she be strong, but inside, she felt nothing but a cold, aching emptiness. As she walked toward her car, the wind carried the faint sound of taps once more, a ghostly echo lingering behind her.

April 3, 2054 – Somewhere in Washington, D.C.

The evening sun had barely cracked the horizon as Jessica sat alone in the backseat of the black sedan, the city slowly walking around her. Outside the window, buildings blurred past in a dull grey rush—monuments to a capital city that had changed as much as the nation itself. Her reflection caught in the glass: silver hair streaked with tired lines, eyes sharp but shadowed with exhaustion. The years of war had carved themselves into her face, an unspoken map of every loss and every sacrifice.

Her hands rested on the worn leather purse in her lap. Inside, notes for the interview, a recorder, her old press badge—relics of a life spent chasing stories, now moments away from confronting one of the most powerful men in the country. She flexed her fingers, trying to steady the nerves coiling in her stomach. Memories bubble unbidden: the funeral where the flag fell from her hands, the call about Mitch, the nights watching the world burn on her screens.

Daniel's voice echoed softly in her mind, a fading warmth in the cold. The weight of years pressed heavy on her chest.

The car slid into traffic, the driver skillfully weaving between early commuters. Jessica closed her eyes briefly and breathed deep, centering herself.

This is it.

The General. The man who had led the Continental Defense Force to victory, the one whose shadow loomed over the nation's fragile peace. The man who, behind closed doors, would soon become something more than just a commander. Her contact at the network had warned her—this wouldn't be just an interview. It was a reckoning.

The car pulled into the press briefing building, glass towers gleaming with sterile authority. She felt the eyes of unseen watchers, the weight of history waiting.

Inside the waiting room, the makeup artist and sound engineer buzzed around her, touching up gray streaks, adjusting microphones, smoothing creases in her jacket. They chatted lightly, but Jessica heard only the roar of her thoughts.

How does one face this man? The one who cost you everything you had left?

Her phone buzzed. A message from Sebastian: "*Dinner later? We need to talk.*"

She stared at the screen, the knot in her gut tightening. Her only surviving son, who had managed to avoid the worst, had made his way to D.C. This was bigger than a family reunion. This was an attempt to salvage all that was left. An uncertain future within a country still healing scars deep as graves.

The assistant producer called out: "We're live in ten minutes. The General will be here in two."

Jessica sat motionless, not answering, steeling herself as she looked toward the door. The next chapter was about to begin.

The studio lights glared down, sharp and unrelenting, as Jessica faced the man who had torn what was left of the country apart and led the Continental Defense Force to wrest control from a government that had betrayed its people. The General sat opposite her, impeccably dressed, his posture rigid with the weight of command—and beneath it all, a deeply rooted faith that shaped his every word.

Jessica's voice was steady but laced with years of anguish. "General, you led an uprising against a government that ordered nuclear strikes on American soil—strikes that devastated millions, including my own family. How do you justify taking up arms and plunging the nation into civil war?"

The General's eyes, steely and resolute, bore into her. "The government's choice was unforgivable. It turned its weapons on its citizens. That act of betrayal tore the nation's soul apart. When law and leadership fail, it falls to men of conviction to restore order, justice, and righteousness."

Jessica's chest tightened, memories crashing in. *The President's orders. The mushroom clouds. Mitch gone. Daniel lost in battle.* She fought to keep her composure.

"But you didn't just react—you led a movement that forced the country into a near decade of bloodshed. How does one reconcile that with the faith you say guides you?"

The General's face softened, touched by a quiet sorrow. "Faith is not blind obedience—it is the compass that steers through darkness. I believe God allowed this trial to purify our nation's sins. The old order was corrupt, immoral, and broken beyond repair. Our rebellion was a divine mandate to rebuild."

Jessica swallowed. *Divine mandate. A cloak for war and death.*

"Millions died because of that 'mandate,' General. My son died on the front lines, before your rise. My husband was also lost, fighting for your cause. How do you live with that?"

He clasped his hands, voice steady. "I do not glorify death. I mourn every loss. But I carry the burden that we fought to save the soul of this country. Without conviction, there is only chaos. Without sacrifice, no redemption."

Jessica's mind flickered to Mitch's last letter, the fear in his words, the hope that this nightmare would end. "You speak of sacrifice and redemption, but what of those who never chose this war—who just wanted to live in peace?"

"The innocent suffer because the world is fallen. Yet, through suffering comes renewal. We rebuilt from the ashes with faith as our foundation. That is why I continue to serve—to guide this nation toward a future where righteousness prevails."

Jessica leaned forward, voice cold. "And what of your righteousness? When you kneel in prayer, do you seek forgiveness for the pain you helped unleash?"

He smiled faintly, unyielding. "I seek strength and clarity. I am no stranger to guilt. But I believe what we did was what we had to do—one that many could not see at the time."

The room felt heavy with the weight of their shared losses and irreconcilable truths. Jessica's eyes burned with the fire of grief and defiance, unmoved by what she heard.

"This isn't over, General. Not while many will resist your 'higher calling.'"

He stood, calm and commanding. "Then they will remember well, for the new America is built on the blood and faith of those who dared to fight."

The cameras cut. Silence settled.

Jessica sat back, the exhausted weight of a decade of war settled deep inside. The nation had been shattered, rebuilt, and forever changed. The interview was over—but the reckoning was just beginning.

April 5, 2054 – U.S. Capitol – Washington, D.C.

The morning air was crisp but carried a softness beneath the sharp edge of early spring. Jessica Parker stood beneath the sprawling canopy of cherry blossoms just outside the Capitol grounds. Pale pink petals fluttered around her like whispered confessions from a world healing itself. The petals caught the sunlight, shimmering like delicate fragments of hope on the breeze.

She inhaled deeply, letting the floral scent mingle with the faint metallic tang of spring rain on stone. The city around her was waking—the distant murmur of voices, the shuffle of footsteps on cobblestones, the occasional clip of heels striking pavement. Washington, D.C. was a city reborn, yet still heavy with its scars.

Jessica's gaze drifted upward, her eyes tracing the delicate branches swaying in the light wind. Each blossom is a tender promise: each petal, a memory falling away. Her silver hair, streaked now with years of grief and endurance, caught the morning light, softening the lines etched deep by war, loss, and relentless nights spent chasing truths. She felt the cool kiss of the breeze on her weathered skin, the subtle ache of bones tired beyond their years.

Behind her, the Capitol dome loomed, regal and resolute, draped in banners and flags. A crowd gathered on the steps—dignitaries, soldiers, citizens—all awaiting the dawn of a new government. The low hum of hushed conversation rippled like a tide, punctuated by the crisp rustle of paper programs and the distant call of a ceremonial bugle.

Jessica let her eyes wander across the sea of faces—hopeful, anxious, resolute. But she did not join their gaze. Instead, she felt the quiet hollow inside, the ache of a decade's worth of war and fractured families pressing down like the weight of these petals on the stone beneath her feet.

A soft voice broke through the stillness.

"Mom."

She turned slowly.

Sebastian stepped into the light, his presence steady and grounding. His dark eyes—older now, haunted yet resolute—searched hers with a mixture of tenderness and shared pain. His wife and two small children lingered just behind, shy but curious, wrapped in scarves and coats against the spring chill.

Jessica's heart caught, a sudden constriction that made her breath hitch. Years of silence, fractured conversations, and now here he was, real and tangible, standing with the family she'd fought to protect.

She stepped forward, folding her hands around his weathered ones, feeling the rough calluses, the quiet strength. His touch spoke of survival, of resilience—a testament to the battles neither of them had fully escaped.

"I... Uh... I am sorry I'm late. I went to see Dad... seemed so peaceful there." Sebastian's voice was gentle, hesitant, as if afraid to open wounds that still bled beneath the surface.

Jessica's throat tightened. She looked down at the petals falling to the ground, the colors changing to red, white and blue. "We had our troubles, but I loved your father. He was a good man. A healer in the worst of times." Her voice was low, almost a whisper, carrying the weight of all the nights spent grieving in motel rooms, the quiet prayers, and a final goodbye she never gave.

Sebastian's eyes glistened. "And Mitch," he said softly, his voice cracking just enough to reveal the depth of loss. "We all miss him."

A bitter, weary smile brushed Jessica's lips. "Too young to understand fully. But he wanted to serve. Fight for something worth fighting for."

They stood side by side, the delicate fall of cherry blossoms like slow tears drifting down, marking time and memory alike. Around them, the world moved forward, yet in this quiet moment, time felt suspended—a delicate bubble protecting grief and love.

"I'm thinking of retiring," Jessica finally said, her eyes distant. "Far from all of this. North Dakota. A place that may be cold as shit, but where the wind blows clean and the past can't reach."

Sebastian nodded slowly, a softness spreading through his face. "I'm coming with you. The family needs that—a fresh start. Something untouched by the war's shadow."

Jessica's lips curved in a tired, genuine smile. "It's time to heal."

They held each other's gaze for a long moment—a shared vow spoken without words. The unbreakable bond of mother and son, forged in fire and tempered by loss. Sebastian ran into his mother's arms, seeking her warmth.

"I love you, Mom."

"I love you, sweetie."

Behind them, the crowd's murmurs rose, signaling the next chapter of a nation reborn. The distant sound of a gavel echoed, firm and solemn. Jessica didn't turn to watch the ceremony. Some truths were better left veiled for now.

Together, she and Sebastian stepped away beneath the canopy of blossoms—petals swirling at their feet like whispered promises.

A new beginning, soft as spring's first bloom.

II.

No Higher Ground

Remember, remember the Fifth of November, Gunpowder, treason and plot. I know of no reason why gunpowder treason should ever be forgot.

November 4, 2049 – Tampa, Florida

The cigar burned slowly in his left hand, trailing a thin plume of smoke into the muggy Tampa air. General Nathaniel Rusk stood on the weathered stone terrace overlooking Hillsborough Bay, the Gulf stretching far beyond it in dusky silence. Below, palm fronds rustled against the wind like restless sabers. The waters were calm, but the continent wasn't. Not anymore.

He exhaled slowly, the smoke rising and dissipating before the breeze carried it away. From this vantage point—just outside MacDill Air Force Base—you could almost pretend the world was at peace. The sun had long faded, disappearing just several hours ago. The shadows of streetlamps over concrete walkways and guard towers now bore the markings of the Continental Defense Force.

But the world was already broken.

Behind him, the thick glass doors slid open with a hiss. The boots came first—four distinct rhythms, all familiar.

"Sir," said Major Derek Ellison, stepping out with a tablet under one arm. "We're five percent into the reporting. They're saying turnout is 'historic.' Whatever that means now."

Rusk didn't turn. "Still pretending the whole damn map is united, I bet."

Ellison glanced over the tablet. "So far, yes. Ohio, Michigan, and Pennsylvania—solid government tallies. Georgia's back under 'federal stabilization protocol.' They're claiming a ninety-two percent turnout in Atlanta. Probably more votes than people."

What a load of shit. Rusk couldn't help but squirm at the politics the United States was playing. Since the nuclear fallout, the *West Coast Alliance* hadn't collapsed as they had hoped. While it kept foreign powers from going near the coasts, it created a vacuum within the country's borders. So, what do you do if you are the government? Simple, you create an illusion of unity behind your decisions. But that was not the case with most Americans, as many found themselves rallying to a newfound army ready to bring down the ones who held the keys to the apocalypse.

A low chuckle came from Colonel Benjamin Beauchamp as he stepped out onto the terrace with his coffee. "You know that old clichéd saying that democracy dies in darkness? Didn't expect it to be broadcast in 4K, with the old song and dance used before the dark times."

Rusk took another drag from the cigar. "They want the illusion. Lullaby the country back into the slumber it has been in since the 1950s. Makes the coming crackdown feel like the righteous cleanup instead of what it is."

The peaceful discussion night soon ended for them—the rest of the war council began to filter in. General Douglas Tavares, recently transferred from Missouri, took his place by the map console inside. Captain Edwin Rawls brought the updated satellite prints. All eyes were on the main screen inside the briefing room, visible through the glass behind Rusk. CNN's polished anchors were smiling too much for a country with two capitals and three armies.

One of the anchors adjusted his earpiece. "We're now getting reports of vote glitches in Tallahassee, Jacksonville, and Mobile—though election officials assure us that these are minor and do not affect the integrity of the count..."

The audio cut abruptly as Tavares muted the feed. "Enough of this shit."

Rusk finally turned. His face was lined but not defeated, his uniform crisp but worn at the edges, much like the country he now fought for. He tossed the finished cigar into a nearby ashtray and stepped inside, Beauchamp and Ellison following behind, shutting the glass door.

"Let's talk reality," he said. "We're past the point where votes matter. What matters now is movement. Where are they sending troops?"

Ellison tapped the tablet and brought up a topographical heat map. "Increased rail and air traffic from South Carolina to the Florida border. Satellite confirms armored convoys outside Valdosta. We believe they're preparing for a push to split the state—cut us off from the rest of the country, our corridor to the western forces."

It was a risky gambit, but the government's move was revealing: Decapitate the command center for the Continental Defense Force and essentially eliminate the bigger threat. Florida played a vital role in the war, as its connection to the states and sea made its location more valuable than any other state.

Beauchamp stepped forward. "It's a classic vice. If they seize Tallahassee and Gainesville, they can choke the supply lines to the panhandle and destabilize the Gulf Command. It's an obvious play."

One that should not have been possible, Rusk considered. Georgia has been a disputed territory since the fallout. While secededing from the government officially, there had been so much chaos within the significant cities that both sides made claims to the land... The government had successfully pushed across the state thanks to control of Atlanta. While going for Florida was the goal, it entailed risk. Alabama, Louisiana, Mississippi, Missouri, Kentucky, Tennessee, South Carolina, North Carolina, Arkansas, Oklahoma, and Texas seceded and were part of the Continental Defense Force. The government's push, in any direction south, was essentially surrounded.

This was not about retaking the states, but to take out what controlled the rebellion and render them headless.

Rusk nodded. "Obvious doesn't mean that it won't work."

He stepped over to the digital map, hands clasping behind his back. "We'll reinforce Tallahassee—quietly. I want two divisions in the tree line west of I-75. No tanks. No aircraft. Just boots, AT weapons, and enough camouflage to make them ghosts."

Tavares raised a brow. "You're baiting them?"

"I'm giving them a tempting gap," Rusk said. "They're counting on a weak link at the center. Let them think they're breaking through and then close the gate. Hard. Let them eat pincer."

The good old-fashioned pincer movement. Something that the Russian Federation perfected in its war against Ukraine.

Ellison swiped the map again. "And Kentucky?"

Rusk paused, eyes narrowing. "That's the real war."

He tapped the map just north of Lexington, near the bluegrass valleys.

"We're not just holding ground anymore. We're preparing to advance. Once the winter muds dry, we move."

Two sides, same strategy. Make a play for a move on each other's capital. Rusk counted on the government's stubbornness to believe the rebels could not mount an offensive. Washington, D.C. was the most protected place in the world; what hope was there to break through? Rusk had a plan, but no one knew what card he would play in this hand.

Beauchamp looked grim. "They'll expect us to stay defensive."

"That's why we won't," Rusk said. "Lexington is the keystone. Take it, and we sever the spine of their Midwestern command. From there, we can force the Mississippi line or even push through West Virginia if necessary. But we hold back until Tallahassee is secured."

Silence followed—measured, thoughtful. Even the hum of the monitors seemed too dull for a moment.

Then Tavares spoke. "There's another problem—the media. The optics don't look appeasing to American eyes. They're building a narrative already—that our states are being 'liberated,' that the election shows people still support D.C."

And that was partially true. The entire northeastern states declared their firm and unwavering support of the government. This was unsurprising to most, as states like New York had always been a thorn in the side of any rebellion.

Rusk stepped closer to the window, eyes tracing the Florida horizon.

"The blind will always follow deception. They think words can fix what bullets broke."

He turned, and his voice lowered.

"People believe in what they see. Believe in the basic necessities of life. Those words thrown around, 'Safety and Security,' they know deep down, they want a country that won't send their boys to bomb their cousins."

He pointed to the screen behind them, where the election map blinked and shifted like a slot machine.

"They can have this staged dog-and-pony shitshow. Come morning, I want every forward unit at readiness."

Ellison stood straighter. "We'll issue the orders tonight, sir."

Rusk nodded, picking up another cigar but not lighting it.

"One more thing," he said. "think about this... Tomorrow is November the fifth."

Beauchamp smirked. "Fitting."

Rusk looked down at the unlit cigar, then back at the map. "Ironic. Four hundred years ago, someone tried to burn down a government for lying to its people. Yet its legacy was its failure."

He tucked the cigar into his breast pocket and looked each officer in the eye.

"We won't fail. Thank you, gentlemen."

January 2, 2050 – Lexington, Kentucky

The land outside Lexington was quiet the morning General Nathaniel Rusk arrived. Low fog clung to the pastureland like breath on cold glass. Cows stood silent beside fences coated with frost. The bluegrass rolled in long undulations toward the horizon, stretching over fields that would, in a matter of weeks, be churned beneath tank treads and soaked in the blood of Americans on both sides.

From the top of the ridgeline where the convoy paused, Rusk stepped out of the Humvee and took a long breath of the Kentucky air. It smelled like tilled earth and damp wood—peaceful. He hated it.

Because peace didn't last. Not here. Not now.

Behind him, a major from the 7th Kentucky Infantry stood at attention, shivering slightly in his camo fatigues. "Sir, your CP is set up about two miles southeast. Forward command is holding the high ground, but we expect another probe by the 3rd Federal Armored within the week."

Rusk didn't answer right away. He had a habit of letting silence do the talking, the way one might let a pack of dogs feel the space before deciding who was the alpha. The major tensed. Rusk finally pulled out a cigar, lighting it.

"Let them probe," he said, smoke curling from his lips. "They're too cautious. They'll feel us out another dozen times before they get the balls to commit."

The major relaxed slightly. "Understood."

"That doesn't mean you don't keep an eye on those sneaky fuckers."

"Yes, sir."

"All right. Let's move out."

The convoy continued downhill.

***

The temporary headquarters had been erected inside a shuttered elementary school just outside the city. Chalkboards still held faded cursive from years ago. The gymnasium was now a war room, stacked with cots and communications gear. Satellite feeds glowed faintly from atop plastic tables. Outside, the howling wind stirred the American flag—the old one, Rusk had insisted—tattered but still clinging to the pole.

A dozen officers stood as he entered, most offering salutes, others nodding. His reputation had grown into something close to legend—the general who said no to Washington. The retired two-star who returned, not for power, but because his conscience wouldn't let him sit out a second American collapse. He didn't need medals. He had mutinies.

"Map," he said.

Colonel Thomas Brandt—a young, lean, eager-to-impress officer—spread out the tactical overlay.

The general studied it with a slow, deliberate motion. He wasn't just looking at lines and markers. He was looking for *weakness*. In their lines. In the enemies. Within the soul of this entire campaign. Within war, there is always something that leads to an advantage.

"Federal 9th Battalion is repositioning north of Georgetown," Brandt explained. "Looks like they're trying to flank us through the hills. We've repositioned the 11th Tennessee to hold."

"They'll roll your flank like paper," Rusk muttered. "Those Tennessee boys aren't trained for this kind of hill fighting. Not like Georgia's boys are."

A moment of silence fell. Rusk looked around, confused at the long faces. Brandt, hesitant: "Sir... we lost Georgia's 4th Battalion a week ago at Paducah."

Rusk said nothing. Just staring at the map, as if sheer focus could redraw it.

"Replace them with Alabama's 2nd Rangers," he said finally. "They've done bush fighting in the panhandle."

"Yes, sir."

He stepped back from the table and looked over the room. The smells of the mountain drifted into his nostrils.

"Any word from the Missouri line?"

"They report skirmishes, but no major movement. We think the feds are concentrating everything they have for a sweep through Lexington."

Rusk folded his arms. "Because of course they are. Lexington is the artery. They cut that, drive us east, take the hills, and push us down into their teeth at Atlanta. By then, it's over."

Nobody spoke. The words stirred troubled minds, working to solve the problem ahead of them. There were no easy answers.

Rusk turned slowly and looked out the window—toward the old road where grey sky met brown hills.

"Start making the necessary preparations," he said finally. "Artillery, armor, recon drones. We're not giving up Lexington. We're burying them in it. Is that understood?"

"Yes, sir!"

"Good. That is all."

* * *

Darkness fell over the mountainous terrain. In the old principles' office, now serving as his quarters, Rusk sat alone with his Bible. The desk was scarred with burn marks from a long-dead electric pencil sharpener. The light flickered every few seconds, a dying LED bulb wired into an old generator. Annoying to his old eyes, but something one must live with.

He didn't pray aloud. He never had. Prayer wasn't theater. It was a reflection.

The first time he read the book of Jeremiah during the war, it felt like prophecy. *"For, behold, I have made thee this day a defenced city, and an iron pillar, and brasen walls against the whole land, against the kings of Judah, against the princes thereof, against the priests thereof, and against the people of the land."*

That's what he had become. Not by choice. By consequence.

He was nearly seventy now. Widowed. His daughter serving in an infantry unit in Alabama. One of his sons—Isaiah—hadn't spoken to him since the day the first federal building was bombed. They said it was a rogue militia, but Rusk knew better. He'd warn them. When the government stripped faith from the schools, silenced dissent, and purged veterans from leadership, something had to give.

And it had. Violently.

Rusk closed the Bible and lit another cigar. The flame burned high for a moment—too high. He held it in front of his face, puffing with delight. *Damn, that is one fine cigar.*

His peace was soon disturbed by a heavy knock at the door.

"Enter."

Colonel Brandt entered, hat in hand. "Sir, comms intercept just came in. The president has ordered that assets from Fort Bragg start being moved north."

"They want to win this in one shot," Rusk said flatly.

Brandt nodded. "Yes, sir."

He exhaled a plume of smoke. "Then let's make sure they miss."

* * *

Classified – Continental Defense Force High Command

From: *Gen. Nathaniel Rusk, Commanding General*

To: *Theater Command Staff*

Date: *January 10, 2050*

Subject: *Strategic Posture and Operational Imperatives – Lexington Defensive Line*

Commanders,

Intelligence intercepts confirm an imminent concentration of federal forces along the I-64 and Bluegrass. Federal 3rd Armored and elements of the 9th Battalion are staging for a thrust through Lexington, with support from airborne units operating from Fort Bragg and Charleston.

Anticipated timetable: 21-30 days to full mobilization.

We assess their strategic intent as twofold:

1. ***Disruption of our Eastern Corridor supply routes****—severing Nashville, Birmingham, and other consolidated southern lines.*
2. ***Psychological and media victory****—a federal triumph in Lexington allows the President to declare the rebellion broken east of the Mississippi.*

In response, we will execute ***DEFENSIVE CONTOUR OPERATION VIGILANT FURY:***

1. ***Ranger units from Alabama's 2nd*** *will embed in the eastern hills to intercept infantry flanking attempts. This terrain favors hit-and-run disruption and denies the enemy artillery positioning.*

2. ***Missouri Mechanized Divisions*** *are to entrench at junctions near Versailles and Midway—early skirmishes suggest they will be the axis of pressure.*
3. ***Reserve artillery units from Georgia*** *will reinforce the western line by day 23. Based on fuel constraints, adjustments to the command calendar may be necessary.*

We do not cede Lexington. There is no retreat—the weight of our campaign and the structural survival of the Southern Coalition rests on this defense. This is our Antietam. Our stand must be surgical.

Coordinate with Civil-Military Liaison units to begin contingency evacuations within a 40-mile radius.

Hold the line.

In command,

Gen. Nathaniel Rusk

Commanding General, Continental Defense Forces

March 10, 2050 – MacDill Air Force Base

The wheels of the blacked-out suburban crunched over the crushed coral lot outside Hangar 3 as the early light of dawn stretched across MacDill. The base was still—silent but not asleep. General Rusk stepped out, stretching slightly before adjusting his service cap. The salty air carried a faint scent of jet fuel and ocean breeze—the perfume of a reclaimed military. Inside the hangar, scattered laughter echoed over the metallic clink of tools. A dozen pilots and ground crew lounged near a half-stripped F-15EX, painted in the subdued gray of the Continental Defense Force. No flashy decals. No tail art. Just a painted number and a prayer.

Lieutenant Jaime Vega was the first to spot him.

"Attention on deck!"

The group straightened fast, but Rusk waved it off. "At ease, gentlemen. I'm not here for ceremony."

He walked past the aircraft and ran his hand along the wing, fingers brushing the fresh paint. "I remember when this bird flew under the Stars and Stripes. Now she answers to something smaller—but maybe more honest."

Captain Derek Darnell, one of the older pilots, gave a tired smile. "We fly whatever still flies, sir. Stripes or no. Paint's paint."

Rusk turned to face them. "I read your sortie logs. Scrambled twice last week on phantom radar contacts. I know the fuel is tight. I know the maintenance team's running with half the parts they need. But we need to hold the skies."

Lieutenant Vega stepped forward. "It's not the gear that keeps us flying, sir. It's the mission. Nobody here defected for glory. We did it because we believe in what this is."

The general nodded slowly, eyes scanning the faces in front of him—ex-Air Force, rogue National Guard, even one civilian crop duster who'd been handed the stick of a recon drone last month.

"This wing may be small," Rusk said, "but you've already done more for this cause than whole armies. You've kept MacDill safe. You've given our columns eyes. And when the skies were dark over Jacksonville last month, your fighters broke the blockade."

Darnell chuckled. "Wasn't pretty, sir. Two missiles and half my HUD gone. Flew blind for forty clicks."

"But you made it back," Rusk said. "That's what matters."

He paused, then looked toward the open hangar doors.

"We're going to need you again. Soon. Kentucky may very well be the next theater—and Tallahassee isn't secure yet."

He turned back, voice low but firm.

"You're not just a wing anymore. You're our air force."

The pilots exchanged glances: pride, fear, steel now running through their veins.

Rusk gave a slight nod.

"Carry on, Captain. I'll see you in the sky."

He turned and walked into the dawn, the sound of tools and turbine tests slowly rising behind him, like a heartbeat.

* * *

The rain tapped lightly on the bulletproof windows of the annex as General Rusk adjusted the reading glasses he refused to admit he needed. A steaming mug of chicory coffee sat untouched at his elbow, getting cold. His speech sat open on the console before him, the words glowing in sterile light. A few lines had been scratched out with a stylus. Others were rewritten, softened, then sharpened again.

Across from him, his longtime aide and acting secretary, Marcy Hart, leaned against a table with a tablet in hand. Rusk would insure his life to Marcy in the worst of situations. They were in this together and would probably die together in glory.

"Sir," she said, "I know you want to strike a balance, but this part—" she pointed with her stylus, "— 'we do not beg for legitimacy from a government that has burned its own Constitution'... that might raise some alarms."

Rusk raised an eyebrow, unamused. "Good."

Marcy sighed but didn't push further. She knew better. He wasn't writing for applause. He was writing about history. The stories of war and what happens in battle always find themselves in conflict, unless you are the victor. The winners write the oldest saying in history, but it remains true. Rusk knew this, so he had to ensure a paper trail of their story existed.

"You know this has to go through secure channels, right?" she added. "No press broadcast. No leaks. The Committee already voted—internal use only."

He looked up from the screen. "You are telling me I have to classify my own damn speech?"

"Technically, yes. They're marking it '*Classified - Internal Dissemination Only.*' They're worried that it will be twisted into propaganda if it hits the open net. 'Rusk calling for a shadow government,' or worse."

Rusk snorted, taking off his glasses and setting them beside the mug.

"We are the damn republic. They don't know it yet."

The door creaked open behind them, and Major Ellison stepped in, sharp as always. His uniform was damp around the collar, Florida's humidity already seeping through.

"General," he said. "It's time."

Rusk stood slowly, picking up the folded hardcopy of the speech and tucking it into his inner jacket pocket. "The pilots already gathered?"

"Yes sir," Ellison nodded. "Air Wing 7, their families, a few staff officers. We've kept it tight. No livestream. Just internal uplink and hardcopy circulation."

"And the plaque?" Rusk asked.

Ellison gave a rare grin. "Mounted this morning. Right below the original MacDill insignia. Says: *'To the Airmen Who Defied Orders and Chose Honor.'*"

Marcy stood as well, smoothing her jacket and collecting her tablet. "I'll send the final draft to encrypted servers when you're finished. We'll seal it behind a CDF firewall, label it EYES ONLY."

Rusk looked between them both, then toward the hallway.

"You know," he muttered, "in the old army, speeches like this would make the front page. Now they get locked in a vault."

Ellison shrugged. "That's how revolutions begin, sir. Quietly. Then all at once."

Rusk gave a half-smile—just enough to crease one side of his weathered face.

"Well," he said, "let's go speak to the ghosts in the sky."

He pushed open the door and stepped out. The storm clouds finally started to part, and the first sounds of the honor ceremony echoed through the courtyard.

* * *

MacDill AFB – Internal Broadcast Transcript – 0900 Hours
Continental Defense Forces
Air Wing 7 Honor Speech
Speaker: General Nathaniel Rusk
Clearance Level: EYES ONLY – INTERNAL DISSEMINATION

Brothers. Sisters. Patriots.

What you did a year ago was not treason. It was a rescue.

You didn't turn your back on your country. You turned your back on a government that abandoned its people, rewrote its laws to suit tyrants, and corrupted the highest calling in our Republic—the defense of liberty.

When you rolled the hangars open, crossed that tarmac with loaded aircraft, ignored the abort orders, and launched for our side, you lit a fire in the heart of this rebellion.

I don't stand here to decorate you. I stand here to acknowledge you. Because without the 45th Bomber Squadron's refusal to fire on civilians in Pensacola, without the silence of radar crews at Hurlburt and Tyndall, without the night sortie out of Maxwell AFB—this movement would have died before it started.

We were foot soldiers and partisans. Now, thanks to you, we are a sovereign air power.

As of this week, we count ***twelve long-range bombers****, including four B-52s and eight B-1s, all under CDF command. Fighter escorts have risen to* ***twenty-eight active birds****—a mix of F-15s, F-16s, and two F-22s that somehow still fly better than Washington's budget priorities.*

We don't match them plane for plane. That was never the point.

The point is: we own the sky ***where it matters****.*

Over our farms. Over our people. Over our future.

You're not mutineers anymore. You are the vanguard of the sovereign South.

When this war ends—and it will end—it won't be the suits who rebuild the country. It'll be the air crews who refuse to bomb their neighbors. It'll be the ones who remembered the difference between orders... and oath.

God bless you.

And may He guide your aim.

* * *

The room was smaller than Rusk remembered—half wood paneling, half government beige. The lights buzzed, and the air reeked of jet fuel, coffee, and Florida humidity. Giving speeches can take a lot out of a person, especially if public speaking is not a skill they hold. This was the case with Rusk, as speeches were a rarity.

Captain Jalen Boone stood stiffly at the edge of the conference table. He was in his thirties, his posture that of a man trying to regain a world taken from him.

Rusk waved him to sit.

"Captain Boone," he said, lowering himself into the creaking leather chair. "Reports say you flew a full bombing run out of Shaw AFB and turned your squadron around mid-flight. Is that true?"

Boone nodded once. "Yes, sir. We had orders to hit a rebel munitions cache near Ocala. Intel said it was a weapons hub. We got eyes on it—sir, it was a refugee camp. Dozens of tents, kids playing in the open."

Rusk leaned back, face unreadable.

Boone continued, voice tightening. "They ordered us to drop. We found out sometime later that a few key figures of the *West Coast Alliance* were at this camp, and that the Government wanted us to murder the refugees to conceal their murder. I broke off and ordered the others to pull back. Three followed. Two went radio silent. I don't know what they did."

Rusk pulled out a cigar, lighting it slowly. "They called you a traitor in Washington."

The cigar smoke began filling the conference room, yet Boone was unfazed.

"Do you regret it?"

Boone's jaw clenched. "I regret not pulling all of them with me."

Smoke curled upward, soft against the hum of air vents. Rusk stared through it. "My nephew flew F-16s. He died overseas. In a war I didn't believe in, for a President who wouldn't shake my hand."

Boone blinked, "...I didn't know, sir."

"He was a good pilot. Followed orders. Trusted the system."

The silence between them stretched long.

"I'm not here for sympathy," Rusk said at last. "I need someone who can fly dirty—low altitude—minimal radar footprint. We've got a resupply run through Mississippi that needs air cover. You up for it?"

"Yes, sir."

"You believe in what we're building here, Captain?"

"Can't say I know for sure, as I am not a political man. War is an extension of politics, that much I know. However, I will not fight for a nation that has me murdering not just citizens, but our people. That's something."

Rusk nodded, slowly. "It is. That's more than most men start with."

He stood, and Boone stood snapping to attention. "Get something to eat. Mission brief is at 1900 hours. Dismissed."

Boone saluted. "Yes, sir."

As the captain exited, Rusk pulled out a folder, staring at the flight roster. Dozens of names, hand-scribbled and updated daily. Some have already been crossed out. Lives. Equipment. Trust.

He stubbed out the cigar, whispering to no one. "God help me, I hope we deserve their faith."

October 28, 2041 – The Pentagon – Washington, D.C.

W*hy am I here?* General Rusk sat stiffly in a chair too clean for comfort. The cold air made the room unbearable, as it usually was within the Pentagon. Rusk was used to the outdoors, or having no air conditioning at all, as he was raised to have it that way in the Army. This was an important day, because sitting across from him was someone who would make anyone stiffen. Across the desk sat then-President Jonathan Keyes, not yet wrapped in scandal, still pretending to be a man of the people.

They hadn't spoken very much over the years, not like it was at West Point. A former officer himself, Keyes was a bright spot but was meant more for diplomacy than fighting wars. However, as president, he did an outstanding job getting America into shooting matches with NATO Allies. Rusk was always amazed that Keyes never got himself run out of office.

"Good to see you again, Nate," Keyes said, his smile tight.

Rusk gave a polite nod. "You asked to see me, sir?"

This piece of shit.

"Yes." The president laced his fingers. "I wanted to talk about your recommendation. You've been nominated for another star."

"I'm aware."

"You've had an exemplary career. Iraq. Syria. The Balkans. Homeland command rotations. I've read the files."

Rusk waited for the punchline.

"But," Keyes said slowly, "your recent briefings to the Joint Chiefs... they've raised concerns."

There it is.

"What concerns, sir?"

"You've been openly critical of the administration's use of air power. Civilian casualties. Target selection. And there's your remarks on 'moral clarity' during a classified ethics review."

"I stand by what I said. We don't bomb refugee columns."

Keyes tilted his head. "We bomb *threats*. That is how we keep America safe."

Rusk's voice dropped. "Is that how you justify burning villages in Algeria? Or drone-striking weddings in Russia? How long we call it peacekeeping before we admit its bloodletting?"

A stiff, unsettling silence fell. Keyes leaned forward. The friendliness vanished.

"You want another star, Nathaniel? You want to command bigger armies? You play by the rules of this war."

Rusk stood. "Then maybe the war's lost already."

He turned to leave.

"You'll never be promoted under my watch," Keyes said, voice flat. "It doesn't take much to revoke your promotion and relieve you of your duties."

Rusk paused, hand on the doorknob. "You always hated being second in the academy rankings."

The president didn't answer.

Rusk exited. He decided to keep walking, even if it meant packing up his office. *I should have resigned on the spot.*

His phone buzzed. He pulled it out to see what it was. Nothing important. Just a daily scripture from a Bible app on his phone. At least, usually it wasn't important, but today it was a psalm. Rusk sighed.

"Psalm 31:24—Be of good courage, and he shall strengthen your heart, all ye that hope in the Lord."

Right on cue, almost as if the app was listening to the conversation.

You aren't going to let me quit, are you...

June 3, 2050 – MacDill Air Force Base

The knock on the door wasn't loud. But it was sharp—a sound that cut through sleep like a scalpel.

General Nathaniel Rusk opened his eyes to darkness. He blinked once, twice, then sat upright, his instincts screaming before his mind could catch up. He'd been a soldier too long to ignore a knock at that hour. No one brought good news at 0430 hours. He sat upright on his bed.

"Enter."

Major Ellen Castor stood at attention, clipboard in hand, her expression pale but composed.

"What is it, Major Castor?"

"It's Miami, sir," she said.

Rusk's gut tightened. "Go on."

"There was... an incident. Civilian casualties in the dozens—maybe hundreds. The unit involved claims they were responding to enemy infiltration. That's... not what satellite footage shows."

"Who did it?"

Castor glanced down at the clipboard, as if saying it out loud would confirm hell had opened.

"The Crimson Reapers, sir."

Rusk's knuckles went white. The Crimson Reapers, the battalion from hell in Rusk's mind. Religious fanatics, flocking to the cause and army that would justify any action they took in the name of God.

Considering themselves as reincarnations of the Templar knights, they flocked to the Continental Defense Force. The only reason they held any power was by distinguishing themselves in battle. Florida would not be in the control of the CDF without the contributions of the Reapers.

"Who's commanding them now?"

"Colonel Isaiah Brand. They were operating under black recon authority—strict comms blackout."

Rusk stood up. He made his way to a desk in the corner of his room. He fired up the lamp and turned on his coffee machine. The folder Castor placed on his desk was thick. Too thick for something that happened in a matter of hours.

"Where exactly?" he asked.

"Little Havana. They went in with word of a brothel serving as a comms point, possibly a honeypot trap operation. They found a small resistance cell. But no weapons. No confirmed arms cache. Rest of—" she stopped, then handed over stills. Thermal. Drone. Satellite.

Images of burned-out tenements. Of women—young, mostly—lined up against walls. Mutilated bodies. Some were executed at point-blank range. One holding a phone in her hand, fingers scorched mid-text.

The header on the report read:

OPERATION LAMENTATIONS

Commander: COL Isaiah Brand

Casualties 46 confirmed (24 Civilian, 22 Undetermined Combatant Status)

Status: Under Detainment Pending Formal Investigation

"Shit," Rusk muttered.

"Sir, there's something else," Castor added. "Colonel Brand says Jesus ordered it."

Tactical Briefing Room – 0630 hours

Hours later, in the Tactical Briefing Room, Rusk stood at the head of the long table. His face was granite. All his senior staff were seated, waiting eagerly.

"The Reapers are being flown to MacDill tomorrow." he said flatly. "Under escort. Disarmed. Stripped of rank."

"Sir," one aide spoke up, "considering what the Reapers have done for the CDF, do we prosecute them in wartime? This'll look like we're fracturing."

Heroes or contributors to your war, it was a bad look. Perhaps in some ways, it was like General Benedict Arnold: a revolutionary war hero turned traitor, selling out to the British due to his disdain for Washington. But this was more than one man; this was a platoon of soldiers following their god-fearing leader into whatever he saw fit.

"We are fractured," Rusk snapped. "This isn't a political question. Based on the evidence before us, this was murder."

"Colonel Brand claims it was biblical," another said. "claiming it was a cleansing, sanctioned by the 'Sword of Gideon.'"

Rusk slammed a hand down, fed up with what he heard. "This army is not a crusade. We are not the fucking Spanish Inquisition. Is that clear?!"

The room fell silent. No one dared to offer any more opinions. Rusk was in a terrible mood, as it was clear this was personal. Brand and Rusk knew each other from the Army, and he was the first to rush to Rusk's side when he was called to lead the CDF.

Then: "What charges, sir?"

"All of them," Rusk said. "War crimes. Breach of the Rules of Engagement. Murder of civilians under occupation."

He paused.

"And one more—because I want the record to be clear."

They looked up.

"Blasphemy."

September 13, 2050 – MacDill Air Force Base – Military Courtroom

The courtroom was makeshift, converted from an old logistics hangar—clean, bare bones, floodlit—crazy times called for crazy measures in such a unique situation. Rows of uniformed officers sat at rigid attention. The press was banned. Only court officials, selected observers, and senior command were allowed entry.

A massive American flag hung behind the dais. Ironic, all things considered.

General Rusk stepped forward to the raised bench. A court bailiff struck the bell.

"All rise!"

He surveyed the room—the prosecution team, the defense, and finally, the defendants in iron restraints. Twenty-two men, seated in formation like a choir from hell. At the front was Colonel Isaiah Brand, expression unreadable, hands bound in rosary-wrapped cuffs.

Rusk's voice rang like thunder.

"This General Court-Martial is now in session under the Uniform Code of Military Justice, convened by emergency order. The charges: conspiracy, dereliction of duty, violation of the Rules of Armed Conflict, and the murder of civilians in a war zone."

Rusk turned his head to the lead prosecutor.

"Is the prosecution ready?"

"We are, sir."

Rusk turns his head to the defense.

"Defense?"

"Yes, sir."

"Very well. Prosecution, call your first witness."

Day 2 – Military Courtroom

"Private First-Class Maritza Gomez, step forward."

She was nineteen, thin, and pale under the fluorescent lights. Her voice shook as she took the oath and sat in the witness chair. The prosecution began its case.

"You served as a comms technician attached to Colonel Brand's unit during Operation Lamentations?"

"Yes, sir."

"Did Colonel Brand brief the unit on the mission?"

"He did. He said... he said we were going into enemy territory. It was claimed to be a honeypot trap operation, that the women were spreading immorality, poisoning the well. He said that the Reapers were commanded to 'purge the camp.'"

A few gasps rose from the gallery. Rusk made no move to silence them.

"And what happened when you entered Little Havana?"

Maritza looked down. "We kicked in the doors. No warning. There were girls... barely older than me. They didn't resist. One of them offered us water. One of the men shot her in the stomach."

"Can you tell the court which man shot her?"

She hesitated, scared to speak.

"Private Gomez, which man shot the woman?"

"Sergeant Anthony Barr, sir."

"Is Sergeant Barr in this courtroom?"

"Yes, sir."

"Did Colonel Brand give the order to open fire?"

"Yes, sir. Before we entered, I heard him mutter something that sounded like 'kill the jezebels.'"

The defense council stood. "Object, the witness is speculating."

Rusk sighed. "Sustained."

The prosecutor turned to the judge's bench. "Let the record reflect that the defendant is invoking divine authority for lethal action outside the chain of command."

Colonel Brand was unmoved. He sat impassive, not flinching. His eyes remained locked on Maritza until she looked away.

"Your witness, defense counsel."

The defense counselor stood. He was a wiry, sharp-jawed lieutenant named Porter. Barely older than some of the Reapers, but already practiced in the fire of controversy. A Yale graduate, serving in a law firm when the war began, now found himself in the service of the rebellion.

"You said Colonel Brand called them jezebels?"

"Yes, sir," Maritza replied.

"Did he ever say fire without cause?"

“He didn’t say *not* to.”

“That’s not the question.”

She swallowed. “No. He told them to kill the jezebels.”

“Were you ordered to shoot civilians?”

“I wasn’t specifically ordered to. But others were. I heard it.”

Porter paced. “Private Gomez, are you a theologian?”

“No.”

“Are you a soldier?”

“Yes, sir.”

“A soldier now charged with desertion?”

“Object!” the prosecution stated. “Irrelevant to the case.”

“Sustained.” Rusk responded.

Porter continued. “Private Gomez, were you present in the building where the RPGs were allegedly found?”

“No, sir.”

“How can you say it wasn’t hostile?”

“Because I saw the girls. They weren’t enemy combatants.”

“But you’re not a soldier now, aren’t you?”

“No, sir.”

“Because you went AWOL a week later.”

The prosecution repeated, “Object!”

“Sustained.” Rusk looked at Porter. “Consider this a warning, Lieutenant Porter. One more time and you’ll be held in contempt.”

"No further questions."

* * *

Florida's night air felt heavy whenever one walked in it, the only refuge being inside an air-controlled environment. For General Rusk, his office was his refuge. The day's activities left him feeling heavier than the humidity outside. He stood at his office window, drink in hand—a stiff drink, bourbon and branch, was called for on this night.

A soft knock on the door pulled him from his thoughts. A chaplain entered quietly. An old friend. "I hope I am not disturbing you."

"Not at all, chaplain. Come on in."

The chaplain pulled up a chair, sat, and stared at Rusk. "It seems you have quite a challenge in front of you. Word on the base is that Colonel Brand may be a martyr," the chaplain remarked, voice calm.

"He's not a martyr," Rusk muttered. "He's a butcher, and a fool with a Bible."

The chaplain sighed, looking at him. "You have to show everyone here that. Separate him from the faith and show reality. Face to face. The men... they're watching you, Nate. They need to see the kind of leader you are."

Rusk didn't answer. He looked out over the base, the humid night swallowing the runway lights. A voice echoed in his mind.

"Kill the jezebels."

He drained the glass, enflaming his mouth, yet it seemed to shut his mind up.

"Thank you, chaplain."

10 Days Later – Military Courtroom

The courtroom was silent as Colonel Brand stood, unshackled at the defense table. After days of testimony, indisputable evidence, and damming forensics, Brand made his choice. He would testify, but not to any prosecutor or defense lawyer. The guards on his sides tensed but made no move.

"Your honor," Brand said, voice clear, deep, and unnervingly calm. "Before this court condemns my soul, I request one thing. A dialogue. With General Rusk himself. Here. In front of everyone."

Gasps echoed through the chamber. This was a strange and very rare request, but these were new times, and nothing had ever been normal in strange new times.

The presiding generals looked at Rusk, seated between them. General Nathaniel Rusk stood, slowly. He looked at Brand, his face impassive.

"Granted," he said.

A low murmur of tension rippled through the gallery as Rusk made his way around the table he sat at. He moved like a man used to leading armies into fire. When he reached the bullpen, he stopped a few feet from Brand, who was also at the front of the defense table. No podium. No armor. Just two men. One in dress uniform. The other, wearing the tattered colors of the Reapers, was adorned with a crucifix made of barbed wire.

Brand stepped forward.

"Tell me, General," he began. "Do you believe God is on your side?"

Rusk didn't flinch. "No. I answer to God. Not the same thing."

"You sit in judgment of me, a faithful man. Dealing with our time's Sodom and Babylon, just as commanded."

He pulled out a bloody page of text, as it was a page from a Bible.

"This was taken from my man, shot in the head by a harlot from that brothel." He looked down at it.

Rusk looked at him. "What was your man doing in that brothel, Colonel Brand?"

"Investigating, sir."

"You sure about that?"

"About as..."

"Are you damn sure? You are certain he wasn't getting his family jewels twisted?"

"Yes, sir. He had conviction. He knew not to let his heart go astray in her path."

Rusk found himself in an awkward situation. Many in that room did not hold the same beliefs as Rusk and Brand, making it difficult for a simple person to understand. Just as Brand wanted it, a chance to perform for those who might set him free.

Rusk folded his hands behind his back. Calm.

"Colonel Brand, may I remind you: He who is without wrong can cast the first stone. It's true. But you haven't shown reasonable doubt in this courtroom. You admit you chose death instead of mercy."

Brand sneered. "Mercy? For traitors who sold their bodies? Inviting back in the rot of modernity?"

"This is not for a select few, Colonel. It's for everyone."

Brand thundered. "If you love him, keep the law."

He turned to the gallery, emboldened. "These people proclaim you the savior of America. But you're no different than me. You wage war. You kill. You punish. You're just better dressed."

Rusk took one step closer. His voice was firm. Cold.

"The difference, Colonel, is that I don't pretend my bullets are sacraments."

Brand shouted now, voice cracking. "This country can't be fixed. It can only be cleansed!"

Rusk answered without raising his voice. "You're right, the country is broken. And it has been for some time. I still believe we can do better. We must do better! That's where you and I part."

He stepped forward again, taking a final breath. This clash of philosophy had reached its conclusion in Rusk's mind.

"You are not on trial for righteousness. You're not here because you feared God. You're here because you are accused of murder."

Brand was breathing hard. Red in the face. But for once, he had no argument ready. No chant. No final line. The Reapers behind him, shaken.

Rusk turned to his fellow generals.

"The court may proceed."

He walked back around the table and took his seat. Outside the courtroom, a brisk, cooling wind blew in. Finally, the beginning of fall was upon Florida.

3 Days Later – Military Courtroom

The courtroom sat silent—dead silent. General Rusk stood up as the generals looked to him. The entire room's eyes were fixed on the General.

Rusk picked up a piece of paper. His voice, when it came, was gravel in a forge. Not thunder. Just heat. Truth.

"I want every man and woman in this courtroom to understand something before I render judgement."

He looked directly at Colonel Brand, then past him to the remaining Crimson Reapers. Their eyes were hard, some bitter, others quietly lost.

"Colonel Brand was correct on one thing; the brothel was indeed a honeypot trap set up by the government forces, through their CIA spy network. I won't stand and whitewash it. The conduct of the women was a violation of both moral and the laws of humanity. As a man of faith, I understand the warnings and shame such a thing can be, simply because my veins run with a thing that causes me to run towards it."

He let a long pause hang in the air. Brand was astonished, as it seemed like vindication was on the horizon.

Rusk turned slowly to the courtroom.

"Temptation is something I carry like all men. I had my way with women as a graduate of West Point."

Murmurs rose in the gallery.

"But I have confessed it. I've never told a soul. Until now. Not because I was ashamed, but because of the clichéd fear of what people might think. I am no better than any of you."

His voice hardened.

"But here is where the road splits, Colonel. You saw sin and chose death. I see it, and choose forgiveness."

He walked a few paces behind the table. Looked at the far wall. Then turned back.

"Those women were still war criminals, but deserved to be treated as prisoners of war. Living by a code is what separates us from the beasts. I do not pretend this war is clean. I am waging this war against this so-called Federal Government because it violated every principle of humanity, dropping nuclear fire upon its own people. I fight them because they violated a simple principle, a right to life."

He took a breath.

"War or not, we are still men. Under the law—*His law*—there was a place for grace."

He turned to face Colonel Brand.

"Mercy does not mean absence of consequence. You led a group of soldiers to execute civilians without a trial. You claimed divine authority to what no general—no king—had the right to do."

He exhaled.

"The court finds the defendants: guilty as charged."

Gasps rippled across the room. General Rusk did not pull a single punch. It was brutal, unflinching. All the Reapers could do was sit in silence, awaiting their fate.

"Colonel Isaiah Brand, you are hereby sentenced to death by firing squad. Sentence to be carried out one week from today."

Rusk banged the gavel down. A wave of reaction surged through the room. He raised his hand.

"Order!"

The room got quiet as Rusk signaled that he had more to say.

"As for the rest of the Crimson Reapers—you followed your commander. Some out of belief. Some out of fear. Most, I believe, out of loyalty. I cannot ignore the blood on your hands."

He looked to them, one by one.

"I will not, however, answer injustice with more injustice. You are hereby sentenced to life at hard labor. You will be transported to the Agricultural Penal Corps in Georgia."

He let the weight of that hang. With the war taking a toll on the country's infrastructure, it made sense to keep the labor force alive to serve in another area, yet never be free to harm again.

"You will feed the army you betrayed. And every sunrise you see will be a gift you did not earn."

He turned and walked out of the courtroom. Behind him, no one cheered. Not a soul. The courtroom sat in stunned, reverent silence.

Only one phrase lingered. Rusk had written in the margin of his journal years ago, underlined in the fading ink:

"Mercy is not weakness. It is discipline in the face of righteous fury."

October 1, 2050 – MacDill Air Force Base – Munitions Storage Area (MSA)

The gray light of dawn barely crested the eastern horizon. The courtyard behind MacDill's old munitions storage area block was lined solemnly. A formation of soldiers, rifles at the ready, stood in silence. No ceremony. No music. Just the wind whispering through the trees and the steady click of boots against concrete.

General Rusk stood with his back straight, his hat tucked under one arm. His face was unreadable, though his eyes betrayed the exhaustion in his soul.

Colonel Brand was marched out between two guards. His uniform had been stripped of rank insignia, but he held his head high. He looked thinner than he had weeks ago, hollowed from the weeks of confinement. Still, he met the firing squad with eyes full of clarity.

The chaplain offered him the final rites. Brand waved him off politely.

"I do not need rituals," he said. "let my words be my prayer."

He turned to the gathered officers, his voice steady and echoing in the cold morning air.

"I did what I thought was right. That's the truth of it. You can call it evil, misguided, or criminal. And you are probably right. I won't fight it. I saw a nation drowning in filth. I saw a world where no one said: enough."

He glanced at Rusk.

"I judged without mercy. Blind to grace, of that I know now. Spoke of law, but forgot humility."

Brand took a slow breath.

"I lost. General Rusk, don't blame my men. Do not curse my men. We chose our path; now we must walk it. Walk yours with discipline. With reflection."

His gaze drifted skyward, then back to the soldiers before him.

"Time to meet God. I am chained to the world, soon to be chained by him. Hell awaits me? So be it."

An uncomfortable silence was felt as a cool breeze blew through. A guard stepped forward with a black bag.

Brand shook his head. "No. Let them see my face."

He looked straight ahead. Then closed his eyes. Whispering something, a prayer perhaps.

Rusk whispered under his breath, "May God receive you, Colonel."

"Ready—"

The order snapped the air. Rifles lifted from the soldier's hands.

"Aim—"

The silence before the final word felt like eternity.

"Fire."

The volley struck Brand square. He fell backwards into the dirt, stiller than a rock. No one moved for several seconds. Then the detail commander saluted. Within a few minutes, the soldiers began removing the body with care.

Rusk remained. Alone. Watching the blood soak the concrete where Brand once stood. And for a moment, he said nothing. He began to whisper again, quieter this time:

"And the greatest of these is mercy."

* * *

It was past noon when General Rusk finally stepped outside for lunch. The courtyard at MacDill began to warm, shaded by swaying palms. A simple meal had been laid out: roast chicken, greens, and cornbread. Rusk sat at a metal table in the garden, away from the barracks, hoping the Florida sun might burn through the shadow in his mind.

He picked at his food, staring at the plate as if it might accuse him.

The plate shattered suddenly under his fist, the ceramic cracking with a violent crunch. A young aide standing nearby let out a startled gasp.

"Sir?"

Rusk didn't respond at first. He lifted his bleeding knuckles, inspected them, then flexed his hand like he couldn't quite believe what he had done.

The aide approached cautiously. "Permission to speak freely, General?"

Rusk nodded.

"Why are you angry?"

Rusk stared at the broken plate. "Because I keep asking myself... What if I made Brand? He was my friend, my soldier... What if all this talk of faith, mercy, and war... What if it just breeds more men like him?"

The aide hesitated. "Sir, with respect... He made his own choices. He took responsibility."

Rusk looked at him, the lines under his eyes deeper than ever. "Sometimes I wonder if all these speeches, the calls to justice, just stir the wrong hearts. This job makes a man second-guess his entire existence."

The aide reached into his pocket and handed the General a cigar. Rusk accepted it silently. He lit it with a flick of a silver lighter, inhaled deeply, and exhaled toward the cloudless sky.

"Maybe you're right, son," he said at last. "Sometimes my thoughts get so loud, common sense goes quiet. And when that happens... Mercy feels like a whisper."

He stared into the horizon for a long moment, the smoke curling above his head.

"Let's make sure the next ones hear it louder."

* * *

CLASSIFIED MEMORANDUM – TOP SECRET – Eyes Only

From: *Gen. Nathaniel Rusk, Commanding General*

To: *CDF Senior Command & Allied Divisional Heads*

Subject: *Repercussions of Court Martial & Strategic Pivot Toward Tallahassee*

Timestamp: *October 2, 2050 – 0400 EST*

Encryption Code: *BLACKROOK-9*

Commanders,

The proceedings of the Crimson Reapers court-martial have concluded. Colonel Isaiah Brand was executed yesterday morning by firing squad for war crimes against civilians. His unit has been reassigned to a permanent labor detail at Camp Gideon, our new agricultural penal colony near Tifton, Georgia. Moral and political fallout is expected but controllable. The trial was public for many on the base, spreading through other units. The sentence was swift. There will be continued whispers—some in trenches, some in barracks—but justice has been seen.

Let this stand as final confirmation: we are not animals. We do not kill without restraint, nor lead men who do. We are not Rome, and we will not become it.

That said, the ideological schisms revealed during this affair run deeper than expected. I'm receiving coded grumblings from faith-aligned militias in Missouri, and signs of unrest from smaller Alabama chapters. I advise <u>extreme caution</u> in how this verdict is framed across our *allied networks. Discipline without conviction risks rebellion; mercy without consequence invites chaos.*

The coming battle in Tallahassee looms large over the CDF, and I advise you to divert public attention away from internal questions. Early reconnaissance indicates that the Federal Army's 3rd Expeditionary Group has been repositioning southward from Savannah. Satellite data suggests logistical staging in Valdosta and increased drone overflights near the Aucilla River line.

Our response must be swift.

Orders:

1. *Begin mobilization of 4th Florida Armored and 2nd Georgia Rangers by midnight.*
2. *Fortify rail lines between Lake City and Monticello for supply transport.*
3. *Activate Civil Defense drills in Tallahassee proper—no civilian execution unless red alert is declared.*
4. *Secure coastal corridors for possible naval intervention support.*

We must meet this head-on, not simply for victory, but for clarity. The men need something to believe in again. Let's give them Tallahassee.

Signed,

Gen. Nathaniel Rusk

Commanding General, Continental Defense Force

October 18, 2050 – MacDill Air Force Base – War Room

The war room inside MacDill was electric with movement. Dozens of analysts, tacticians, and communications officers hunched over flickering displays. Maps of northern Florida were stretched across every screen, red icons for government forces inching steadily toward the panhandle. The capital—Tallahassee—was circled in a thick green flag. That was the line. It could not be crossed.

General Rusk stood at the center, hands clasped behind his back, eyes locked on a digital projection of the city. His uniform was crisp, and his expression was harder than ever. Behind him, a wall-sized tactical screen displayed topographic overlays, showing elevation, river networks, and troop movements updated in real-time from battlefield drones and satellites.

The doors opened with a hiss, and a junior intelligence officer approached, breathless. "Sir, latest satellite imagery confirms two columns of armor pushing through Apalachicola. The target is the coastal road. Slicing the state in half—cutting us off from Gulf supply lines."

Rusk's jaw tensed. "That road gives them Panama City and an open line to any holdout Navy units. We hold it, or we lose the whole damn peninsula."

His aide, Major Ellison, stepped forward with a tablet. "Air recon from Eglin confirms drone swarms on their vanguard. Cyber teams are attempting a wave-two disruption with signal spoofers."

This was the CDF's first real test. Holding Tallahassee meant keeping the government forces out of range of the Gulf. The navy's blockade of the West Coast stretched them thin, leaving the Gulf completely exposed. When the CDF rose and overtook several bases, the government had no choice but to blockade the Atlantic coast. The iron-clad grip on Florida prevented the Navy from entering the Gulf, thanks in part to the defense capabilities in Pensacola and MacDill. It also didn't help that the CDF had an aircraft carrier, the USS *Benjamin Franklin*, awaiting any visitors who attempted to breach the coast.

"Deploy Falcon Group south of the Suwannee," Rusk ordered. "Let's bring a welcoming mouse trap—anti-armor mines, tank busters in the tree line, and shoulder-fired MANPADS on standby. A nice, pleasant little kill box. We bleed them on the way in."

"Yes, sir." Ellison turned, barking into his headset.

Rusk turned to his top field commander, General Kravitz, who had been quietly observing the map. "You have the authority to commit the 6th Armored. We own the tree line before they crest I-10."

"Tanks are already positioned there, sir."

"Good. And I want a ghost flank out of Wakulla. Special forces. I think it's time we make the terrain our ally."

The room buzzed with renewed energy. Radios cracked with bursts of code. Officers moved between digital sand tables and real-time strike feeds. Through the chaos, Rusk remained centered.

"They want Tallahassee? Let them come and die for it."

October 20, 2050 – MacDill Air Force Base – War Room

It had been thirty-six hours since the battle began. The war room had thinned, but Rusk remained. The lights were dimmed now, most of the illumination coming from the wall-sized tactical map. It blinked and pulsed with updates every second, a living portrait of war.

Rusk decided to get some air and headed to his office. He stood by the window overlooking the tarmac outside, where emergency medical helicopters landed in intervals. *Poor bastards.* He had a cigar between his fingers, the embers flaring red as he took long, deliberate draws. Smoke curled around his face, blending with the stale tension in the air.

He hadn't slept or eaten in over thirty hours—his stomach in knots. For hours, he waited and clung to every report coming out of the panhandle. It made him sick at the prospect of losing so many men and equipment in battle. *Losing men in that shithole of a city, disgusting*.

His concentration was soon interrupted by a knock at the door. It was Major Ellison, who entered, wiping sweat from his brow. "Sir. Reports from the 6th just in—enemy armor took the bait and rolled into the trap at I-10. We've confirmed that thirty-four vehicles were neutralized, with minimal Continental losses."

Rusk nodded, not taking his eyes off the window.

"Wakulla's ghost flank was a success," Ellison continued. "They blew the lead supply column and scattered the rear guard. Commanders on the ground say enemy comms are in complete disarray."

"Good," Rusk muttered. "Fear's a contagion. Once it spreads, the whole line breaks."

"Sir, this makes a person wonder if this attack was in haste."

"Explain."

"This doesn't feel like it's a surgical attack. Almost as if it's a political attack."

"Internal pressure?"

"Possibly. Because doesn't the Pentagon war game these scenarios out?"

"Yes, they do."

"And yet this attack is about breaking the CDF more than anything else."

A notification bell rang from Major Ellison's tablet. He opened it and scanned it, grimacing.

"Report from the Bonehunters: enemy drones regrouping south of Perry. Fast-movers might be incoming. We've scrambled three birds from Homestead to intercept."

Rusk turned to him. "Let's light the bastards up. Bonehunters can bait them into the open with decoys."

Ellison hesitated, "Sir, one more thing—the chatter on the radio frequencies. Discussion with high command to use gas."

Rusk's eyes narrowed. "Are they that rattled?"

"Apparently."

"Put it in the record. If they go chemical, I want full confirmation, and I want the footage stored in five separate blacksites."

Ellison nodded, saluting him, then left.

Rusk took another drag from the cigar, pacing slowly. The air in the room was cooler now, but heavy. His boots echoed on the concrete floor as he circled his desk again. His office was dark and somber, in contrast to the theater of light and shadow that was the war room. A battlefield ingrained in the digital landscape.

He exhaled smoke and muttered, "This country was split long before we drew these lines."

* * *

Sitting upright in his desk chair, a knock startled Rusk awake. He looked at his watch, 0330 hours—almost five hours since Major Ellison left him. *Dammit, I fell asleep.* He straightens his uniform out, clearing his throat.

"Enter."

The doors opened, and General Kravitz stepped in.

"Sir," he said quietly. "Tallahassee holds. The enemy is withdrawing."

Rusk stared into the light that filled the room through the door. He said nothing, tapping the desk with his fingers.

October 23, 2050 – Tallahassee, Florida

It had been only a few days since the battle's conclusion, but the battlefield lay smoking. Government armor had been lured into the choke point along I-10 and cut to pieces. The terrain, seeded with mines and lined with missile nests, had turned their advance into a meat grinder. Drone strikes had been repelled by scrambling towers and surface-to-air missile volleys. Infantry columns, once so confident, now lay scattered in disarray among the tree trunks and road ditches.

The forest south of the highway was littered with husks of machines and bodies. Burned-out tanks smoldered next to blackened corpses. A handful of prisoners had been taken—most shell-shocked, others too wounded to speak. The Continental Defense Forces had held the line. Tallahassee stood tall—and Florida would not be divided.

From high above, a single B-1B Lancer roared through the morning sky. The strategic bomber cut through the clouds like a blade, its massive wings gleaming in the red dawn. It banked low over the smoldering wreckage, trailing twin plumes of exhaust that rippled the air behind it.

Inside, Rusk sat beside the flight commander in the cockpit's jump seat. The air was dry and cold, filled with the faint scent of hydraulics and oil. He adjusted the mask, held tightly around his face.

"Target site confirmed, sir. Zero movement from hostiles."

Rusk leaned forward, scanning the ground through reinforced glass. Fires still burned in the distance. Black smoke drifted into the horizon. Small figures—medics, recovery teams, engineers—moved among the wreckage like ants cleaning up after a thunderstorm.

"Hell of a waste. They really thought we would fold," he muttered, his voice low and rough.

"No, sir," the pilot replied. "Not while you're in command."

The jet thundered past the state capitol building, circling Tallahassee's dome like a guardian angel. Below, troops still lining the street raised their weapons skyward in salute. Some clapped. Others sighed. A few simply stood still, gazing up.

Rusk pulled out a cigar from his pocket, eager to light it. He didn't smile. His mask would not allow it to be seen.

"Kravitz may need to push west in 72 hours. Panama City may be where it's going next. And then..." he paused, watching the curve of the coast. "It's to the heart."

The jet pulled up and climbed toward the heavens, slicing through the dawn.

October 24, 2050 – Tallahassee, Florida – Landis Green

The sun crept cautiously over Tallahassee's broken skyline, as if unsure it had permission to shine on such a place. Its golden light filtered through a layer of lingering smoke, bathing the ruins in an eerie amber glow. The palm trees that once swayed outside Florida State's dormitories were now nothing more than blackened trunks or snapped stumps, their fronds curled and crisped like the pages of an old book caught in a fire.

General Rusk stepped out of the Humvee and into the wreckage of the campus. His boots sank slightly into the wet, muddy earth where sprinkler systems had burst from shellfire. The ruins of the Wescott Building loomed nearby, scorched and pocked by mortar hits, the once-proud university seal barely visible behind soot-stained columns. A gaping hole had torn through the front rotunda, exposing steel bones and broken stairwells.

This wasn't a campus anymore. This was a wound.

Landis Green had been transformed into a field hospital that existed only when civilization failed. Rows of stretchers lined the field, some shaded by hastily erected canopies, others exposed by the morning sky. Medical personnel worked in perpetual motion—nurses with dark circles under their eyes, combat medics red up to their elbows, and orderlies moving from cot to cot like grim reapers running out of time.

The cries of the wounded echoed like ghosts under the colonnades.

"Clear this lane for surgery!" a woman shouted nearby. "I need a transfusion unit and clamps—now!"

Rusk kept walking, his stride slow, heavy. He passed a body covered in a white sheet. Flies buzzed around the edges, but no one had time to move it yet. A tag was tied to the man's boot—his name smeared in dried blood. Someone scrawled "CAME IN SINGING DIXIE" beneath it.

He walked on. He passed a teenage rifleman with a missing hand. His eyes stared at nothing. Next to him, a combat nurse whispered lullabies to a man whose intestines were held in by a compression wrap. Nearby, a girl no older than nineteen sobbed as a chaplain gave her last rites beside her lover, who had already gone cold.

Rusk didn't speak. He just let it soak in. Every step he took felt heavier.

He reached a line of amputees sitting up against the side of a wrecked vending kiosk. Their laughter caught him off guard. They were joking about prosthetics— "I want one with a bottle opener," one said. Another nodded. "And a fishing pole attachment. Why the hell not?"

They noticed the General.

"Attention on deck!" one of them barked, trying to stand. His leg stumped and thudded back to the ground. "Sir!"

"At ease," Rusk said, his voice a low growl. "You've earned the right to sit."

He crouched beside them.

"We held 'em, General," said a lance corporal, his eyes rimmed red but proud. "They threw everything they had, and we held."

"I'm so damn proud of you men," Rusk said. "You buried them in their own arrogance."

The corporal grinned. "Damn right, sir."

From farther off, a harmonica began to play. Slow, trembling notes of "Wayfaring Stranger" drifted over the wounded. The harmonica was cracked and imperfect, but it hushed the sobs around them like a prayer.

Rusk looked across the green, where ivy used to run and students once napped between classes. Now it was a graveyard with IV lines and tourniquets. In a quiet moment, he could still hear the mortar strikes, the whirring of drones, and screaming.

He saw his reflection in the cracked visor of a dead combat medic. It stared back at him like a question he couldn't answer.

A nurse approached him. Her face was smudged with ash and dried tears. "Sir, we're low on everything. Morphine, dressings, and antibiotics. I've got people being stabilized with chewing gum and pressure bandages."

"I'll get you what you need," Rusk replied. "Tell the quartermaster I want a full requisition from every medical depot between here and Ocala."

"Yes, sir." She left, limping slightly from a bruised hip.

Finally, he sat on a splintered park bench that had miraculously survived the shelling. He pulled out a cigar, lit it with shaking hands, and stared at the horizon.

The leaves were falling from the trees by Dodd Hall, reaching the ground like survivors in the wind.

Rusk exhaled smoke and thought about the cost. He thought of the men who followed him and would never see another sunrise. Of the children they left behind. Of the quiet price no general ever got to admit he paid.

"General?"

It was Major Ellison. His face was pale from sleepless nights.

"I thought I might find you here," he said.

"Where else would I be?" Rusk muttered. "This is the true battlefield."

Ellison nodded. "You should rest, sir."

Rusk didn't answer. He took another puff from his cigar, eyes locked on a stretcher where a wounded soldier gripped the hand of his younger brother—barely sixteen, with eyes too old for his face.

"Tell the boys to dig in," he said after a long silence. "We're not done yet. And send word to Panama City."

Ellison nodded. "You think they will make a play for it?"

"I doubt it, but I'm not about to let those slippery bastards get their claws into any part of the panhandle."

Rusk glanced back at the field—this garden of pain, this cathedral of valor.

The trees swayed again, leaves falling all around. Fall was in the air.

* * *

CLASSIFIED – EYES ONLY

From: *Gen. Nathaniel Rusk, Commanding General*

To: *High Command, Continental Defense Force*

Subject: *Strategic Update – Post-Tallahassee Consolidation / Gulf Axis / Eastern Preparations*

Date: *October 26, 2050*

Location: *MacDill Command, FL*

Summary:

Following the successful defense of Tallahassee and subsequent expulsion of federal forces east of the Apalachicola River, I submit the following summary for battlefield losses, strategic assessment, and projected action along both western and eastern axes.

1. **BATTLE DAMAGE AND CASUALTY ASSESSMENT – TALLAHASSEE SECTOR**
   - *Confirmed 6th Armored Battalion losses: 42% operational strength.*
   - *Falcon group sustained 17 KIA, 61 wounded in initial trap engagement at I-10 chokepoint.*
   - *Bonehunters report 22 casualties, mostly from proximity drone retaliation near Perry.*
   - *118 confirmed civilian casualties in Tallahassee proper; the majority due to federal chemical munitions deployment before retreat.*

Morale remains strong, but exhaustion is evident. We have rotated three companies out for R&R and reassignment. Psychological support personnel are being dispatched from Georgia and Texas sectors.

2. STRATEGIC HOLDINGS – GULF AXIS

Despite the victory, ***our position remains precarious along the Gulf Coast.*** *Federal naval forces continue to attempt to penetrate our defensive line west of Tampa and Mobile Bay.* ***We assess four destroyers and at least one guided missile cruiser remain on station in the Eastern Gulf.***

The ***primary goal of the Tallahassee campaign*** *now is about re-establishing ground-to-coast connectivity with our Panama City and Pensacola garrisons, which currently house key missile defense infrastructure and deep supply reserves. While we achieved partial success, sustained resupply by sea remains untenable without naval parity or air superiority over the Gulf.*

Recommendation: *Begin accelerated talks with sympathetic North Carolina and Mississippi naval commanders. We regain a temporary corridor if even one vessel defects or disables federal radar buoys. Emphasize honor, not politics—some of them still listen to oaths.*

3. OPERATION FIREBIRD – PRELIMINARY

Intel suggests the Federal 5th Corps is regrouping in southern Ohio and western West Virginia. Satellite imagery confirms new fortifications near Lexington, KY—possible staging for a counteroffensive aimed at splitting the Georgia-Tennessee link.

We will not allow that. *I intend to strike preemptively. Rail and armor relocations begin westward under night movement protocols. All special* *forces from the Alabama theater are to be reassigned for infiltration and sabotage operations near Fort Knox and Louisville.*

Lexington will not be a defense. It will be their downfall.

4. FOLLOW-UP ACTION – WESTERN GULF CAMPAIGN

Lastly, while our next full-scale operation lies inland, I will be dispatching limited recon detachments and special forces to begin probing operations west of Panama City. We need to know what we're dealing with. If there is an opportunity to cut the enemy off from Mobile and Biloxi via inland maneuver, we must take it—even if it's a long shot. Pensacola cannot stand forever alone. And with their defeat in Tallahassee, I will leave nothing to chance regarding the safety of the panhandle and the CDF.

If Lexington breaks them in the heartland, ***Panama City becomes our anvil.***

-End Transmission

March 3, 2051 – MacDill Air Force Base

ALERT... INCOMING TRANSMISSION...

Classified Operational Memo

From: *Chief of Staff, Command Group Alpha*

To: *Gen. Nathaniel Rusk, Commanding General, Continental Defense Force*

Subject: *Operation Silent Thunder – Strategic Bombing Outcome and Implications for Lexington Campaign*

Date: *[REDACTED]*

Clearance Level: *Omega-Black*

Executive Summary:

Operation Silent Thunder, carried out under strict blackout conditions, has achieved a decisive strategic breakthrough. The coordinated airstrike involving the 3rd and 7th Bomber Wings penetrated deep into government-controlled Kentucky airspace and successfully neutralized the central logistics hub outside Lexington—codename: "Depot Griffin." The strike has not only disrupted forward supply chains to the capital defenses, but also severed the eastern rail line and destroyed over 90% of their fuel reserves staged for counteroffensive operations.

Strike Details:

- ***Aircraft involved:*** *6 B-1B Lancers, escorted by 15 F-35s operating under ECM cover.*
- ***Entry Vector:*** *Low-altitude infiltration via Appalachian corridor.*
- ***Target Time:*** *0310 hrs local*
- ***Payload:*** *5,000-lb. JDAMs, fuel-air bombs, and anti-runway penetrators.*
- ***Casualties:*** *CDF: 0. GovForces est. 430+ (direct), 800+ (logistical)*

Secondary Effects:

- *Massive fires triggered secondary explosions in the ordinance depots.*
- *Psychological disruption recorded via SIGINT chatter. Morale appears fractured across eastern Kentucky brigades.*
- *Government command nodes now issuing redundant and erratic orders to frontline units. Confirms comms relay hub loss.*

Witness Report:

General Rusk was in the command observation deck during live drone feedback of the operation. His exact quote following confirmation of Griffin's destruction.

"Broke your spine, you bastard."

Following the strike, confirmation was received that the Continental Defense ground forces from the Tennessee border initiated a rapid westward advance through the shattered corridor. Early estimates suggest a 30-mile breach in government lines with minimal resistance.

Implications for Lexington Campaign:

This action has effectively compromised the government's ability to reinforce or resupply Lexington. We estimate a 48 to 72-hour window before the enemy attempts to consolidate remaining forces at the state capital or withdraw toward Ohio.

Recommend immediate exploitation:

1. *Mobilize the 15th Infantry to seize crossroads at Richmond.*
2. *Push artillery brigades into Garrad County.*
3. *Drop tactical airborne units behind the Bluegrass parkway to sow panic.*

Expected enemy fallback point: Frankfurt or Cincinnati.

Final Note:

Recommend Panama City campaign units remain on standby. Navy blockade pressure remains a factor; further Gulf operations must be postponed until Lexington is secure. Civilian morale in Florida is stabilizing following Tallahassee, but resources are tight.

This memo is to be destroyed within 48 hours unless refiled under Ghost Archive Alpha.

-End Transmission

* * *

"Dad," she said, glancing over a tablet filled with requisition numbers, "you must push for medical airlifts from Texas. We're overloaded in Pensacola."

General Rusk listened to a lot of advice and wisdom but held his daughter's advice close to his heart. Lieutenant Elise Rusk, of the 2nd Alabama Infantry, sat with folders in her hand, intent on winning the war for her father.

"I know," he replied, voice rough. "But the skies are watched. We're stretched thin already. I'll handle it though."

There was a lull. Birds chirped, distant rotors hummed somewhere overhead. Rusk stirred his coffee absently, watching the ripples.

"You look tired," Elise said finally.

"I'm always tired."

They sat in silence until an officer knocked on the door and entered the office. It was his aide, Major Ellison.

"Sir," Ellison said with a salute. "Apologies. A message just came through from the 7th Bomber Wing. Operation Silent Thunder is complete."

Rusk set his mug down as Ellison handed him the classified transmission. His eyes sharpened like iron catching fire.

"Casualties?"

"None. Depot Griffin has been erased. From the report, it seems that secondary explosions confirm the destruction of the logistics hub. SIGINT shows a complete collapse in communications. It's a mess on the ground, sir. Our breach unit from the Tennessee line moved through within minutes. Thirty miles in and growing."

This was it—the breakthrough the Continental Defense Force was looking for. Catching the government off guard was a rare feat. Rusk and his commanders had pulled off the impossible. The government's ineffective air defense around its units had paved the way for a possible assault, yet it was never considered serious in their eyes. It's a rebel force with ragtag Americans, not bread for war. They could not pull off an air assault so large that it could be decisive in a battle.

Rusk leaned back, letting the weight of the moment settle.

"Have Command draft a new campaign line."

Ellison hesitated. "And Panama City?"

The risk of diving in. If the CDF was caught sleeping at the wheel south while focusing north, the risk of losing the panhandle was still in play. But the decisive breakthrough was too significant to ignore.

"On hold," Rusk said. "The Navy's blockade makes that a chessboard of its own. Lexington is the priority."

Ellison nodded and stepped back, making his way out. Rusk stood. Elise looked at him, worried.

"You okay?"

He placed her hand on her shoulder. "I will be. Tell the guys in Logistics... they're about to be busy."

March 10, 2051 – Undisclosed Location – Somewhere in Kentucky

The morning skies over Kentucky were veiled in smoke. For General Rusk, the war had stretched beyond geography—it had become spiritual. He stood in the mobile command center positioned south of Lexington. Since adversaries closely watched his position, he kept it secret and away from battle. Too stubborn to stand beside them, Rusk ensured it was within spitting range. Maps and satellite feeds flickered before him, but his mind was elsewhere.

The room was buzzed with quiet urgency. Radios squawked with positions, casualty updates, and last-minute calls for air support. Rusk didn't speak. He watched, arms folded behind his back, until the voice of Major Archie Fallon finally broke through.

"Sir," Fallon said, "We've confirmed the 15th and 22nd have cut through the outer line. The gap we opened near Richmond is holding. Lexington is folding in."

Still, Rusk said nothing. He looked out the narrow window slit, past the oak tree line, toward the fading skyline where the final act of a long war was unfolding.

A young officer approached. "General, shall we begin phase three?"

"No," Rusk said. "Let them retreat. The ones that don't want to die for the President don't have to. Perhaps they sense defeat."

Fallon waited, unsure. "And those who fight?"

Rusk turned his full gaze on the map—his old classmate's name still attached to the central node, "Executive Command – D.C."

"Well then, we do what they want: we fight."

* * *

FIELD LOG – WEEK TWO OF LEXINGTON CAMPAIGN

Written by: Lt. Samuel Laird, 1st Recon Division.

They say the fighting started as a sweep and turned into a trench war. The hills outside Lexington are stained like Gettysburg: forest fire smoke and phosphorus haze. We buried men with bayonets still in their grip.

But then came the air. I'll never forget the scream of our bombers—low, fast, dropping thunder across their rear guard. When Griffin went up, they didn't have a fallback option for resupply. Half of 'em started eating cold beans and panic set in.

High Command sent down the order: 'Advance; show no fear.' We took the courthouse soon after approaching this battle's third week.

* * *

FIELF COMMAND LOG – BATTLE OF LEXINGTON

DATE: *[REDACTED]*

LOCATION: *Near Fayette County, KY*

FROM: *Gen. Nathaniel Rusk, Commanding General, Continental Defense Force*

DAY ONE: *At 0500 hours, Continental Defense Forces began a coordinated advance from the south and southeast. Artillery batteries began shelling outer government entrenchments east of Richmond, and fighter wings ran suppression missions over eastern skies. No serious resistance was encountered until reaching the Jessamine County line.*

DAY THREE: *Government Forces regrouped and deployed air defense units. A drone strike hit our forward operating base outside Nicholasville. Casualties: 24 dead, 53 wounded. Civilian buildings were destroyed. We responded at midnight with an armored surge, catching enemy tanks out of position. Town secured by 0400. Interrogation of prisoners reveals desperation among regular troops—many are unaware of Lexington's dwindling resources.*

DAY EIGHT: *A surge from our right flank breaks into the city via New Circle Road. There are reports of snipers on rooftops. The enemy has resorted to civilian disguises and basement bombs. We initiate loudspeaker broadcasts: surrender and be treated under the Geneva Conventions. Some comply. Others ambush our medics. Rules of engagement bend, then break. We lost three officers in a cleared building that detonated as they radioed in.*

DAY TEN: *Downtown falls just after midnight. City hall burned down in the final defense. Lexington is ours. The enemy command attempted to escape towards Cincinnati but was intercepted by airborne units. Their commander, Brigadier General James Moffet, was taken alive.*

Exhausted and defeated, his men are being processed under standard wartime procedures.

I stood outside Rupp Arena this morning. Light snow had started to fall, something rare for this time of year. There were no cheers, just the sound of trucks, moaning generators, and stretcher wheels grinding gravel.

War is a grave. Today, we dug it deeper.

April 4, 2051 – Undisclosed Location – Somewhere in Kentucky

The command center buzzed—not with anxiety or anxious waiting, but with the sound of an oiled machine proceeding with its task. Rusk sat alone late into the morning, staring at a still frame of the courthouse. No lights in the windows. Just one flag—his flag—raised by a private whose name he didn't even know.

Fallon returned quietly. "Sir, mop-up operations complete. It seems some of the troops are calling it a victory."

Rusk lit a fresh cigar, slow and deliberate. "It's not victory. It's surrender. There's a difference."

He stood and walked out of the tent. The air was cold. Cherry blossoms did not yet bloom in Lexington, but he thought of them anyway.

* * *

The air in Lexington was heavy with the scent of scorched stone and torn soil. Despite the storm of battle now behind them, the streets still echoed with the ghosts of war—broken glass under boots, burnt-out storefronts, and fluttering flags, half-ripped, tangled in the wind. The sky was still stained with smoke, and the guttural sound of distant artillery thundered like an echo from another time. General Rusk stood near the city's war monument, newly cracked by mortar fire but still tall, symbolizing resilience. His long coat fluttered in the breeze; his boots caked with mud and ash.

Around him, the 91st Combined Division gathered—battered, weathered, but unbroken. These men and women had held the line during the darkest weeks of the Lexington campaign. Faces caked in soot, some bandaged, others missing pieces of themselves they could never regain. Yet they stood straight. Not for cameras. Not for social media. Not for history. But for each other.

"You've done more than history could ever ask of you," Rusk said, standing on a low truck bed, refusing a megaphone. His voice carried, rough and unyielding. "You've cracked the spine of the old world. But ahead lies the final part, the head. You aren't marching for vengeance. You are marching for rebirth. We are not tyrants. We are liberators. Let no one forget that."

The soldiers remained quiet for a beat, then a cheer rolled through them—not raucous, but firm, grounded, earned.

Major Fallon approached from the side, a tablet tucked under his arm. "They're moving out in a couple of hours, sir. Intel says that they are consolidating a defense line around Roanoke. From the chatter, D.C. is in chaos. They weren't expecting us to push so fast."

Rusk nodded. "Have them take their time. Our march on Washington now begins."

As he stepped down, a young private approached—barely nineteen, uniform two sizes too big. He handed Rusk a letter from home. "My mama says you're doing God's work, sir."

Rusk took it slowly. "No, son. We do the work of man now. But we pray he is watching."

June 23, 2052 – Naval Station Norfolk – Ceremony Grounds

The ceremony was held under bright summer skies—the kind that mocked the memories of war. American flags—now bearing thirteen bold stars in a new constellation—fluttered from every corner of the base. In the heart of Naval Station Norfolk, an open parade ground had been cleared, lined with folding chairs, military brass, and war-worn veterans. Some stood on canes, others in wheelchairs, but all with straight backs.

A choir sang a solemn rendition of "America the Beautiful" as the honor guard marched. At the podium, General Rusk waited. His once dark hair had gone silver, the lines on his face carved by battle and grief. He no longer needed to wear medals—his presence alone was the badge of a thousand memories.

Before him stood a row of soldiers clad in formal dress, bearing the ribbons and scars of the war's final chapter. Among them was Sergeant Manuel Ortiz, whose arm had been rebuilt from fragments after pulling three comrades from a burning tank; Lieutenant Erin Baird, known as the Angel of the Potomac for her defense of the river line; and Corporal James Westfield, a scout who vanished behind enemy lines and reemerged three weeks later with the intel that turned the tide.

"You were there fighting for victory," Rusk said, his voice even, slow, and reverent. "You watched a country burn and held the line so a new one would rise. This medal isn't for glory. It's for endurance. For pain. For choosing to keep going when every part of you wanted to stop. For carrying others when you could barely move yourself."

He stepped forward, one by one, pinning the Medals of Honor onto their uniforms. His hand lingered on each. They saluted; he returned it with solemn gravity.

"I remember what it felt like to lead the charge into that city. But you... You were on the edge of the spear. And the ones who came after will never forget your names."

"Anything but being a meme, sir."

"Indeed, soldier."

As the applause rippled, Rusk turned slightly. Beyond the crowd, beyond the cameras, he saw a young girl sitting on her mother's lap. Her father, one of the honorees, knelt beside her and let her touch the medal.

Rusk's jaw clenched. He turned away slowly, his gaze drifting up to the sky. Behind him, a vision started to blur his eyes. Cherry blossoms... pink petals dancing like spirits in the sun.

I wonder why... what do they mean?

April 3, 2054 – Washington, D.C.

Washington, D.C., bloomed in defiance. The cherry blossoms at the Tidal Basin flared in soft shades of pink and white, clustered like living clouds against the branches of trees that stood sentinel through the fall of a nation and the rise of something new. Wind stirred the blossoms into the air like confetti from heaven—graceful, silent, indifferent to the blood that had soaked the soil years before.

General Rusk walked slowly along the basin's curved path; hands folded behind his back. To his left, Elise, now an incoming junior senator from Alabama, kept pace in low heels and a grey overcoat, her dark hair tied back in a practical bun. On his right, Luke Rusk, his estranged son, now a Captain in the newly reformed Continental Defense Forces, kept one hand near his belt as if still expecting combat. Their father moved more slowly these days, the limp in his left leg more noticeable, the creases around his eyes deeper.

Crowds were light. Most recognized Rusk immediately, but few dared approach. Secret Service agents kept the General under a watchful eye, walking behind the family. A reverent hush hung around him now—part awe, part grief.

"I used to bring mom here," Elise said, her voice quiet. "She loved the blossoms."

Rusk nodded. "She called them God's soft surrender. Said even death deserved beauty."

Luke exhaled slowly, his breath fogging in the spring air. "You think she would be proud of how things turned out?"

"I think," Rusk replied, "she'd cry daily. Then get back to work."

They passed a group of children on a school tour. Their teacher whispered something, and the kids turned to stare. One little girl waved. Rusk nodded toward her, but his eyes lingered too long—perhaps seeing the ghosts that still whispered in his memory.

Elise broke the silence. "The talk of D.C. seems to be your title... Lord Protector of the United States of America. British roots returning into the new republic."

"I hate that title, I am no lord." Rusk muttered.

Lord Protector, a title that had not been held in almost three centuries, was not American. However, like Oliver Cromwell in 1653, Rusk felt it was still an appropriate position to lead the country through the transition process.

"Would you run for president though?"

Rusk stopped at the edge of the water. Cherry petals drifted past like little ships with no harbor.

"I've led men to their deaths," he murmured. "That's enough power for one lifetime."

Luke adjusted his collar. "You still smoke that same cigar?"

Rusk looked at his son and smiled faintly. "Not during cherry blossom season. Doesn't seem right."

* * *

They gathered in a private dining room at the Jefferson Hotel. The lights were low, and the windows were open just slightly to let in the scent of spring. Outside, D.C. buzzed in its strange post-war hush—no longer afraid, but not quite healed.

The table was set for six, but only three seats were filled. Elise poured wine. Luke cut into his steak. Rusk toyed with a plate of roast duck, the skin crisp and untouched.

"Will your sister be joining us?"

"Anne said she would be running late."

The night continued, and silence had settled like an old quilt over the table.

"Simon called," Elise finally said. "NBC wants an exclusive on the tenth anniversary of the war's beginning."

Rusk blinked slowly. "I gave them everything in the interviews. Jessica Parker will get the last word."

"She will?" Luke asked. "She will flail you alive. Bleed you on camera."

"She lost her son years ago, her husband died at Lexington," Rusk said, his voice low. "She can bleed me all she wants."

The silverware clinked. No one else spoke. Elise refilled her father's glass, even though he hadn't touched the first one. "Do you remember what Mom used to say before dinner?"

"That no meal was holy unless we argued first?" Luke offered.

Elise chuckled faintly. "No, stupid. She'd say: 'Eat like it's your last, laugh like it's your first.' I think she hated silence more than she hated war."

"I think she hated both equally," Rusk replied.

They ate, though only half-heartedly. When dessert came—a simple apple tart—Rusk waved it off.

"Save it for after," he said, rising. "We got a storm to walk into."

* * *

The studio was modest, tucked into an old press building away from the public eye. It wasn't what it once was—no grandeur, no ceremonial polish—but it was enough to broadcast across the still-reuniting states.

Jessica Parker sat in silence, her silver hair softly curled and pinned, her face framed by the soft glow of studio lighting. She wore black again, though no one had died recently—not recently enough. Her hands trembled once, then went still. The teleprompter glowed with a blank screen.

"Two minutes out," said the producer.

Across the room, Rusk walked in slowly. He wore a dark blue uniform coat with no insignia; his only decoration was a simple silver star on his lapel—the New Nation's symbol. He nodded, his eyes locked on Jessica. She stood. They shook hands with deliberate slowness.

"Thank you for your time, General."

"Thank you for having me."

Silence. The loudest noise that overwhelmed the room. The red light blinked on, and it was off to the races.

Jessica opened with the expected line. "You have been called many things, General. Liberator, traitor, war criminal, and now Lord Protector. You have led millions through fire—and some say into it."

He nodded, listening intently to every word spoken.

"You have also been called many things, Ms. Parker. A patriot, propagandist," Rusk replied. "Yet here we are."

Back and forth it went. Two heavyweights battling over conflicting beliefs and incidents that forever changed their lives—the nuclear strikes, the rebellion, God, and power. Jessica challenged him on Daniel, Mitch, and the cost of it all.

"If you were still in government, would you condone the use of nuclear weapons?"

"Absolutely not."

"And why is that, General?"

"Because it was unnecessary, barbaric, and a telling to our allies that we don't care for the people. And that built within me something fierce; the will to act."

"By spilling more blood?"

"Blood will be spilled within the confines of any war, Ms. Parker."

"My son died for the government. Where is his justice, General?"

"A tragedy. And I am sorry it came to that. The failures of this government will haunt us for centuries."

"Do you hold the *West Coast Alliance* responsible for their part in this, General?"

"All parties are responsible to an extent; no one person shares the blame. This was a complete failure of governing."

"Does that include you, General?"

"Not for these decisions that occurred before me, perhaps when I was in the Pentagon. But I was exiled from D.C., if you know anything about my history."

"How do you intend to help those within the states of the *West Coast Alliance*?"

"That is a bridge we have yet to cross. Once we assess the inhabited areas, we'll start the cleanup and create blocked-off zones. I will help them rebuild."

"You intend to be merciful to those who started this war?"

"I feel we must. They are Americans. We were supposed to fight for them, and we failed them."

"You told the world to show mercy," she snapped. "And then you ordered men to their executions."

"I showed mercy to the innocent," Rusk said calmly. "I showed judgment to the wicked—those who betrayed the American people."

She stared hard. "And you think you get to decide which is which?"

"No," he said softly. "But I carry the burden because no one else would."

The interview soon raced to its conclusion, not fast enough for Rusk and Parker. The crew shut down the set around them, packing up ever so silently as the grave.

Jessica finally asked, "Do you sleep well?"

Rusk looked away. "I don't sleep, Ms. Parker. I never do."

***

The evening air blew from the east. The worst had passed, and the family gathered in the hotel suite's sitting room. A fire crackled softly. Luke flipped through the channels, paused on reruns of the interview. Elise poured a small glass of bourbon.

Rusk sat in a comfortable leather chair, finally smoking that cigar. The window beside him was open just enough to let the breeze stir the curtains.

“I didn’t expect you to be that open,” Elise said quietly.

“What do you expect? He’s honest.” A voice shot through. The family turned to see a familiar face. Anne Rusk walked in with her suitcase in tow, as she finally arrived, albeit late.

“Glad you can make it, sweetie.”

“I wouldn’t miss this for the world, Dad.” She softly replied, walking over to her father to give a hug.

Luke crossed his arms. “You didn’t answer the question about her son, Mitch.”

“I answered how I always do,” Rusk said. “Sometimes that says more.”

Elise leaned forward. “You think she’s right about us? That we became what we hated?”

Rusk took a long draw. “Maybe. But we didn’t lie about it. We didn’t hide behind politics or slogans. We bore the ugliness openly.”

Silence fell again. Outside, a single blossom floated through the window and landed on the armrest of Rusk’s chair. He looked at it for a long moment. Then crushed it gently between his fingers.

“Cherry blossoms,” he muttered. “Always bloom after the fire.”

“Deep, as always,” Anne replied.

“I don’t know how else to be.”

Elise scoffed. “You can be a golfer.”

Rusk let out a small chuckle. “Ok, now you are just lying.”

"We should take him to the golf course when this settles down." Anne snapped back.

Luke raised his hand. "I would 100% be down with that; the air is getting too heavy in here."

"That's just you blowing ass, Luke."

"Anne, what did I always tell you about speaking that way?"

"Don't do it in front of you?"

"Yes. Please and thank you."

"Same as always, old man."

Rusk gave his daughter the side-eye.

"Hey, who are you calling old?"

They all shared a laugh. For the first time in what felt like years, happiness seemed to overflow within Rusk at that moment.

April 5, 2054 – Washington, D.C.

The cherry blossoms had come late that year, but in the end, they bloomed all the time.

Washington, D.C., wore the silence of early spring like a funeral shroud. The wide avenues that once bore tanks and protestors were quiet now—swept clean but not forgotten. Down the National Mall, beneath the soft pink canopy of flowering trees, General Rusk walked alone, his boots crunching over gravel damp with morning dew. The wind was cool, not cold, brushing past his cheeks like an old friend. The scent of blossoms mingled with a faint tinge of smoke from distant ceremonial fires, kindled across the city in remembrance.

In one hand, he carried a dog–eared manila envelope sealed with a red wax stamp, its corners smudged from countless hands. In the other, he carried a half-smoked cigar, its cherry pulsing softly like a quiet heartbeat. He moved slowly, deliberately, like a man with nothing to outrun. He was careful to smoke it away from the trees.

His doctors warned him to quit smoking, yet Rusk refused to stop. In his mind, he figured his lungs were too far gone to reverse. If his death were to be in the form of lung cancer, so be it. As far as he was concerned, his life was on the cusp of running its course. Although, he wanted to live more for his children, grandchildren, and country. Yet, he was unmoved by the prospect of falling into the void, perhaps to heaven or hell.

He paused at the edge of the reflecting pool. It was still and glassy, like a mirror held up to history. The Capitol dome shimmered faintly in its surface, blurred by a drifting blossom. Behind him, the broken republic stirred a new flag atop a new building, a new oath awaiting the rise of a new nation.

Not a word was uttered by Rusk. Words, after all, had torn nations apart. Today was for silence.

A steel bucket sat nearby, nestled beneath a crooked cherry tree—the same tree, it was said, that had once been planted in honor of Lincoln's second inaugural. Rusk knelt slowly, groaning at the tightness in his knees, and opened the envelope with a single flick of his thumb.

Inside were documents that no history book would ever print: orders from the early years of the war, kill lists, maps of the failed airlift in Colorado, coded correspondence with the *West Coast Alliance*. There were two letters he had written but never sent—one to his daughter on the eve of Lexington, and one to the President of the United States, begging him to call off the nuclear strike.

He fed them into the bucket, one page at a time.

The fire sparked from a match struck against steel, catching quickly. The edges of the paper curled, blackened, then flared bright before collapsing into glowing orange threads. The pages made no sound as they died, except for the whisper of ash folding into itself.

He puffed his cigar slowly, the smoke curling up and around his face. The ember glowed red against the soft pink petals floating in the air. He squinted into the flame, watching his past disintegrate. He found himself remembering to respect the cherry trees, and he promptly put out his cigar. After so many years of having a steel mind, forgetting himself now was slowly becoming a part of his life—a price to pay with age.

Behind him, footsteps approached—measured, hesitant.

Ellison, his longtime aide, and Fallon, his trusted operations officer, emerged through the blossom haze like ghosts returning from war.

They wore their full uniforms, hats under one arm, and one carried a tablet like they always had.

"Lieutenant Colonels Ellison and Fallon. Gentlemen?"

Ellison and Fallon stood to attention, issuing a salute. "General Rusk, sir."

"At ease, gentlemen. The war is over, let us breathe a little bit."

Fallon looked at him. "Of course, sir."

Ellison lowered his hand, pulling up his tablet. "General, it's almost time. They're waiting for you."

"Because of course they are."

"It seems we face another type of battle, sir."

"Politics. The one thing that wars are an extension of. Now it must be fought in conference rooms."

Fallon turned slightly and observed the cherry blossoms around him. He couldn't help but take it all in. He followed the little fire, but thought nothing more of it.

"What time is it?" Rusk asked.

"Seventeen-thirty hours. Your swearing-in will be in approximately three hours. Then, sir, all eyes will be on you."

Rusk chuckled once, low and tired.

"All eyes have always been on me, Ellison. I just stopped caring."

A blossom drifted into the flames, curling into cinder. Rusk watched it as it died.

"Lord Protector. They want to turn back the clock and crown me a founder." He muttered. "Give me statues. Paint me like some damn

Moses. Yet they didn't see what I did, what we did. They didn't sit in the room where we toyed with people's lives on a map. They didn't bury boys whose names I never learned."

"You gave them something to believe in, sir."

Rusk turned slightly, glancing over his shoulder. "No, Colonel. I gave them something to survive through. Belief that came after blood."

Ellison nodded. "Still... they're waiting."

The general exhaled smoke into the morning air. It hung there, briefly caught in a ray of sunlight. He stood.

His back cracked, his joints protesting, but he was upright—tall and solid, like the statues he now despised. He took one final look at the fire. The last page crumbled in on itself—a sketch of the Lexington strategy map, penciled by his own hand.

He crushed the cigar under his heel.

Fallon stepped forward and handed him a small box. Rusk opened it. Inside was the new insignia of the Commonwealth—thirteen stars arranged not in a circle but in a soaring arc. The country may have still had 50 states that were coming back together, but this was a representation of the victors. Although the government loyalists would insist it was a draw, as the government wasn't entirely disassembled, it was now under a new regime.

"Have the new elections been set?"

"Yes, General. It seems many states don't like the idea of re-electing all 435 members from scratch."

"Many should be grateful it didn't mean a more dire fate. Besides, you can't reset if the same people are allowed to get back in again."

He pinned it to his lapel, without another word. The window picked up slightly, stirring petals all around them. Fallon and Ellison stepped aside as Rusk began walking down the path.

"General..." Fallon said.

Rusk stopped, half-turned.

Fallon gave him a faint smile. "Let's go finish what you started."

Rusk's eyes scanned the horizon—the Capitol glowing in the sunrise, the Mall filled with hushed anticipation, camera crews, soldiers, families, survivors.

"I didn't start anything," he muttered. "I just picked up what someone else broke."

As they walked on, silence fell between them. The ash from the fire swirled into the breeze, rising alongside the petals. Then, behind them, a young soldier jogged up. Nervous. Out of breath. He saluted.

"Sir, I have been tasked with escorting you."

Rusk didn't stop walking.

"No need, soldier. I have my trusted people with me to escort."

"Yes, sir."

And so he walked—into the wind, into the light, into the waiting arms of a country desperate to believe again. The blossoms rained around him like confetti and dust and memory. And the last line, heard only by the cherry trees, was this: *"Let history judge me. I served my God, my men, and my conscience. The rest is ash."*

III.

Upon This Soil

March 26, 2050 – Somewhere near Tifton, Georgia

The morning mist clung to the earth like a veil, soft and cool against Liam Sullivan's skin as he knelt in the rows of tilled soil. He pressed a calloused hand into the dark, moist, and fragrant dirt. It gave just enough under his palm, like bread dough on the rise. *A good spring,* he thought, wiping sweat from his brow though the sun had barely cleared the pine line.

Birdsong echoed through the pecan trees behind him, and far off, a rooster crowed as if late to the morning. He stood slowly, his back crackling like dry branches. Liam may have been getting up there in age, but he had the muscles of a farmer, built to last forever. From here, he could see the old farmhouse—white paint chipped and sun-faded—with a worn wooden porch that leaned slightly westward like a tired man. Five pairs of boots sat on the stoop, evidence that his children were already out and about, doing chores or sneaking off into the woods. Probably both.

He let out a slow breath and whispered, as he always did when alone, "Oh God, give me strength for today and grace enough for the rest."

He walked back toward the barn, boots squelching softly in the dew-soaked grass. His youngest son, Ethan, no older than nine, was chasing a barn cat with a stick. "Leave him be, boy!" Liam called. "A cat's no match for your trouble."

"I'm just trying to see if he can jump higher than last time!" Ethan shouted back, laughing as the cat darted up the nearest hay bale and out of sight. The furry creature was considered lucky that it was faster than the nine-year-old boy, as it was no match for his hands.

While one was racing the cat, Liam's middle-born son, Garrett, was atop the tractor, fiddling with a stubborn ignition switch. "She isn't turning over, Pa!" Garrett grumbled.

"Talk to her nicely," Liam said with a grin. "These old girls don't take kindly to impatient hands."

Garrett grumbled, but he started touching the controls calmly. Within seconds, the tractor coughed to life. Garrett gave him a mock salute.

Despite the peaceful life on the land, Liam felt unease rising in him—a pressure building behind his ribs. He couldn't place it. Maybe it was the chaos of the world he'd overheard on the radio the nights before: mass resignations in Congress, the Government Forces siege of Atlanta, strange words like "blockade" and "secession" cropping up on every station. Or maybe it was something older, something instinctual, the kind of dread a man of the soil learns to recognize before a bad harvest or an unexpected frost. *I have kept my family away from war... but how long can I keep that up?*

By late morning, he was in his rusted F-250, driving along cracked county roads. The fields gave way to a pine forest, then finally, the outskirts of Tifton. The town looked as it always did—stubbornly outdated, fiercely proud. The American flag flew above the post office, but a second flag—a navy-blue banner with a white cross, the symbol of the growing Southern Restoration Movement—now fluttered next to it. Liam frowned. He didn't like politics, and he liked factions even less. When they knocked on his door, he turned them away. Liam was just one farmer. But his contribution to agriculture did not go unnoticed by the powers of the newly formed world.

The county store sat on the corner of Main and Railroad, its screen door creaking like an old hymn. Inside, it smelled of oil, dust, and sugar. Locals stood around the old Coke cooler, murmuring about "something happening down near Valdosta" or "CDF forces also on the move." Liam didn't say much. He gathered fencing wire, some extra seed, a case of motor oil, and—on a whim—two pounds of salted peanuts. You never know when you'd need protein on the move. With the blockades in effect, many products were now unavailable or simply too expensive to obtain.

Liam found himself grateful that he had no desire for many of the products affected by the war. At the counter, the purple-haired girl smiled at him like he was a local celebrity.

"Mr. Sullivan," she said cheerfully. "You ever think of getting on TikTok?"

He raised an eyebrow. "What on earth would I do on there?"

"Talk farming. Give life advice. Make the kids cry with dad jokes. Make more money?"

"I don't need TikTok to do that, Suanna," he said, handing her exact change. "Got a living room full of unpaid critics at home."

She laughed, bagging his things, and said, "Still think you'd blow up on there. You've got that 'wise old man in a post-apocalyptic drama' look."

"Let's hope the apocalypse stays on the screen."

"Don't know it's that simple, Mr. Sullivan. California is breathing it now. It seems things are picking up all around us."

"There is nothing here for either side, honey."

"You never know. Seems there is movement near Valdosta."

"Well, just keep the apocalypse off my farm."

But even as he stepped outside, that word—apocalypse—stuck to him like the red dust rising off the road. He put his supplies away, still hearing the hum of the word. He was just about to crank the engine when he heard it: the low thrum of diesel engines, the rhythmic chop of rotor blades overhead. He turned and squinted toward the tree line. There, the convoy came cresting the distant hills like a steel river.

Armored trucks—real ones, not National Guard hand-me-downs—rolled through the two-lane highway just north of town. Their paint was unmarked, matte gray, and dusty. Each vehicle flew a familiar but altered flag: thirteen stars, a horizontal tricolor of red, white, and blue.

A group of townspeople gathered on the sidewalk, some waving, others simply watching silently. Liam's stomach dropped. He knew what this was. Not the Guard. Not feds.

Continental Defense Force.

"Jesus, Mary, and Joseph," he whispered, throwing his truck into gear. He tore down the backroads at forty over the limit, past wildflowers, fence posts, and rusted signs. In the passenger seat, the bag of peanuts rolled off and spilled across the vinyl floor. Despite the mess, that seemed to be the furthest thing from Liam's mind.

* * *

By the time Liam reached the farmhouse, the horizon had shifted. The sun was lower now, casting long golden rays across the fields. Birds still chirped, and the cattle lowed in the pasture, but everything felt... off and irregular. The trees were too still. The wind still carried a scent of fuel and dust, not spring and pollen—not uncommon, but strange.

He parked behind the barn and climbed out of the truck, nearly tripping over the spilled peanuts. *Dammit.* A few hens scurried at his sudden approach. From the porch, his eldest daughter Molly called out, "You all right, Pa? You're white as a sheet."

He looked up, frantic, but remained composed. "Yeah, sweetie. Just a little amped up. Is supper ready?"

"Yes, Pa."

"Good. Get everyone inside now."

Molly went out to the barn to get her other siblings. Liam paced up and down the porch, waiting for all his children to enter the farmhouse.

By the time the family gathered around the large, hand-carved dining table—built by Liam's own father decades ago—there were many Sullivans in one room. All but one chair was filled, and a few kids shared the old bench. The clatter of silverware was met with whispered jokes and inside references, and Liam only understood half.

The smell of buttered cornbread and fried venison hung in the air. Steam rose from a pot of mashed sweet potatoes. Liam was hungry, but his mind was distracted by the larger issue. He carried on as normally as possible, so as not to alarm the children. But he realized he had to tell them the truth.

"Lord, we..."

Liam's prayer was interrupted as Ethan, raced inside to the table. He quickly sat down and bowed his head. Liam stared, giving him the 'you've got some explaining to do' look.

"What did I do, Pa?"

"It's what you haven't done, boy. Not washing your hands. And then, running inside the house."

Ethan got up, rushed to the sink to wash his hands, and then rushed to sit back down, taking care to walk fast but not run. Once he returned, the family bowed its heads, and Liam continued.

"Lord: we cleared this land, we plowed it and sowed it, and it wouldn't be here if we hadn't done it all ourselves. But we thank you for this food all the same, amen."

The sounds of kitchenware and clanging of dishes overfilled the room. Each was eager to dig into a dish that overwhelmed the senses. Liam's mind caught up to him, and he found himself looking out the window again.

"Pa," Molly said softly, passing him a plate. "What's going on?"

He didn't answer at first. He looked down the table, his gaze settling on each of his children—from his youngest boy, gangly, to his eldest son and his wife.

"I saw 'em," he finally said. "The rebels. The Continental Defense Force. Rolling in by the dozens. Military grade trucks. No federal markings."

Silence settled like ash. Even the youngest stopped chewing.

"They're heading this way?" asked Ronan, the oldest son at twenty-two, a wiry boy with clever eyes.

"Hard to know where they are going, but they may be here by morning," Liam replied, reaching for a roll but not eating it. "And when they come, anything could happen. Wanting our farm supplies, maybe more."

His wife's seat remained empty. The silence around it was always loudest at dinner.

"Should we leave?" Molly asked, trying to sound calm.

Bethany, his middle daughter, looked at Molly with agreement. "Leaving wouldn't be the worst thing, Papa."

"Leave?" Liam scoffed. "Where would we go? Gas shortages within a hundred miles. The cities are worse. This land has been ours for four generations. No one is taking it from us."

Liam hated it when people considered him a doomsday prepper with his meticulous preparation of survival supplies, but things like this war made it all the more justified. When the first reports of riots breaking out in the major cities and the home improvement stores being looted and destroyed, Liam decided it was time to take action.

"Papa," piped up Ethan, barely tall enough to be eye level with the family, "are we going to be drafted?"

A hush fell over the room. Even the youngest could sense it. The hens must have also sensed it, as they were quieter tonight.

Liam leaned back in his chair and crossed his arms. "I don't know. But I do know one thing—if you feed an army, you don't starve. And if you look afraid, you might lose everything. But they'll call you their neighbor if you stand like a man."

His phone buzzed. He pulled it from his pocket to look. A message from his neighbor across the county. "*Hey Liam, just a heads up: CDF sighted near the old cotton gin. They're stopping at each farm.*"

Bloody hell. This is not good. Liam knew what this meant. The CDF was looking for something, or perhaps pressing into service. With how contested Georgia had become in the last few years of the war, it wasn't surprising that the CDF was securing resources. Despite housing a heavy presence of government forces, Atlanta remained a gray zone. They maneuvered as if they were not planning a long-term occupation.

Liam pocketed his phone without a word.

Then—suddenly—Bethany said with a grin. "Papa, you know you're trending on TikTok again, right?"

Oh, that was quite a pivot. Everyone turned to her, confused.

She held up her phone. "Someone from town filmed you at the store, yelling about the apocalypse. It's already at 48,000 views."

Liam groaned, pressing his hand to his forehead. "That damn Suanna... I ought to tell her mama."

Ronan snorted. "You're famous again."

"I've never been famous. I've been known, which is a curse in its own right."

Molly giggled. "People are commenting that you're like if Cormac McCarthy and Gordon Ramsay had a baby."

"Aye, and that's the problem with this world," Liam said dryly. "No one listens unless you're loud or dead."

The humor blasted the graveness of the situation, bringing them a little peace. But deep down, they knew this peace was always a short-lived one.

* * *

Nightfall soon fell, and the crickets and animal life came to life within the trees. Liam sat alone on the porch, deep in thought in his favorite rocking chair. He sipped coffee from a chipped ceramic mug. Out past the tree line, he could see them now. Lights. Headlamps. A convoy on the far road. Rolling slowly. Deliberate.

He didn't wake the kids. Instead, he got up from the porch and walked toward the steps. He thought back to something his father told him before he lay his head down most nights, something his father read to him from a book whose leather cover was cracked, the gold leaf fading. A psalm that brought familiar comfort when conflict loomed.

"Though I walk through the valley of the shadow of death, I will fear no evil."

He closed his eyes, thinking on that phrase as the night air filled his nostrils. War may soon be at his doorstep, but he always took comfort in what his father taught him in confronting fear.

"My plow will be close, just in case."

March 27, 2050 – Near Tifton, Georgia – Sullivan Farm

Dawn broke slowly and blood-orange rose over the Georgia horizon, creeping across the rows of cotton and corn like fingers testing the earth. The morning was still, but not quiet. A low rumble—a vibration that didn't belong—shivered the farmhouse walls before any birds sang.

Liam had been awake before sunrise. He hadn't changed from the flannel shirt he'd worn the day before, now rumpled and sweat-stained. A mug of coffee steamed on the porch rail beside him, half drunk. His Bible lay closed on his lap, a red ribbon marking Proverbs.

The rumble grew louder.

By the time the first truck came into view, the children were awake and peering from windows, sleepy-eyed and curious. Molly was already dressed, arms crossed tight across her chest. She didn't speak. She just watched.

"Do you want us to arm?"

"Don't bother. It's futile. However, if they do something to me, do what we trained for; doomsday protocol."

"Yes, papa."

A half-dozen military trucks came into view—no U.S. flags, but not bandit trucks either. The lead vehicle was a heavily modified Ford with armor plates welded crudely to the sides. A flag fluttered from the antenna: thirteen stars in a circle on a dark blue field.

Continental Defense Force.

The convoy stopped at the base of the driveway. Dust rose like mist. The Sullivan family's worst fears had come to pass; war had reached their doorstep.

Three soldiers stepped out of the first truck—one in full camouflage, another in desert fatigues, and a third in a clean gray uniform with a chest full of ribbons. The one in gray was tall, bald, with hard blue eyes and a voice rough as gravel.

He approached slowly, no weapon drawn. Liam was relieved, but nervous. Just because weapons were not being pulled out did not mean they were out of the woods. Many scenarios ran through Liam's mind as to the motive of their arrival. Was it to question loyalty? To fight? To question? So many different theories, but no answers at that moment. Until he spoke to them.

Liam met them halfway down the steps.

"Mr. Sullivan," the man said, extending a hand. "Colonel Wyatt Sloane. I'm here on behalf of the 3rd Logistics Division. We're establishing supply routes for the Continental Defense Forces."

Liam didn't shake his hand. "What do you want from us, Colonel?"

Sloane gave a thin smile. "Your country needs you. It means opportunity and inevitability."

He reached into a pouch on his belt and pulled out a folded map marked with red zones and blue lines.

"You are located in one of the highest-producing agricultural quadrants between Macon and the Alabama line. Your land is fertile, your water is clean, and your silos are full. We want to requisition you formally for your services—either as a direct supplier under Army contract, or..." He paused. "Under conscription orders."

Liam's jaw tightened. "War has already taken my wife, Colonel. And you bring it to my doorstep?"

"You had to know it would be sooner or later, Mr. Sullivan. If you decline, you'd be offered relocation to a secure facility further north, and your land would be placed under provisional military management."

"A polite way of saying you'll take it, regardless of what I say."

"This is the fight of our lives, Mr. Sullivan. The old world being clung to is gone. Unlike our enemy, you will be compensated—gold, not paper. Or... You can refuse and let the harvest rot under someone else's care."

Molly opened the front door behind them. "Papa?"

Liam turned slightly. "It's all right, girl. Go back inside." He did not use their safe word. In a world where all words, actions, and motions are watched, moving without others seeing is essential. Liam trained his children to act if he ever used a distress word they all knew to use if they were ever in an emergency. In this case, he didn't use it. Molly went inside without saying another word.

The Colonel raised a hand, backing off slightly. "We don't want to fight. But this is war. And in war, every army needs resources."

Liam looked down, lost in thought. He knew this day would come, yet he still felt the urge to resist it from consuming his family. "I've got kids," Liam said. "This land has been there's since before the war started. I've buried kin in that field over yonder. You think I would let someone else sow it?"

Colonel Sloane didn't blink. "Then fight with us. Keep your land. Keep your say. Hell, we'll even make you a quartermaster. You'll manage the supply for half the county. Report to MacDill directly."

"I want my children to live in peace, Colonel. I buried scavengers that killed their mother already."

"Mr. Sullivan, you know peace hasn't been possible since the nuclear strike on California. This won't end until the current D.C. regime collapses."

Liam stared at him. "You say MacDill? You talk to Rusk himself?"

General Nathaniel Rusk's name and reputation had made themselves known in Georgia. This didn't surprise the Colonel, as the propaganda machines on both sides made him both savior and traitor in the same digital spaces.

The colonel smiled faintly. "I've heard him pray."

That earned a dry laugh from Liam. "And what about the federal boys? You think they'll just let you walk off with Georgia's abundant resources?"

The colonel was surprised but unfazed by Liam Sullivan's extensive knowledge of the reports from the front.

"They have no interest in occupying Georgia. They blazed down to the panhandle from Atlanta. If they wanted the agriculture here, you'd have this conversation with them, not us."

Silence passed like wind through dry stalks. Liam hesitantly reached out and took Sloane's offered folder—a thick packet of forms, hand-signed orders, payment estimates, and military logistics charts. Among the papers, one thing stood out—a small velvet pouch. He opened it to find several gold coins, stamped with a phoenix.

"First payment," the Colonel said. "The rest comes as the supplies move."

"If I do this," Liam said slowly, "You'll leave my children be?"

"They'll be protected. And they'll have a nation's gratitude."

Liam turned toward the porch, where all his children now stood behind the screen door, quiet as ghosts. His eyes lingered on each face.

"All right," he said at last. "But I do this my way. On my terms."

Colonel Sloane nodded once. "As long as you get us what we need."

Liam stood on the porch as he observed the convoy beginning to move again, and the soldiers pulled away to the next farm. Liam stood alone in the rising sun, coins clutched tight in one hand, papers in the other.

From behind, Garrett stepped beside him. "Are we at war now?"

Liam didn't answer right away. Then he murmured, "Yes, son. We're at war."

No one knew what their father felt in that moment, but they were sure of one thing: they were in it now.

April 4, 2050 – Sullivan Farm

The farm was no longer just a farm.

In less than a week, Liam Sullivan's quiet patch of Georgia soil had been transformed into a supply hub for the Continental Defense Force. His farm was enough to feed his family and turn a small profit, but now, it was being expanded to feed an army. The wheat fields still shimmered under the April sun, the irrigation pumps hummed, and the livestock stirred in their pens—but the rhythm of life had shifted. Where tractors once rolled, now military trucks thundered. Where silos once stood untouched, now men in fatigues climbed ladders and loaded grain by the ton.

The Continental Defense Forces sent two dozen men, mostly logistics hands, to oversee the transition. They pitched canvas tents near the barn, erected temporary fencing, and brought in field radios that crackled through the day with orders from MacDill.

Liam hated the noise.

He stood near the gate at the edge of his property, smoking a corncob pipe and staring down the convoy lined up along the dirt road. The sky was thick with dust from the wheels, and a heavy haze hung in the air. His sons were already out in the fields, helping haul crates of corn and potatoes.

Molly and Beth directed the kitchen staff—two neighbors who'd come to help—as they baked flatbreads and dried meat for preservation.

"Morning, Quartermaster," called Private Larsson, the youngest of the soldiers, barely older than Molly.

"Don't call me that," Liam muttered. "I'm a farmer."

But the title was already being whispered across the farm. *Quartermaster Sullivan*. The man who fed a rebel army.

Inside the old barn, a small command table had been set up with manifests, grain charts, and route planning documents. Liam refused to sit at it. Instead, he stood and pointed, grumbled and ordered, and scribbled notes into a little pocket journal bound in leather. He ran everything with the same stern precision he used when raising his children—feed what grows, cut what rots, and never waste a seed. But the stress was mounting.

On the third day of deliveries, a flat tire delayed the shipment. On the fourth, a group of federal scouts was spotted near the southern road—they vanished before soldiers could respond, but the message was clear: they were watching.

On the fifth, the grain silo jammed. Liam worked through the night with Ronan, clearing it manually.

By the sixth day, he was starting to feel like a commanding soldier of sorts—his war was fought not with bullets, but bushels.

That evening, as twilight fell, the convoy was ready. Five trucks lined up before the gate with crates of sweet potatoes, onions, carrots, and grain sacks. Much of the supplies were harvested before the arrival of the CDF, and some were pulled from the reserve stocks of the Sullivan family. A hand-painted placard sat atop one of the crates: "*Property of the Continental Defense Force—Supplies for the front.*"

Liam stood before it all, arms crossed. Colonel Sloane had returned to oversee the departure. The two men locked eyes.

"First shipment on time," the Colonel said. "Impressive."

"Don't thank me. Thank the soil, and my bountiful harvest." Liam said, though even he knew the soil didn't harvest itself.

Sloane stepped closer. "General Rusk has been briefed. Your name came up in the dispatch. You've made quite an impression."

"I'm not in this for medals."

"No," Sloane said, looking past him at the farmhouse where Molly and the younger children were waving goodbye to the drivers, "You're in it for them."

"You have kids of your own, Colonel?"

"Four. They are in hiding somewhere in Texas. Three girls and a boy. I miss 'em something fierce."

Liam lit his pipe and said nothing more.

Sloane mounted his jeep and raised a hand. The trucks roared to life. They rolled off in the orange dusk one by one—a serpentine lifeline winding toward the front.

The dust had barely settled when Molly came to stand beside him.

"Is this going to be every month now?"

He looked at her—freckles across her nose, sleeves rolled up, hands still dusted with flour.

"Every week. Every day. Until it ends."

Molly's voice was low. "And it never ends?"

Liam took a long draw from his pipe, then exhaled slowly.

"Maybe. Maybe not. But we keep working."

May 16, 2050 –Sullivan Farm

The stars above the Georgia countryside shimmered in eerie stillness, cloaking the earth below in a quiet too deep for comfort. The crickets had stopped singing, and the frogs at the nearby creek fell silent. Only the faint rustling of wind through cornfields betrayed any movement.

Liam Sullivan stirred from his sleep before the dogs even started barking. He knew something was wrong.

He slipped out of bed, shirtless and barefoot, his chest rising and falling as he moved toward the window with the instincts of a man who'd lived off the land his entire life. His eyes scanned the blackness—and then he saw them.

Parachutes.

Ten or twelve, maybe more, descending like silent ghosts from the heavens, lit dimly by the crescent moon. They glided lower and lower, black canopies nearly invisible against the sky. Liam raced to his daughter's room, shaking her violently.

"Molly," Liam whispered, snapping into motion. "Get the kids. Hide them in the root cellar."

"What is it?" she asked, already sitting up. Her hair was tangled, voice shaking as she asked.

"Possibly an attack. Soldiers. Move now."

Liam grabbed an old shotgun from beside the door, then changed his mind and went for the scoped hunting rifle above the mantle. No time to grab boots as he sprinted across the porch and into the shadows near the barn, just as the first boots hit the soil.

The commandos landed with precision—smooth, quiet, like wolves on the hunt. Black uniforms, night-vision goggles, suppressed weapons. They were as quiet as a church. The CDF guards were not even alerted by their presence. A fundamental weakness in training was that the CDF was unlike the U.S. Military.

They moved toward the barn first, aiming for what they assumed was an ammo stash. They had been briefed on this target: a farm suspected of harboring a Continental Defense Forces supply chain—food, vehicles, maybe fuel. The strike team was a force known to the world as elite: Special Tactics Group Delta, chosen for their efficiency and silence.

But what they didn't account for was Liam.

Two stepped on a pressure plate buried years ago—part of an old boar trap Liam had long forgotten. The explosion tore through the silence, lighting up the trees, throwing blood and bone into the soybean fields.

The team froze in shock. It was too late. The CDF forces on site were awake and alerted to their presence. Shots began to ring out at the Delta Forces, realizing they had entered a trap.

Liam was already in position on the ridge just north of the barn. His first shot, with precision, dropped a soldier trying to flank the chicken coop. The second pierced the chest of a radio operator, who had just opened his comms channel. Silence again—except now the dogs howled like banshees. The floodlights snapped on, bathing the fields in golden light.

From the house, Molly opened fire with the old double-barrel shotgun Liam's grandfather used in the Korean War. She was careful to remain behind the glass and in cover, as even someone as naïve as a farmer could be killed quickly in the open. Disoriented from being hit, the Delta Force commando pointed his weapon at the house, turning his back to a CDF soldier aiming his gun at him. The glass windows shattered from the gunfire; Molly hit the deck with glass slicing her face.

A CDF soldier pointed his weapon at the Delta Force, shooting him repeatedly. The third commando fell screaming into the bush.

Still, the rest of the team pressed forward. They breached the barn and found nothing—just hay and empty crates. The team had not been briefed that the CDF had already moved out the vital supplies and that soldiers remained on site to assist with building the farm's infrastructure further for future supplies.

Suddenly, the lights inside flickered. An industrial-grade cattle prod, hooked to a makeshift car battery trap Liam had rigged years ago to keep raccoons out, snapped to life. It struck the intruder square in the back, paralyzing him mid-scream.

Another tried to breach the main house through the side window, unaware it was nailed shut and booby-trapped with barbed wire. He tumbled back, bloodied and screaming, into the arms of his own team.

One by one, each started to panic. They had entered a trap, and now half their unit had been wiped out. A simple seek-and-destroy mission with ten Delta Force specialists had now turned into a fight for survival. What they'd walked into wasn't a simple farm—a centuries-old homestead fortified by a deeply paranoid and clever man.

Of course, he wasn't paranoid enough not to inform the Continental Defense Forces of each of the traps when they first arrived. One of the most painful things Liam found himself doing was informing every CDF soldier who walked through of the dangers of his farm. This was something he did not want to volunteer for, as it was his farm's life at stake, but he felt it was better than being executed for killing their people with his traps.

In the chaos, Ronan ran to the stables, AK-47 in hand, climbed onto the roof, and began firing at the intruders, shouting insults in Gaelic. *What does that dumbass think he's doing?!*

It drew enough attention for Liam to line up one final shot and remove the leader—an officer marked by a subtle patch on his sleeve. With that, the last four surviving Delta Force soldiers vanished into the darkness, retreating the way they came, silent shadows again.

Ronan made his way down from the barn, as did Liam.

Liam shoved his son. "Are you out of your damn mind?!"

"I was trying to help, Papa."

"I was in cover! You were out in the open with trained killers aiming at your dumb ass!"

Ronan looked down in silence. Liam grabbed the AK-47 from him in anger, but was careful enough to know it was a loaded weapon. The last thing needed was more foolishness.

"Don't you ever pull a stunt like that again! You hear me?!"

"Yes, Papa."

A silent shush fell over them both in that moment. Every Sullivan was shaken, but grateful to be alive.

* * *

By dawn, the farm was quiet.

Blood seeped into the soil near the barn. Two bodies lay sprawled by the chicken coop. One was impaled on a jagged fence post, victim of his haste. Another had been buried in the hayloft after succumbing to internal injuries. The commanding officer lay lifeless in the middle of the dirt road, a shot to his neck.

Liam stood in the yard, still barefoot, rifle resting on his shoulder.

A Continental Defense Force jeep rolled up just after sunrise. To his surprise, Colonel Sloane stepped out, jaw slack as he looked at the mess.

"We got reports that you were attacked. The hell happened here?"

"Based on my research of their patches, it looks like Delta Force. I believe the word I found online was... a commando raid?"

"Son of a bitch..."

"They know the CDF is here, Colonel," Liam said plainly. "They seem to be targeting everything connected to them."

Sloane stepped carefully over a body. "We thought this place might stay off their radar."

"So did I."

A long silence held between them.

"This farm is one of several contributing to our units holding the line in the Panhandle. We can't afford to lose it. You will be assigned a couple of units for protection."

Liam looked out over his hand, then at the broken bodies. "No. Just give me the tools. I will protect this land like I've always done."

Sloane looked at him. "This is not up for debate, Sullivan. You may have fought off one of the best units in the military, but you can't possibly hold up against a lot more of them."

"I'm a farmer," Liam replied. "I know how to handle pests."

"It's done; this is not a debate. You will have units assigned before the end of the week."

Sloane returned to his vehicle, ordering men to clean and clear the area. Liam walked off toward the barn as the sun rose behind him, its light catching on the darkened rows of corn.

* * *

Diary Entry – Liam Sullivan

May 17, 2050

One day after the raid

I can still smell the gunpowder. It's settled into the walls, the dirt, the skin under my nails.

I buried four men today. Didn't know their names, as it seems they scrubbed their identities for their mission. I didn't care much about learning them, regardless. They came to kill, and they died for it.

The kids hardly slept last night. Ronan won't stop talking about his heroics from the roof like David fighting Goliath. He's proud of his heroic act, but I see it in his eyes. Something inside him shifted.

I told him he was not allowed to go back on the roof. He was stupid for exposing himself up there, risking sure death against someone as skilled as a soldier. When he created a distraction, however, it felt like he was doing something right—like protecting our home was something he was capable of.

The commander he hit looked closest in age to my son. It is incredible that someone so young could be in command of such a dangerous mission.

Ronan mentioned hearing him cry for his mother as he breathed his last. I find it hard to sleep knowing that now.

I pray every day, asking why this land can't stay peaceful. No answer. Just the wind through the pines.

Colonel Sloane says he is deploying multiple units here. Hell no.

No matter how big their army is, I won't let my field become someone else's barracks. I don't want uniformed men using my soil for war. They track blood and orders into the very land my great-grandfather tilled. Despite my protests, I know this is just the first wave of change.

I've started reinforcing the north fence and moved the bee hives closer to the irrigation ditch. One wrong step, and someone will find out how angry bees can get.

I pray we're not preparing a battlefield on the farm.

I pray... but I keep building anyway.

October 4, 2050 – Sullivan Farm

The morning sun hung low in the Georgia sky, barely above the tree line, casting golden shafts of light through lingering smoke. Dew clung to the grass as Liam walked the path he'd taken a thousand times before—boots crunching over gravel, the leather strap of his worn tool bag slung over one shoulder.

Something was wrong.

He smelled it before he saw it. Burnt metal. Oil. Char. Then came the shape—twisted, blackened, and half-sunken into a muddy rut.

His Autonomous tractor was smoldering in the field, its green paint now blistered and curling off in sheets. One rear tire melted into a deformed puddle. Smoke hissed softly from beneath the cracked hood. The engine compartment had been tampered with—sabotaged from within.

Liam's breath caught. He dropped the bag. His fingers trembled as he stepped forward, reaching for the scorched metal before instinct pulled his hand back.

He let out a low, animal grunt before suddenly kicking the machine with a fury that startled the birds from the trees.

"DAMN—YOU—DAMN—YOU!" he shouted, his thick Irish brogue sharpened by rage. He kicked again. And again. Dust flew from the ground as his boot struck the melted tire. "I give you everything—*everything*—and it's not enough!"

He dropped to his knees, his fists clenched into the soil, and his head bowed.

"Why, God, why?" His voice cracked. "Why is this happening to us? Haven't I been faithful? To everyone, does that matter? I've given all that I have! Every breath of my children, every callous on my hands!"

A silence filled the air. Just a stillness emerged. Only the wind answered—rustling through the pines like a whisper of a God too far to hear.

Liam uncurled slowly, breathing hard. He pulled off his wide-brimmed hat and hurled it into the dirt. For a long moment, he knelt there—sweat mixing with tears he didn't bother to wipe away. He stood strong for many he loved and would refuse to show weakness so that his children might witness and learn. But on this day, he couldn't hold it in, and with no one watching, he felt like it was time for him to unload.

He stood with the strength of an unbroken spirit, too stubborn to fall. Liam walked to the smoldering tractor, laid a hand on its side as if apologizing, then turned toward the barn in the distance.

"I'll fix you, old girl," he muttered. "Or we'll use the old ways. This land won't break before I do."

He retrieved his hat, brushed the dirt off, and placed it back on his head. Then he walked back down the path—slower this time, but with purpose in his step.

* * *

Liam was back in the barn by mid-morning, the scent of scorched rubber still thick on his clothes. His children had seen the wreckage and kept their distance, offering no jokes or questions—just quiet glances through the windows. Ronan wordlessly brought him coffee in a worn mug, then returned to help the younger siblings sort the tools and seed inventory. Harvesting season had arrived, so the farm was buzzing, bringing in the much larger harvests planted in the wake of the Continental Defense Forces' arrival months earlier.

Even amidst the morning activities, the children knew something had happened to Liam. And something had risen in its place.

The news came just after noon.

An old blue pickup, coated in road dust, rolled into the yard. It bore the insignia of the Continental Defense Forces—a grey and black American flag painted hastily in place of the normal red, white, and blue. Two soldiers climbed out. One was young and pale, his helmet slightly too large. The other was an older man with a clipboard and sun-scarred skin. A third remained behind the wheel.

"Liam Sullivan?" The older man asked as he approached.

Liam set his mug down on the fence post and nodded. "The one and only."

"I'm Captain Albert Hayes. I have orders here. Command has made some changes after the last few months of commando raids on the farms within this region." He handed over a sealed folder. "Effective immediately, your farm is being granted regional status. That means added resources. Labor. More protection and oversight than already added."

Liam raised an eyebrow. "Oversight?"

Hayes nodded, glancing around. "You're getting prisoners, Mr. Sullivan. Ten of 'em, from a recent court martial. The rest of them were sent further north to another farm. You'll have them under guard here and put them to work."

Liam stiffened. "Criminals?"

"Soldiers, technically. But they're under sentence of hard labor. You'll have authority over them for the duration of the war." Hayes handed him another paper. "In exchange, the Army is granting you emergency requisition status. You can request supplies directly. And your promotion has been processed and confirmed. The provisional rank: Civilian Quartermaster."

Liam didn't blink. He looked past Hayes toward the fields, some still half-burnt in some areas from last night's flare-off.

"I suppose I don't get to say no."

"You could," Hayes sent gently. "But you know what they did. And you know what they could do for your fields. If you want to reach your current quotas on time."

Liam stood there in silence. He knew that the extra hands would be an immense help. With the constant raids and sabotage units lurking around the area, he knew that he would never meet his quotas unless he had the help of the Army.

Finally, Liam took the papers, scanned them briefly, and signed. "Fine. I'll take 'em. But you tell whoever's listening—I won't have beatings or screams on my land. They break the rules, I'll deal with it my way."

Hayes nodded. "Understood."

* * *

That night, the family sat around the table. The mood was tense. The children spoke softly, and Bethany leaned into her older sister Molly's shoulders. Cherry pie with whipped cream was passed to each member. Liam took his plate, eager to dig in. The stress of the outside world made him very hungry, especially with how many calories a farmer can burn.

Liam took advantage of the calm mood as the family dug into the dessert.

“They’re sending prisoners,” Liam announced, breaking the silence.

“I heard,” Bethany murmured. “Are they dangerous?”

“From what I can tell, they are broken,” Liam replied. “But they seem to be loyal soldiers. We should still be wary of them.”

“Why do you think they are broken?”

“Just a sense from reading their file. Not much different from the land, same as me.” He paused and looked down at his hands. “But we’re given broken things, and it's up to us to plan what we do with them.”

“Does this mean we need to carry guns around, Papa?”

“Possibly. But I want to understand what they are before we do anything further.”

“Yes, Papa.”

“Head on a swivel!”

October 7, 2050 – Sullivan Farm

Morning rose, and the truck returned, with a cage in the bed. Inside were ten men. Filthy, standing in silence. Staring through the mesh with eyes that had seen war, death, and something darker still.

Liam stood in the gravel driveway, arms crossed, eyes like flint. He didn't flinch when the cage door opened. He didn't flinch when the soldiers stepped out, each chained at the wrist, heads low.

"Welcome to the Sullivan Farm," Liam said. "This may be crawling with the CDF, but this is my farm. You work hard, you will be treated well. You try to escape; you'll be hunted down. You cause harm to anyone here, I'll put you under the farmhouse."

The prisoners stared at him, not responding in any way.

He nodded once, then pointed to the burned field. "There. That's where we will begin. One row at a time. One row for each sin we carry."

The sun rose behind them, hot and merciless. Just like that, the work was about to begin.

"Corporal Reynolds!"

"Quartermaster!"

"Show these men their quarters, brief them, and prepare them for the field!"

"Very well. Come along, gentlemen."

Corporal Reynolds escorted the chained-up prisoners to a newly built temporary housing area that would house the disgraced soldiers of the CDF.

* * *

Liam Sullivan stood near the edge of his barn, arms folded across his chest, watching the prisoners shuffle by under armed control. The morning sun cut harsh angles through the mist, casting long shadows over the fields. Among the prisoners stood the Crimson Reapers—zealots once feared across the countryside, now reduced to shadows of themselves, covered in ash and dirt, wrists chained and backs bent from the days of toil.

He had been told that one of their former leaders had demanded to speak with him. Against his better judgment, Liam agreed—only if the man was shackled, watched, and permitted no privacy.

The guards led the man forward. He was gaunt but stood tall, his eyes flickering with a strange light. His name was Anthony Barr. Once a firebrand zealot-turned-sergeant, he was known for beliefs laced with brimstone and blood. Now, he wore a torn prison uniform, his beard overgrown, his gaze unflinching.

Liam motioned toward a bench under the old pecan tree near the workshop. He didn't sit. The former soldier did.

"You asked for me," Liam said flatly.

Barr nodded. "Yes, sir. You're now our guardian. They say you're a man of faith."

Liam's jaw clenched. "I am. They say you use your faith for... misplaced actions."

Barr looked up, calm as the wind before a storm. “I believed I was doing the right thing. This country has fallen into something grim. Immorality and debauchery. We were taught to be soldiers in the war against Sodom.”

“As far as I was briefed: you murdered innocent people,” Liam snapped. “Women. Justifying actions by twisting a proverb into poison.”

Barr didn’t react. “Mr. Sullivan, there were things about that mission that were briefed to us that didn’t make it to trial. I can never tell you of course. But I can say this: The jezebels were the way to hell; it went down to the chambers of death.”

“Is that so?” Liam’s voice dropped into a cold, quiet fury. “There is one simple thing you forgot, Sergeant Barr, something that everyone forgets when war is declared: shalt... not... murder...”

Barr stared at the earth. “Maybe... We clumped together instead of separating. You weren’t there to know, though. Justice is all we have left in a world burning.”

Liam stood there, stone-faced. For the first time in his life, something he had always believed was being used against him. He never imagined that the conflict of his beliefs would reach the hills of his farm.

Liam stepped closer. “You and your men will never touch another innocent again. You’ll break your back in my field. Eternal damnation passed by your superiors. And if I find out you so much as glanced at any of my daughters in a way I don’t like... I will personally cut off the thing that leads men astray.”

Barr’s hand moved toward his crotch. He knew what the warning meant deep in his heart, and saw in Liam’s eyes it was not just a warning, but an ultimatum. Barr raised his eyes. For a moment, he seemed smaller. Human.

"It never even occurred to me to look at them, Mr. Sullivan," he said. "I give you my word, none of my men will cause your family any trouble."

"I will hold you to that."

"I take responsibility," Barr replied. "I don't expect forgiveness from anyone either."

"You won't get any from us here," Liam said. "But I will give you this: a chance to live, work, and make use of what little of your life is left."

He nodded to the guards, who pulled Barr up and silently led him away.

Liam turned to the rising sun, the heat already pressing against his weathered skin. The rows of corn shimmered in the light, and behind them, the prisoners moved like shadows. But the land still stood—his land, his law.

And this time, no devil would cross it unscathed.

October 16, 2050 – Sullivan Farm

The wind had changed.

Liam stood at the fence line with his youngest son, Ethan, watching the horizon. Thick clouds gathered in the west—not the kind that promised rain, but the kind that made the dogs restless and the chickens silent. The humidity clung to his neck like a wet rope, and even the birds kept quiet.

"It's too still," Ethan murmured, scanning the sky. "Feels like the start."

Liam nodded slowly, chewing the inside of his cheek. "It's not the weather that's the worry. It's the silence." He turned his head toward the south field, where the prisoners worked under watch. Even the Reapers, broken as they were, seemed anxious. Something was coming. And Liam had learned by now that when the air warned you, you listened.

Liam had suspected something was amiss. The units assigned to protect the Sullivan farm had been ordered to protect the nearby railway stations. When Liam pressed the commander on what was happening, the response was that there had been reported movements of artillery heading south. They were coming from Atlanta, he said, and they seemed to be searching and destroying while heading south for the coming offensive. Of course, he replied that it was classified as to where the target they were after was located.

He walked to the barn and called out for Molly. "Get the kids inside. Tell your sister to lock the back doors and close the cellar just in case."

"What's happening?" she asked, brushing flour from her apron.

"I don't know. But I don't like how the air feels. If the CDF left anything of importance behind, we might be next on someone's list."

* * *

The kitchen was quiet. Too quiet. The family sat around the table, eating quickly. Outside, the wind howled through the shutters. Liam's youngest daughter, Bethany, said grace in a whisper before supper, and even the children didn't interrupt.

In the distance, something echoed. A low pop. Then another.

"Fireworks?" Ethan asked.

Garrett stood up, tense. "That wasn't fireworks."

Liam pushed his plate away. "I need to check the road." He grabbed his coat and rifle, then kissed Molly's forehead. "Keep them inside. Stay near the cellar."

Out on the porch, Liam listened. The sounds were clearer now. Gunfire, distant but steady. A skirmish. Maybe more. The sound of artillery explosions in the distance soon became noticeable. While scary, it was not something many feared. There had been no reports of artillery units making their way towards Tifton, at least as far as the commanders who briefed Liam knew. Considering that he spoke with MacDill regularly, there had been no evidence of an offensive heading in their direction.

The radio in the kitchen crackled to life—an emergency bulletin flickered though:

"This is a regional emergency broadcast. A series of coordinated raids have been reported across northern Georgia and parts of Alabama. Remaining supply routes are under attack. Citizens are urged to shelter in place..."

Liam returned to the porch as headlights blinked on the distant road. Two CDF trucks, covered in mud and scorched at the edges, screeched to a halt in front of the farmhouse.

A familiar face jumped down—Colonel Sloane, the commanding officer of the CDF's logistics corps.

"Colonel! What's happening here?"

Colonel Sloane caught his breath. "Drone and artillery attack. They hit a supply train west of here. We've got wounded and no stable station within thirty miles. We need the barn."

"Colonel, it's got the equipment set up in there."

Sloane looked at him. "Clear it, dammit. We will pay you anything we aren't already paying."

Liam didn't hesitate. "Worry about that later. Right now, just bring them in, and we'll handle what we can."

"Medics are on their way—we need to set up somewhere."

Liam soon called over his children, the guards, prisoners, and everyone else to help bring out the wounded from the trucks.

* * *

For Liam, the hours felt like weeks. For the wounded, it felt like eternity. The barn had been transformed into a makeshift medical shelter. Blood seeped into the straw. Soldiers lay on every surface—some conscious, others barely breathing—a medic barked orders, using duct tape and morphine like magic tricks to buy more time.

Liam stood at the back, covered in sweat, handing over clean towels, rags, and whiskey jars. His kids fetched water by the bucket, while Molly boiled bandages in the kitchen. Liam could not have been prouder of his eldest daughter, who had taken complete control of the situation and led the charge with their family since their mother passed. *Nora would have been so proud of you, Molly.*

One soldier, no older than eighteen, clutched Liam's hand. "Am I going to die, sir?"

Liam kept his gaze steady. "Not tonight, son. God willing, you will live to see the sunrise."

Outside, the wind howled louder. Another battle was on the horizon. Not a commando raid. Not saboteurs. A full front. And Liam Sullivan—farmer, father, man of God—was now once again about to be on the front lines.

October 18, 2050 – Sullivan Farm

The morning broke blood-red over Georgia hills. Liam didn't sleep a wink. None of them had.

The barn still reeked of whiskey, sulfur, and sweat. Soldiers moaned softly beneath heavy quilts and makeshift bandages, while crows circled overhead, drawn by the smell of death in the nearby fields.

A convoy of CDF vehicles rolled up to the gravel path just past dawn, wheels kicking up plumes of dust that hung in the humid air like fog. At the front rode Lieutenant-Colonel Jericho Maddox, a tall, wiry, officer whose right arm was in a sling. His uniform was stained and wrinkled, his eyes sunken with lack of sleep.

Liam stepped off the porch and met him halfway. "I was expecting to see Colonel Sloane, especially after what happened."

"Colonel Sloane is coordinating out of a command center right now."

"I suppose you bring news in his place if you're here."

Maddox shook his head. "We're here to move out the wounded, yes. But we're forming a line here. The drone attack was feint. Real push is happening today. They're heading this way."

"My farm?" Liam frowned. "Why?"

"Because it's a logistical artery now," Maddox said flatly. "And we made the mistake of letting the whole world know it. Government satellites picked up our movements, along with social media tracking our presence. They know. You and several farms here are the bloodline for the central supply route between Macon and Pensacola. They cut this off; it creates a crisis for the CDF."

Liam exhaled. "So, I guess you're not just here to move the wounded."

"No." Maddox looked over his shoulder at the tree line. "We're here to fight."

* * *

Liam stood with Maddox on a hill above the pecan grove. He had never seen so many soldiers—some dug into shallow foxholes, others manning sandbags and rusted tractors refitted with machine gun mounts. Teenage boys from the town were helping carry boxes of ammo. Many protested their help, but they insisted, as this was an all-hands-on-deck situation.

Liam's family, however, was not present with him. Deciding the risk was too great, they headed to the cellar to wait it out.

"Rifles?" Liam asked. "You got enough?"

Maddox gave a humorless smirk. "We've got enough bullets. It's bodies we're short on. They are all around us forming a defensive line."

Liam rubbed his jaw, staring toward the horizon. "What direction are they coming from?"

"All of them."

And in the moment, they heard it—faint at first, like distant thunder. But it grew. The whir of drones, the low rumble of APCs (Armored Personnel Carriers), and the unmistakable crack of long-range artillery firing from far beyond the tree line. The ground shook beneath their boots.

"Positions!" Maddox barked. "Everybody get down!"

Liam didn't run. He turned to the barn one last time, to his children waiting and praying inside the cellar. His eldest son, Ronan, stayed by the barn with a rifle. Before taking positions, Liam watched as Molly took the kids to the basement. She peeked from the storm door, her face pale.

He gave her a nod. Just a nod. It had to be enough.

* * *

The assault began with an artillery barrage. Shells cratered the upper pasture, sending soil and limbs skyward. One landed in the irrigation ditch, erupting in a geyser of water and steel. Then came the drones—small, fast, deadly. CDF soldiers fired back with everything they had: rifles, hacked signal jammers, and anything else that could take them out.

A drone clipped one of Liam's silos and it exploded into a fireball, taking the corn bin with it. Maddox's men scrambled into firing positions, shooting at muzzle flashes in the tree line. Return fire came in red-hot arcs.

Liam fought, too.

He wasn't a soldier but a farmer—and in war, farmers became dangerous men. With a scoped rifle given to him by Maddox, he climbed into the hayloft of the now ruined barn and picked off an advancing enemy scout emerging from the tree line. He prayed as he fired. Not for his aim—but for his soul.

The CDF's unit led a flanking maneuver down in the orchard, surprising an enemy detachment trying to breach the livestock gate. The soldiers opened fire with semi-automatic and fully automatic rifles, forcing them back. Debris flew all around the trees from the bullets raining down. They had pushed the enemy back with many casualties, but there was no cheering. There was no glory in this.

By dusk, the smoke had turned the sky a sickly bronze.

The enemy had pulled back under heavy fire, abandoning their vehicles in the field. Continental Defense Forces had managed to reinforce their battalions already on station in Tifton. Maddox's final radio call summoned a squadron of Apache helicopters from Macon. Their rotors sliced through the air like judgment itself.

As Maddox had indicated, this seemed to be a search-and-destroy objective. Once it became clear they could not fully achieve their goal while also making their way south, they withdrew. By nightfall, the battle was over.

The grove was half gone. The barn was a shell. Blood sank into the soil, deeper than the rain.

* * *

Liam sat on the porch, a blanket over his shoulders, staring at the wreckage of his land. Ronan walked up, rifle slung low. "We held up."

"Yeah," Liam said hollowly. "We did."

Silence passed between them. Molly interrupted it as she emerged from the front door, bringing coffee in his old chipped mug. She placed it beside him, then sat at his feet, leaning against his legs. "Tell me it's over, Papa."

"For now," Liam whispered. He looked at his hands—dirty, scraped, shaking. "Maddox is supposed to update me soon. But nothing really ends anymore. It just goes quiet."

Liam began to cry, looking down. "Thank you, God. You protected my family on this day."

Ronan and Molly looked at him, also teary-eyed. Despite the carnage, they were lucky to be alive. War had arrived at their doorstep, yet they were unharmed, all things considered.

The wind picked up, swirling embers skyward. The war had not touched the house, a miracle on this day.

November 19, 2050 – Tifton, Georgia – Railway Station

Weeks soon passed.

The land never slept. It groaned, limped, and bled—but it endured. The front had now shifted west, with the repelled assault at Murphy Grove, the Continental Defense Forces had held the region. But they were stretched thin, and the wounded kept coming. Resources were tighter than ever. Liam found himself in meetings with officers twice his age and half his humility, debating logistics and land use like he was some kind of quartermaster general. He held the title, but it was name-only most days when it was the high command.

He wasn't a quartermaster. He was a farmer with a ruined barn and half a harvest. And he was out of workers. His neighbors had fled, been conscripted, or killed in the chaos. His oldest sons were still there, but exhaustion had left them moving like shadows. Help was desperately needed.

The answer soon came on a warm Tuesday morning, in the form of a convoy arriving at the train station. Liam had found it strange that Sloane had ordered him to be at the train station by 1300 hours instead of just receiving a truck convoy as it had always been. But it seemed that in the wake of constant attacks, the need to be near the air defense set up in the town was now necessary.

Liam had just finished patching a fence line when he got the call from the colonel. He drove down to a half-standing Tifton, and waited eagerly for the train. He was met with a large number of soldiers coming off the train, but noticed at least ten in chains. An officer with a clipboard approached him.

"Mr. Sullivan."

Liam wiped his brow. "That's me."

The officer tilted his head back toward the second railway car.

The prisoners emerged one by one, chains clinking, boots scuffing the dry dirt. There were eleven of them—filthy, malnourished, but still carrying the unmistakable edge of violence in their eyes.

Across their uniforms, a red marking had been stamped: CR.

Crimson Reapers.

Liam froze. *More of them? But I already have six.* He realized that this was what remained of the platoon that slaughtered civilians in Miami—those who were tried and convicted under General Rusk. And now... They were here. About to be on his farm.

"Hell no," Liam said. "I already have six Crimson Reapers. I don't want more."

"We picked them up from the Jackson and O'Malley farms," the officer replied coolly. "You lost four due to drone attacks. Your farm is considered a strategic logistics site. These men will be under watch by armed supervisors. They work. Nothing more."

"I will have seventeen Reapers total. What if they try something?"

The officer gestured toward another railcar. "You'll have a platoon on-site. This is not negotiable."

Liam stood silent, the hammer in his grip flexing white-knuckle tight. "Fine. But they're not returning to those railway cars if they step out of line."

November 22, 2050 – Sullivan Farm

The Crimson Reapers worked under the sun like ghosts—silent, quick, efficient. They were no strangers to orders. Most obeyed without protest, though Liam kept a Glock 17 pistol on his hip and a double-barreled within reach at all times.

He didn't speak to them, except one.

Sergeant Anthony Barr. Clearly older than the rest of the platoon, he now sported grizzled features and spoke with a southern drawl. His hands were calloused, and scriptures tattooed on his collarbone shone in the sun. He worked without complaint and always finished first. One evening, as Liam watched him haul crates alone in the old hay barn, he looked up.

"You still believe in redemption?" he asked.

Liam didn't answer.

Barr smiled faintly. "You talk like a preacher when you're yelling at your kids. Figure you must practice what you preach."

Liam stepped forward slowly, still watching for sudden movements. "I believe the guy upstairs watches everything."

"Even us?"

"Especially you."

Barr leaned on the crate. "If he is watching. What does that make you? A warden? A shepherd?"

Liam took a moment to consider the question. “I am a farmer. A father. This is my land. You and your men alone are to blame for why you’re here. You got that?”

Barr nodded. “Understood.”

* * *

Liam sat on the porch. Bethany and Garrett were beside him, the stars bright and sharp overhead.

“Do you trust those men, Papa?” she asked.

“No,” he replied plainly. “But I trust the Lord to handle them. I’ll handle the fieldwork.”

She gave him a look. “You really think they will change?”

Liam sat in silence for a moment. He was astonished at how grown up his children had become, deep in thought to ask the tough questions.

“I don’t know,” Liam said, swirling the dregs of coffee in his mug. “But I know what it’s like to carry shame. You get lighter when you pray about it. Some men though, never let it go. But some… they do.”

He looked toward the dark silhouette of the barn.

December 14, 2050 – Sullivan Farm

Just weeks after the prisoners arrived, Liam finally began to see results. The back field—once overgrown and forgotten—was now cleaned and furrowed. Rows of early winter wheat had been laid under moonlight, and the repaired irrigation system pumped with rhythmic confidence. The prisoners worked without protest. Not out of kindness, Liam suspected, but out of exhaustion and routine.

Still, something in the air had shifted. It was easier to breathe until the night of Broken Hollow.

The day had been unusually warm, the kind of southern December day that tricks you into thinking that winter won't come. The sun dipped early, though, and the wind carried the scent of woodsmoke that wasn't theirs.

Liam was finishing his evening routine of playing with the younger children when the dogs started barking—deep, guttural growls that froze every motion inside the farmhouse.

"Cellar. Lock the doors," Liam said, already moving.

He threw on his coat and grabbed the rifle from above the mantel. He cocked his pistol, holstered, and made his way out.

Outside, the shadows danced across the distant pine tree line. The CDF platoon was already on alert, running around setting up for a potential attack. He scanned with binoculars from the front porch, hands steady despite his heart hammering. Nothing. Then—

The sound of a silo in the distance.

A grain silo.

He ran...

By the time Liam reached the silo, flames had begun to flicker from the cracks—small, surgical, not chaotic like a wildfire. Controlled. Intentional. That's when he knew.

Saboteurs.

A second explosion blew out another grain silo. He dropped flat as metal screamed overhead.

Soldiers in dark fatigues returning fire at the CDF platoon swept across the property like shadows, parachuting in—six in total. They moved low and fast. Silent.

But they weren't the only ones in the dark.

The prisoners had been kept in makeshift bunks in the south granary, under heavy guard by the Continental Defense Force troops stationed on the property. When the gunfire broke out, the guards assumed it was another failed escape attempt. But the alarms quickly shattered that illusion.

Incoming strike team. Black ops. U.S. government signatures. Likely sent to once again destroy the Sullivan Farm—logistics, storage, and if necessary, the farmer himself.

The commanding black ops officer made his way to the granary, killing the two guards. He made his way in... inside, he saw prisoners chained to their beds. He made his way to the lead bed, that of Sergeant Barr, and released him from his chains. He turned and faced the rest of the men.

"Destroy the farm," the commander announced. "And you will be free again."

As he made his way to another man, he was caught off guard as powerful arms made their way around his neck. Sergeant Barr choked him with all his might, depriving him of his life.

"We may be prisoners," he whispered to the commander. "But we are the CDF, and I'll be dammed if I align with you."

Snap.

The black ops commander fell to the ground, motionless. Barr breathed heavy, calming himself. He grabbed the keys from the commander's hands, releasing his men.

"We defend this farm," he declared. "With our lives!"

The Reapers never questioned Colonel Brand, and in turn, would never question Sergeant Barr. They didn't understand the loyalty, but they followed orders.

"Yes, sir!"

The Reapers soon made their way out of the granary. Grabbing the weapons of the dead guards. They ran towards the tree line, where muzzle flashes had emerged from enemy combatants.

The former Reapers had smelled it before Liam had. Combat.

It had been months since they'd seen it—but their instincts hadn't dulled. As the firefight erupted near the orchards, three prisoners opened fire at the ghosts in the trees. They didn't try to escape at all.

They had joined the fight. *I'll be damned*.

Gunfire continued through the night, but with no air support or reinforcements, the commandos were once again at a loss. No element of surprise would allow them to complete their mission and escape to a rendezvous point.

By dawn, all six saboteurs were dead or captured. Three Reapers had been shot. One died crawling to help a wounded comrade. Another took a bullet protecting a medic saving a wounded CDF soldier. Prisoners of war, yet loyal to the cause, right until the very end.

Two grain silos were destroyed. But the barn and several other silos were safe, thanks in part to the CDF helping contribute to building many more of them for the logistics supply—still, a massive setback with the destruction of two.

Liam stood in the smoldering ruins, rifle slung on his shoulder, looking down upon the corpse of what looked to be possibly another Delta Force commando.

A silver eagle was stamped into the man's chest plate. It meant only one thing: government-issued. His mouth tightened at the sight.

Liam made his way to the remaining Reapers—back under guard. They were bloody, winded, yet still standing.

"Why didn't you run?" Liam asked.

Barr looked at him—his scripture tattoo again showing in the light—shrugged. "Because this is home now."

Liam stared at him for a long moment.

* * *

Liam returned to the house as the first light broke over the peach orchard. Molly stood at the door, eyes red from tears but determined as ever.

"You're alive?" she asked.

He kissed her forehead gently. "Barely."

She looked past him, toward the charred silo in the distance. "It never ends, does it?"

"No, not yet," Liam said quietly. "But we've endured. More than I thought we ever could."

He looked toward the fields, where the prisoners were already being sent back to work. They gathered their tools, and the guards escorted them to their assigned area. They walked like free men—not with orders but by habit. The wind carried the faint sound of an engine convoy in the distance—another wave of change coming.

But for now, Liam Sullivan had the only things that mattered: his God, his family, his land.

December 21, 2050 – Sullivan Farm

The first frost hit on a Sunday.

It coated the tops of the pasture grass in silvery lace and turned the plowed rows brittle. Chickens froze where they slept. Pipes groaned under the weight of late December wind. The sky was gray, low, leaden—as if the whole world held its breath.

Winter had come to the Sullivan Farm, and it would be cruel.

By midweek, the stores of canned food began to shrink at an alarming pace. Eggs became a rarity, and salt pork was down to the final slab. Liam had ordered rationing across the board—his family, his workers, the guards, the prisoners—all ate from the same pot.

The lines between captor and captive began to blur. Despite the promise from Rusk that a Christmas supply run would be delivered before Christmas Eve, Liam did not count on it. With how much things were delayed, he knew it could be January at the earliest before it arrived.

Nights were the worst. Even inside the farmhouse, the cold pressed through the floorboards. They burned wood so fast that Liam had to choose between heating the barn or the bedrooms. Some nights, he slept beside the children with his arms stretched over them like a blanket. It wasn't necessary with how many blankets they had, but it made him look good in their eyes.

The prisoners made do with the winter gear distributed to all soldiers. Their military-standard coat wasn't warm, but they didn't complain. They took turns feeding a fire outside their quarters. There were no complaints about that either, just silence and the occasional hymn hummed under their breaths.

The evening air was still, and Liam took this opportunity to chop up some fire wood. While chopping by lantern light, Liam noticed a prisoner—his name was Davis, a quiet man in his thirties—moving slower than usual. His hands trembled, breath from his mouth came ragged.

"Get inside, soldier. Get warm," Liam ordered.

But Davis shook his head and tried to lift another log. Moments later, he collapsed into the snow. Liam dropped his ax and rushed over to the man. His head was burning up, and his breathing wasn't good. He soon realized it.

Pneumonia. He lifted Davis and got him into the house. He used his radio to call for a medic and tried to revive him, as he realized he wasn't breathing.

Within minutes, the CDF Chief Medical Officer assigned to Tifton arrived from a nearby outpost. But he arrived too late; Davis was already gone. All Liam could do was pray and hope that his mind had been at peace.

The next day became a very somber one, as the prisoners learned the news of their comrade's passing. Liam declared a day off for the Reapers, allowing them to have a service for him.

By sunrise, they buried Davis near the tree line. A small wooden cross made by Liam would be all that marked where he lay. No family. No flag. Just Liam, his son Ronan, Sergeant Barr, and three prisoners standing shoulder to shoulder.

Sergeant Barr read a line from Ecclesiastes, from the heart:

"To everything there is a season... A time to be born, and a time to die."

Liam folded his hat to his chest, staring down at the frozen soil.

"He seemed like a good man," he said softly. "Followed orders. May he find peace."

* * *

The day carried on, and so did the Sullivan family. But with winter, some Christmas miracles seemed necessary for them. Ethan and Bethany were helping move hay bales in the back of the barn when one of the upper stacks shifted. The entire top level came tumbling down, burying the children in a wall of straw and timber.

The screaming echoed across the field.

Liam sprinted from the house barefoot through ice and slush. By the time he reached the barn, the structure groaned under the weight of the collapse. Two CDF soldiers tried lifting timbers—but it was the former Reaper, Jeremiah Evans, who dove straight into the pile without waiting. He tore through the hay like a man possessed.

"I got them!" Jeremiah shouted, pulling Ethan and Bethany from the wreckage, cradling the siblings' limp frames as Liam dropped to his knees beside them.

Bethany was crying, as was Ethan silently. They were shaken, but breathing. Liam gripped Jeremiah's forearm hard.

"You saved my son, my daughter."

"I saw the barn go. Just ran," the man said, his voice low. "Didn't think twice."

Liam stared at him. Then put his hand on his shoulder.

"Neither would I."

Liam choked up. It was a Christmas miracle that he never knew he needed in that moment. The rhythm of winter had been a tough one. Long days of brittle cold, and nights warmed by shared verses and flickering firelights. On this day, there was something that warmed them more than a fire ever could.

Angels. Watching over them.

* * *

Later that night, Liam walked over to the granary. He sat down in the place where the prisoners bunked since arriving. He didn't bring a rifle or pistol. Just a lantern. And a card.

No one spoke as he entered. They watched him sit cross-legged on a straw mat and open a card in an envelope.

"This is a card my son and my daughter made for you, Jeremiah," Liam announced. "I wanted to read it to you and the rest of the men."

Jeremiah looked to Sergeant Barr, who nodded, signaling it was okay.

"Yes, please, sir."

Liam looked down at the card.

"To Jeremiah: thank you for your bravery in saving us in the barn today. We are alive because of you. You are a good man. God bless you. From Ethan and Bethany Sullivan."

Liam closed the card and handed it to Jeremiah. He looked at it, giving a small, weak smile.

"I am low on many things, as you all know. The war has taken a heavy toll. But on this Christmas, I also bring you fresh bread made by the Sullivan family with care. Some butter to make it tasty as well. And a little bit of meat that we could scrounge up."

He handed them a large pan of bread, and the men eagerly gathered around to collect it. For the first time since arriving, their eyes filled with life.

Barr looked at Liam. "Thank you, sir. I mean it."

"We're all in this together."

Barr was handed a piece of buttered bread. He stood to attention, saluting Liam.

"Merry Christmas, sir."

Liam nodded silently.

"Merry Christmas, Barr."

* * *

Diary Entry – Liam Sullivan

December 25, 2050

Today is Christmas. We gathered in the parlor with what little we had. We decorated a thin tree, half-lit with some bulbs we salvaged. We lit candles against the frost-colored windows. I made the kids some wood-carved toys and decorations. My daddy taught me well in woodwork, I assume perhaps because if the day came when we had to make our own stuff, this was the occasion.

They loved them, and that was all that mattered to me.

As we drank our hot cocoa, the prisoners began singing carols in the granary. Bethany ran outside to listen, and I followed.

"They're singing 'Silent Night,' Papa," she told me. I just picked her up, listening as their voice carried into the night.

I told her, "Let them sing." My voice was thick with the memories of singing it with Nora.

It is amazing how the Christmas spirit causes you to reflect on love and joy, even in war. I think of that story my daddy always told of the First World War: The Christmas Truce, a story of how British, French, Austrian, German, and Russian troops stopped fighting for just a little while to celebrate Christmas Day.

Soldiers who had spent every waking moment trying to kill each other exchanged gifts like families do around the tree. They played games in the snow and sang carols—a sight like none other.

I wonder if that is happening somewhere... maybe up north, where the fighting is at a standstill. I don't know, but one can hope.

My heart feels full in this moment. Because for just a few hours, on a cold Christmas night, it feels like there is peace on earth.

March 7, 2051 – Sullivan Farm

The first green shoots appeared in March.

It began as a shimmer of color along the edges of the field, so faint it could have been mistaken for memory. Then it grew—grass pushing through frost, the dogwood trees near the road blooming white like a baptism, and the soil softening beneath boots that had grown so used to the crunch of ice.

Winter was ending.

Liam stood on his porch at sunrise, cup of weak chicory coffee in hand, and breathed in the scent of damp earth. For the first time in months, he wasn't bracing for pain. The air was still cold, but it no longer bit. It just reminded.

"Spring's early," Ronan said, stepping beside him with a spade over his shoulder.

"Or maybe we're just late," Liam replied. "Feels like we lost something we can't name."

The first day the plows returned to the field, Liam called all hands—his family, the guards, and the prisoners. He drew a line in the thawed soil with his boot.

"The time for just surviving is over," he said. "Now, we start again."

It wasn't a campaign speech to a crowd of eager followers. It was a vow by a man ready to move forward.

Everyone was assigned a section. They mended fencing, tilled furrows, and planted seedlings. Even the younger prisoners smiled as they moved—their chains still locked but looser, less cruel. The rebuilding of the grain silos had lifted the men's spirits, as it meant progress was once again rolling.

The man once known as Sergeant Anthony Barr, now just Barr, helped fix the irrigation pump. When asked how he knew how, he shrugged.

“Farmed with my grandfather before I became a soldier.”

Liam watched him. “You’re good at it. Perhaps it’s time you find it again.”

The hum of the diesel engine soon echoed down the dirt road. A Continental Defense Force truck pulled into the drive, and a major stepped out, flanked by two MPs.

“We came to assess the status of your prisoner work program,” the major said, flipping through a leather folder.

Liam looked him up and down.

“Well, Major, if you’re here to ask if they’re still under guard, the answer’s yes. If you’re here to ask if they’re still men, the answer’s also yes.”

The major frowned. “We’ve received word that you’ve been... less strict with protocol.”

Liam’s hand twitched near his belt. But instead of raising his voice, he gestured to the barn, the granary, the freshly seeded rows.

“You see any signs of escape? Are they starving? That man over there,” he pointed to Jeremiah, “saved my son and my daughter’s lives. Another is buried over there, died of pneumonia just before Christmas. Many more are buried over yonder, died defending this land from enemy combatants. If protocol means treating them like animals, I’ve broken it daily.”

The major said nothing. Just scribbled a note, snapped the folder shut, and left without further comment.

Sometime later, Liam sat down and wrote a letter to General Rusk. He was not writing something long, just a paragraph about what was troubling him. And about what was still worth fighting for.

To: General Nathaniel Rusk

From: Liam Sullivan – Tifton, Georgia

Dear Sir,

The next time you send men to question me again about my treatment of the prisoners, come here and do it yourself. I humbly treat these men the way my father would have done it. I haven't forgotten that they committed an atrocious act, but I also know that they have saved the lives of my children. They have helped you in your quest against the government.

Fight your battle, and I will fight mine.

Sincerely,

Liam Sullivan

March 10, 2051 – Sullivan Farm – Oak Tree

Liam called everyone to the old oak tree one Sunday—his family, guards, and prisoners. He set his Bible on a stool and cleared his throat.

"I'm a stubborn man," he said, looking at them. "I'm proud, arrogant at times. I used this book too often to justify anger. But if this war has taught me one thing: strength isn't about standing tall, it's about kneeling low."

He looked each one of the people before him in the eye. All listened with intensity.

"I don't care what uniform you wear or wore. You're on this farm now. You work, eat, and do what you do in your private time. I pray and seek favor against the wind and rain. I welcome those who wish to follow what I do. But now, we're done sorting the wheat from the tares. We will plant. And God as my witness, we will finish this."

Everyone stood there in silence. Liam soon went down onto one knee on the thawed ground. His head bowed. Muttering something under his breath. What he said was anyone's guess. But he moved on the hearts of those around. Slowly, one by one, they joined him.

Sometime later, a sealed envelope arrived by courier. It bore the insignia of the Continental Defense Force High Command. Inside was a simple message.

To: Liam Sullivan

From: General Nathaniel Rusk

Dear Mr. Sullivan,

I received your letter and have thought about what you said. Your handling of the growing conflict has served the CDF and your country. I appreciate the humility you have shown when you didn't have to.

You've done more than feed an army, Mr. Sullivan. You've tended to a nation's soul. I am grateful, and have made a point to visit your farm and tell you in person.

With regards,

Gen. Nathaniel Rusk

Liam read it three times before setting it down on the dinner table. His hands shook—not from fear, but from something older. Something he hadn't felt in a long time.

Hope.

April 6, 2051 – Tifton, Georgia – General Store

It began with the distant sound of laughter.

Liam had driven the battered pickup into town for seed nails and tractor bolts. He didn't expect music. He didn't expect *dancing.*

As he turned onto Main Street, the town was unrecognizable—lined with banners, bunting, and Continental Defense Force troops hooting from the backs of their transports. People were on rooftops waving flags, men and women raising jars and clapping each other on the back. Music played from an old radio on a general store windowsill—Glen Miller's "In the Mood" somehow cut through the years and the war.

Liam parked near the post office and stepped out, blinking. A corporal passed him by with a bottle in one hand and a cigar in the other.

"What's with all the commotion?"

"You ain't heard?" the soldier beamed. "We broke 'em! The government forces fell at Lexington! Their lines snapped like twigs under a truck tire. Rusk's men are marching towards Washington, D.C., now, sir. Reports going around that the President's bunker isn't answering. Some rumors are that they're drawing up a surrender treaty now."

"Oh my god."

Liam's mouth opened slightly, words failing him. He looked across the town square and saw folks hugging in the streets, others crying, soldiers writing messages in chalk on old storefronts: *VICTORY COMES SLOW BUT IT COMES*. One said, *ON TO WASHINGTON.*

He felt the weight in his chest loosen, like a yoke unclasped.

* * *

That night, Liam broke the news to his children. Screams of joy and excitement filled the house like he hadn't seen since before the war started. The end of so much pain was finally reaching its end, and a new dawn could be seen on the horizon.

He sat on the porch with his family, smoking a pipe and watching the stars. Molly emerged from the front door and handed him a bowl of peach cobbler.

"You cried earlier," she said, sitting beside him.

"You saw no tears from these eyes, little lady," Liam grunted.

"Yes, you did, Papa."

He said nothing in response. How could he? For something he had longed for and wanted for his family had finally come. "The war is over, or near its conclusion."

Molly looked at him. "Wasn't sure we would ever get there, honestly."

He nodded, quietly.

"Neither did I. These years felt like decades."

Molly let out a big sigh.

"You think things will be normal again?"

"I honestly doubt it. All we can do is hope for the best."

"You're not wrong there, Papa."

"Perhaps now, you can find yourself a young man, and start giving me grandkids."

"Now let's not get ahead of ourselves, Papa."

"What do you mean? Gotta start pulling the weight of the country again."

"Now hold on, who would want to marry a daughter of a tough farmer like you?"

"Plenty, dear. Plenty."

Both began to laugh. The cringe in their stomachs overpowered their ability to maintain this very stupid conversation. Soon after, they sat in silence, observing the night sky. A shooting star darted across the sky, racing into the next galaxy.

August 15, 2053 – Sullivan Farm

The next few years brought word from the capital: peace talks were underway, the old government fractured, and foreign alliances began dissolving. It was as if the world was drawing in a breath and didn't know whether to exhale or scream.

One morning was different from the others. Just after dawn, a convoy visited Liam's farm. This was not new to the Sullivans, as it had been the case for several years. Three dark green trucks and a pair of escort Humvees crested the dirt road, raising a cloud of chalky dust behind them. At first, Liam thought it was another requisition—some final demand before the end.

Then he saw the flag on the lead vehicle—thirteen stars in a staggered, bold arc—and the man who stepped out.

General Nathaniel Rusk, in full-dress uniform. He brought no camera crews, no ceremony. Just a man walking the last mile himself.

Liam stood at the gate, wiping his hands on his trousers. "Well. Didn't expect you today, sir."

"Didn't plan on being expected," Rusk replied. "I figured if I showed up unannounced, you'd be less likely to rehearse bullshit lines."

Liam chuckled dryly. "Don't care much for those."

Rusk looked over the fields, then at the row of prisoners—still working, still guarded. But looser, freer. Some of them waved as they passed.

"What will happen to them, sir?"

"They will be transferred upstate once things are settled down. They are still convicted prisoners. But they will be properly treated for what they have done here."

"Thank you, General."

Rusk walked around, looking at the barn and silos in the distance.

"I've read the reports," Rusk said quietly. "And your letters. I know what you lost. What you endured here. And what you chose to become instead of what the world tried to turn you into."

He paused, then took a small wooden box from his aide.

"You're being formally recognized in the capital in the spring—Civilian Medal of Honor. Compensation approved by the newly formed treasury. They're building a museum about all this. You'll be part of it."

"I don't need a medal," Liam said, voice rough. "Or a damn museum."

"Yes, you do," Rusk replied, firm. "And your kids deserve to see them."

They stood in silence for a time. In the silence, Rusk decided to light a cigar, and Liam, in turn, pulled out his pipe and lit it.

"You ever think about what happens now?" Liam asked. "Now that the war's over."

Rusk exhaled slowly. "Every damn night. All I do is think about it."

"You carry such a prestigious title now: Lord Protector of the United States of America."

"A temporary title, a stupid one at that."

"Not sure people care anymore, General. They want their lives back to normal."

"That may not be possible for a while, but I'll make things happen."

"You think this peace will hold?"

"I think it has to," Rusk replied, sticking the cigar in his mouth as he spoke. "Because we've all bled enough. And because too many decent men like you are tired of war. Tired of planting crops in a graveyard."

"Damn right."

The wind rustled the pines. Both men couldn't help but enjoy a sliver of the wind brushing their faces.

Finally, Liam extended his hand. "You're welcome to supper, if you ain't in too much of a hurry."

Rusk smiled, clasping it. "I'd be honored."

As the sun sank behind the pine trees and smoke curled from the farmhouse chimney, the war—though not officially over—felt distant. As though it too had been harvested, buried deep in the soil, and left behind with the winter frost.

April 4, 2054 – Washington, D.C.

Spring arrived with dignity in Washington, D.C.—not in trumpets or parades, but in soft petals and a chill wind that hinted at rebirth. The cherry blossoms had bloomed early that year, as if the trees knew peace had finally settled over the land. Their pink-white flowers drifted like snowflakes, covering the National Mall in a soft carpet of forgiveness.

Liam stood on the steps of a refurbished marble building—once a federal office building, now the seat of the interim national assembly. He felt uncomfortable in his pressed gray suit. His collar itched, his boots didn't fit right, and his hands kept fidgeting with the cloth-bound program folded in his breast pocket.

A crowd had gathered for the inauguration of the new American Republic's first Lord Protector of the United States of America—General Nathaniel Rusk. Banners fluttered with the latest national symbol: thirteen stars arranged in a circle, a laurel branch beneath them, no eagle, no olive branch—just strength and rebirth. The plan had been made clear a while ago; the states would be annexed into this new government, and reformed elections and administrations would take effect.

Liam's medal hung heavily on his chest. His children had cried tears of joy when he received it, back at the reception in the Capitol's restored rotunda. Dignitaries, veterans, and even a few of the prisoners he once guarded, Sergeant Anthony Barr and Corporal Jeremiah Evans had been in attendance. But now, outside, alone in the crowd, he felt small again—just a farmer from Georgia, boots caked in memories.

He found a spot beneath a cherry tree and leaned back against the trunk, breathing in the scent of blossoms and new-cut grass. His cane rested against his knee—his hip still stiff from that winter fall in the barn. He looked over the crowd, watching their eyes fixate on the distant podium.

A woman beside him cleared her throat gently.

"Mind if I sit?"

He looked up, surprised by the silver-haired woman with the camera slung around her neck and notebook sticking from her satchel. Her eyes were tired but sharp, and she moved like someone who had learned not to flinch at sirens.

"By all means," he said, gesturing.

She settled beside him with a slight grunt, stretching her legs.

"Ever been to D.C. before?" she asked.

"First time. You?"

She smiled faintly. "Not my first... but maybe my last."

They sat silently as the national anthem played softly in the background and General Rusk stood at the podium.

Rusk looked older and slower. His once-black hair had turned silver, and his uniform was crisp but worn at the cuffs. He began to speak, his voice rasping across the crowd like scripture carried on the wind.

"...This is not a victory for one side. This is a resurrection. We tore apart the old world, not because we hated it—but because we could no longer live inside the lies it told. We were promised transparency. Now, we demand liberty and accountability. We have not replaced one empire with another. We have replanted the roots of our republic in better soil..."

Liam looked at the woman. "You believe him?"

She tilted her head. "I used to ask if I trusted the speaker. Now I ask if I trust the silence that comes after. This one... he speaks like he believes it. That counts for something."

"What did you do in the big war?"

She hesitated. "Witnessed it, wrote about it, endured... too much of it."

He nodded slowly. "Sounds terrifying. I farmed... Just uh... grew food. Until they knocked on my door and said the war needed me."

She chuckled softly. "It needed all of us, didn't it?"

"I suppose." He looked at her again. "You lose anyone?"

Her expression faltered. "My son. My husband."

"I'm so sorry, ma'am."

"Thank you. What about you?"

Liam swallowed. "I lost my wife in the earlier years, but my children made it through, thank God. But I lost good men on my land. Men I buried. Lost a kind man to sickness. One of the ones they said deserved to die. But I came to believe differently."

She looked at him with new eyes, then held out her hand.

"Where are my manners. I'm Jessica."

He took it. "Liam."

The two shook hands, callused and weary, beneath the drifting petals.

Up on the stage, General Rusk's speech rose to its conclusion.

"...We fought not just for a nation. We fought for the soul of our neighbor. And though our sins are many, they do not outweigh our capacity to change. May this new dawn be lit not by the fires of vengeance, but by the mercy of memory."

Applause rolled across the Mall. Liam and Jessica stood in silence as the crowd around them erupted.

Jessica turned to him. "What will you do now?"

"Go home. Fix my fences. Raise my grandkids."

She smiled. "Sounds like heaven."

"And you?"

"I'm thinking... North Dakota. I hear its quiet."

Liam chuckled. "Yeah, when you're freezing your ass off. Sounds nice. Perhaps I'll visit. I could use some quiet."

Jessica smiled again. "I would like that."

The petals fell around them like confetti, not for victory—but for peace.

April 12, 2054 – Sullivan Farm

The farmhouse had changed. The war had stolen its quiet, but time was slowly returning it.

Liam stood at the fence near the edge of his land. The wood was new—cut from Georgia pine and freshly sealed. A slight wind stirred through the budding trees, rustling the fields where young corn pushed up through the tilled soil. It was spring again. Not the violent bloom of cherry blossom in Washington, but the grounded, familiar reawakening of Georgia farmland.

Beyond the fence, Ethan and Bethany ran barefoot through a pasture, laughing as they chased chickens that didn't much care to be chased. The sounds were life. And life had finally returned.

Inside the house, the old cross above the door had been dusted off and rehung, and the walls were covered with a new coat of white paint. The prisoners who once toiled his fields were long gone—pardoned months after the Treaty of Washington was signed. Some had sent letters. One being Jeremiah, who asked if he could return, not as a laborer, but as a worker. Liam wrote back with a job offer and a handshake in words.

He stepped onto the porch, cane in hand, and grunted as he lowered himself into the chair. The seat creaked with familiarity beneath him. He lit his pipe, the smell of cherry tobacco filling the air.

On the small solar-powered radio beside him, the announcer spoke softly.

"As it was centuries ago, and again ten years ago, today is the anniversary of the Civil Wars that began in America. Today, Lord Protector Rusk prepares to mark the anniversary with a speech in the restored Capitol building, millions across the new republic are gathering in quiet reflection..."

Liam puffed the pipe, eyes half-lidded. He didn't need the radio to remind him. The land reminded him. The trees remembered. The wind carried ghosts. He hoped, however, that the ghosts would go somewhere more pleasant.

Molly stepped out with a mug of coffee as she always had. "Papa, they're starting."

He nodded and stood, following her back inside. Ethan and Bethany ran past him, making their way inside. The family crowded the living room—knees on floors, elbows on couches, kids perched in laps. On the television, the cherry blossoms of Washington framed the Capitol steps.

Lord Protector Rusk stood thinner but no less commanding before the nation. Behind him stood war heroes, now senators, and a generation born after the worst had passed.

"We came through fire and shadow," Rusk said. "Not as conquerors, but as stewards. Today is the first day we dig into the problems we face and start piecing together the puzzle that lies before all Americans. We survived a reckoning. And what we do now—what we build now—must be better than what we buried. May the God of peace walk with us into this new dawn."

Silence filled the room. Eyes glued to the television.

Liam got up and turned off the TV. That was enough for one day.

Ronan looked at him. "You all right, Papa?"

Liam gave a tired smile. "Just thinking. All those years... and it all came down to the basic human rights. Mercy."

He looked out the window. A single blossom from the dogwood tree floated past. He walked to the table, reached for his hat, and placed it firmly on his head.

"I've got a fence to finish. Sit if you want, but work is calling."

He walked out the door, slow but steady, the sun warm on his face.

And behind him, his family followed.

IV.

Echoes of the March

July 17, 2046 – Somewhere near Pensacola, Florida

The storm rolled in from the Gulf like a living thing—low, slow, heavy, static, and wrathful. Wind slashed across the water, and sheets of rain bled down from the gray sky. Beneath it, four AH-64 Apache helicopters knifed through the clouds in tight formation, their rotors chopping the air like war drums.

Inside the lead gunship, Captain Jonah Reece gritted his teeth behind his visor, eyes locked to the glowing HUD. Rain streaked the reinforced glass. His fingers hovered just above the trigger controls. Just below him, in the copilot's seat, Warrant Officer Kelso tapped the comm panel and brought the music feed back up.

The 1980s super band Asia's *"Who Will Stop the Rain"* hummed through the flight helmets—not loud enough to distract, just loud enough to remember what this was. What they'd become. The words settled in the bones like prophecy.

"Still poetic, sir?" Kelso muttered.

Reece didn't smile. "Just timing."

Ahead, through the curtain of storm, the glow of the Naval Air Station Pensacola flickered like a wound in the dark. It sprawled across the coast just north of the water—fuel depots, shipping containers, flatbed launch pads, and warehouses packed with government ordinance. The site pulsed with activity despite the hour. Trucks moved beneath sodium lamps. Cranes swung lazily. The war machine was wide awake.

"Visual on target," Reece radioed. "Confirm thermal lock."

One by one, his wingmen crackled back.

"Viper Two, lock confirmed."

"Viper Three, weapons hot."

"Viper Four, tracking north grid."

Lightning cracked over the sea, revealing the target in stark, shadowless clarity for half a second. Then came the dark again—and the first missiles.

THOOM.

Two Hellfires streaked from Reece's wings, cutting downward in a hiss of fire and smoke. They struck the far end of a depot, where fuel drums lit up like Judgment Day. The explosion ripped the silence apart, and the shockwave slapped back against the cockpit like a giant's breath.

Alarms screamed from below.

"Multiple radar pings," Kelso barked. "SAM's going active—east block."

"I see it." Reece banked hard left, weaving through rain sheeting sideways across the canopy. A plume of smoke rose from a burning stack of shipping crates. Behind him, Viper Three let loose a second volley—rockets tearing through a row of semi-trailers loaded with mortar crates.

The song continued playing, haunting and slow, clashing with the violence unraveling below. It was the wrong tempo for war—but maybe that made it right.

"Air defense tower on the ridge," Viper Two called out. "Painted and tagged."

"Viper Four, you're up," Reece ordered.

A few seconds later, a chain of 30mm cannon fire buzzed out from behind and shredded the structure. Concrete burst apart like an eggshell. The radar array folded backward, toppling into the flames.

From the ground, tracer fire stitched into the air— very sloppy, a shocking display of desperation. Reece flared upward, gaining altitude just enough to fire again. A side-mounted Hydra rocket pod loosed a final volley into the east quadrant, where the last fuel tank went up in a blast that lit the sky like sunrise.

“RTB,” he said into the comm. “We’ve done our bit.”

One by one, the Apache’s peeled off and vanished into the night, ducking low to avoid return fire. The storm swallowed them up once more. In the cockpit, Reece leaned back and let out a breath he didn’t know he’d been holding.

“Who will stop the rain...”

The line drifted through the static, softer now. Melancholy. Broken. He glanced at Kelso, who looked out into the dark like he was watching something that wasn’t there.

“We merely dented them,” Kelso said, voice low.

“Maybe,” Reece replied, staring out into the smoke-choked horizon. “But it’s a start.”

October 16, 2050 – Somewhere outside Tallahassee, Florida

The Florida sun was already burning hot despite the early hour. A sticky fog clung low to the ground, evaporating slowly as the boots of the 3rd Infantry Brigade tramped over cracked rural highways and dusty roads overrun with vines. The trees thinned ahead, revealing the sprawl of Tallahassee. Plumes of smoke rose like accusatory fingers from distant buildings.

Field Log – 0900 hours

Location: Somewhere near I-10

Unit: 3rd Infantry Brigade

Commanding Officer: Lt. Col. Lucas Raines

We are less than ten miles from the Capitol. Our boots crush dry pine needles and broken asphalt. The air smells like hot metal and swamp rot. We're the tip of the spear here, it seems. The objective is simple: push through, hold the line, and bleed them dry until the CDF can strike them closer to D.C. I'm not sure we'll live to see that day, though.

* * *

Lieutenant Colonel Lucas Raines trudged near the front of the formation, his rifle slung, his eyes scanning the tree line like it was wired to his heartbeat. Tall, wiry, with a hollow-eyed intensity carved into his face, Raines had become a legend among his men—not because of any speech or bravado, but because he kept surviving—because he kept them alive.

Behind him marched a battalion that was equal parts seasoned veterans and frightened kids barely out of high school. Their boots scaped along the edge of County Road 219, flanked by ditches that had long since been filled with stagnant, mosquito-rich water. A few carried scraps of old Confederate flags as patches—not for heritage, or that they even agreed, but as a joke. As if irony could shield them from bullets.

Now and then, they'd pass burned-out trucks, some civilian, some military. A cat darted across the road, feral and lean. Someone in the ranks commented, debating whether it meant good luck for them… or bad. It wasn't the color black, so that was a good sign.

Raines didn't respond to any of the chatter. His mind simply could not break from being locked into the mission.

They were just a few miles from the city's outer edge when the call came over the radio:

[Radio Transmission]

"Command to Raines. Got eyes on a government armored column southbound from I-10. ETA to your position: 36 minutes. Air cover is tracking. Standing orders: engage if provoked. Maintain pressure. Repeat: maintain pressure."

Raines clicked his receiver.

"Raines to command, roger. 3rd Brigade will hold ground. They want hell, we'll give it in buckets."

They briefly halted near an abandoned gas station—half-collapsed, its canopy twisted like a crumbled soda can. He watched as their field medic assigned to his unit distributed iodine tablets, and re-wrapped a wounded man's leg.

Raines walked over. "Are you still sure you want to go in, Doc? Won't your wife leave you?"

The medic looked up with a faint trace of a smile. "Jessica and I don't speak much nowadays anyway. Not since our son died."

Raines respected that. He knew that the great Dr. Daniel Parker wasn't the same man from the Texas hospitals. Something had hardened him. Maybe it was the war, the death of his son, his estranged wife. Perhaps this war was a crucible that no one escaped unchanged.

Raines scanned the treetops again. "Tell the boys to be ready. Once we hit the edge of Tallahassee proper, it's house-to-house. I want every member of this unit ready; Today we hold them by the nose, and stick our iron boot up their fat ass."

The commander knew that the world's complexity changed as war reached the civilians. He thought back to a few years earlier in rural Mississippi, sheltering from bombings that took place. The ground shook from distant explosions as he clutched his rifle like a rookie, a scared lieutenant surrounded by screaming children and panicked families. His own father had died in the first airstrikes, crushed under debris when a government missile hit the town hall. That night, Raines had vowed he'd never be caught unprepared again, that the fire would forge him into steel.

His mind returned to the present, as the brigade resumed movement, they neared the outer edge of Tallahassee and came upon an old banner lying in the street. The soldiers looked at the torn, battered banner that had seen better days. Vines climbed over it like veins running across an arm. The words it carried were where it really stood in their minds.

RUSH FOR CHI OMEGA. One of the younger soldiers, Private Sam Kilpatrick, paused.

"Sorority rushing... talk about throwba—wait a second... Chi Omega? Isn't that where..."

Raines stopped. "Yes. A slimy son of a bitch murdered two women in their sleep in their sorority house."

Kilpatrick narrowed his eyes. "You seem to know all about it."

"Of course. He was the reason my father made a point to tell my sisters to lock their doors. Especially when they went off to college."

They fell silent at his answer. The banner sat in the street like a fallen monument to a wound the city and the college never bothered to suture.

Raines looked at it for a long moment, then muttered to no one in particular, "Every object here has a ghost in it."

Kilpatrick grabbed a lighter and set the banner ablaze. His act hadn't been sanctioned, but no one reprimanded him. The fire was small, yet it held a small roar in its flame, cracking the material of the banner. Some of the soldiers nodded to themselves. A few whispered among themselves. Others just watched, glassy-eyed.

"All right, men. Let's move out."

* * *

Hours had passed since the sighting, yet it appeared to be a false positive. With reported sightings deep in the city's heart, orders were given to move closer to the city center. The 3rd Infantry Brigade had just entered the zone when a frantic radio call pierced their ears.

[Radio Transmission – Bravo Squad]

"Contact! Grid 4-E. Movement in the trees—possible drone recon or light armor scouting element. Awaiting orders."

Raines grabbed his radio. "Stay low and observe. Do not fire until fired upon."

His jaw flexed. They were getting close.

The brigade moved again, now cutting through Stadium Drive—just west of Doak Campbell Stadium. The massive red letters spelling "FLORIDA STATE" still hung across the arch, though chipped and darkened from months of abandonment.

Suddenly, the rumble of jet engines broke overhead—a split-second scream of incoming death.

"DOWN!" someone yelled.

As a government fighter screamed past, the unit scattered across the road and ditch lines. But then—an eruption in the air. A streaking missile lanced from a tree line and met the jet's payload midair.

The air-to-ground missile exploded prematurely—its warhead sheared in half, tumbling like a wounded animal. Spiraling down, the jet slammed directly into the crimson *FSU* signage above the stadium's main gates.

The resulting fireball lit up the surrounding blocks. Glass shattered from abandoned windows nearby. The massive "F" cracked and fell forward, crashing to the pavement like the fall of an iconic statue.

Everyone lay flat, as still as possible. Silence fell over them as the minutes rolled on. Only the echo of the burning metal groaning overhead.

Raines stood slowly, brushing dirt from his flak vest. "So much for subtlety," he muttered.

Parker jogged over, checking for injuries. "Everyone good?"

"All good over here," Raines replied. "Possible civilian casualties, if any, are still in the city."

The soldiers chuckled grimly, breaking the tension for a heartbeat. One man spat into the dirt. Another crossed himself.

* * *

By nightfall, the brigade took up positions on the west side of Tallahassee, establishing a forward operating point out of a former middle school. Chalkboards still bore lesson plans from years ago—one scrawled with "INDUSTRIAL REVOLUTION."

Raines sat in what had once been the principal's office, spreading out topographical maps over a duty desk. The memories of children filled his memory of Denver. Raines had been there to recover bodies. He remembered lifting a child no older than his niece, charred and clutching a stuffed rabbit. Her mother had been fused into the floor tiles of a train station bathroom. That was the day he stopped believing the war could ever be clean.

Parker entered with two mugs of instant coffee. Raines never liked instant, as he considered it the shittiest coffee one could ever drink. But in this case, he would gladly accept it.

"Got you one, sir."

Raines took it silently.

"We lost five scouts today," Parker reported. "Two were ambushed near the mall. Three to a buried IED."

Raines stared into his mug. "That's only the start, unfortunately."

Parker didn't answer. Raines rose and pulled open the blinds as the stars emerged from the clear sky.

He turned to Parker. "They're going to throw everything at us before we break this line. I hope you're prepared to be a grave keeper again."

Parker sipped his coffee. "Just as long as I don't end up in one."

Raines nodded. "First light. We hit them before they regroup."

He stepped outside to find the unit quiet. Some sharpened knives, others cleaned their rifles, or thumbed through small, worn books. One soldier played a harmonica softly near the gymnasium doors.

Raines stood in the dark for a long time, watching smoke drift from the city ahead. He lit a cigar, the flame briefly illuminating the worn edges of his scarred face.

Then he whispered to the night:

"This is their making, fire and brimstone. Let them burn in it."

October 17, 2050 – Somewhere in Tallahassee, Florida

It was just past dawn when Raines' boots hit the gritty clay of a half-collapsed parking garage near the hospital district. The once-busy downtown corridor had turned into a grim trench line—broken asphalt, overturned ambulances, medical gloves fluttering like ghostly petals in the early wind.

Field Log – 0800 hours

Location: Monroe Street, Northern Tallahassee

Unit: 3rd Infantry Brigade

Commanding Officer: Lt. Col. Lucas Raines

We've dug into the northern ridge above the Capitol. Enemy UAV activity is high. Sniper nests in the Leon Heights buildings. Holding pattern until armored support arrives. Morale is holding, barely. We lost twelve men crossing Thomasville Road last night. One of them was seventeen. No name tag. God help us.

* * *

"I want eyes on every rooftop. Swann, take your squad and sweep the west flank."

Sergeant Henry Swann nodded. He moved like a man who hadn't slept in three days, which was the case with all the men. His helmet was nicked from shrapnel, his uniform crusted in blood—not all his own. Dr. Daniel Parker jogged beside him with a med-kit slung low. His brow was furrowed with dread.

"We've got wounded stacking up at the county courthouse," Parker said.

Raines didn't respond immediately. He pulled a pair of binoculars from his pouch, scanning toward Gaines Street. A low hum vibrated the horizon. Drone? Or a city's final heartbeat?

"Well doc, set up triage under the old law library arch," Raines muttered. "That stonework's thick enough to stop small arms."

Swann grunted, then paused. "Did you hear?"

"Hear what?"

"They hit Cascade's Park last night. CDF forces pushed in. Half of them got wiped out in a friendly fire airstrike."

Raines looked at him. "Jesus Christ on a motorbike."

"Respectfully, sir, he isn't here. And he sure as shit ain't on a motorbike."

Before Raines could respond, a low whistle interrupted them—radio static burst in Raines' ear.

[Radio Transmission]

"Command, be advised. We've got thermal pings near College Avenue. At least six, possibly eight hostiles. They're not ours."

"Copy that. Intercept and identify. Watch for sleepers."

The word made Raines flinch. *Sleepers*. Scum of the earth tactics used in city warfare. Dressing like civilians, hiding weapons, using suicide tactics to lure in troops, while using civilians as meat shields.

He waved forward his squad. "Let's clear this street."

They pushed through Monroe Street. The destruction grew denser the closer they got to the Capitol's perimeter. Apartment complexes were half-shelled, balconies turned to jagged concrete mouths. A burnt SUV still smoldered at the corner, the charred skeletons inside curled against each other. A child's toy rested on the dashboard—melted plastic that once had eyes.

"Contact right!" a soldier yelled.

Gunfire burst from a second-floor window. Parker dove behind a bench, firing upward. Another soldier dragged a wounded comrade behind a cement barrier. All around them, chaos.

Raines spotted movement. Quick in his own actions, he grabbed a frag grenade. He pulled the pin and tossed it as hard as he had ever thrown an object. It landed and bounced, causing an explosion that blew out the window—flame, smoke, and a screaming body tumbling to the street.

"Clear it, get those motherfuckers!" he shouted.

They stormed the building. Floor by floor. Room by room. The smell of rot and cordite fused in their lungs. Heavy gunfire blew through the walls, but they surrounded the enemy, and it didn't take much to overpower the forces within the building. Inside one apartment, they found a makeshift sniper's nest had been carved into what once was a child's bedroom. Stuffed animals lined the walls. A crib was riddled with bullet holes.

Swann stood frozen in the doorway. "Dear God... why?"

Raines whispered. "Seems war doesn't care where it sleeps."

* * *

The push through the southern edge of the university campus came just before noon. By now, the midday sun cast a cruel light on what was left of Tallahassee's heart. Smoke bloomed from where Doak Campbell Stadium once stood. The ground trembled every few minutes—government forces' artillery from the west, pounding the CDF front like the drumbeat of an executioner.

The 3rd Brigade held the line near Stadium Drive. Raines crouched beside a rusted transformer box, checking the new position with a bloodied map. Sergeant Swann limped up beside him, clutching a half-empty magazine and looking like he hadn't blinked in hours.

"We've secured the west halls," Swann reported. "But we had to burn Pike's."

Raines looked up, confused. "Why?"

Swann shrugged. "One of the kids. A Private David Ellis. Suspected possible hostiles in it, so we blew it to hell."

"You let them torch it?"

"I didn't see a need to stop them."

Raines stared toward the smoke curling over the horizon where the house once stood. "Hell of a war for it to die in."

They moved down Stadium Drive, past the hollowed remains of classroom buildings and campus shops. An overhead roar sent everyone ducking.

A loud, incoming fighter jet.

"AD team, eyes up—!" Raines barked.

A fighter buzzed the sky, streaking low. Moments later, a missile shrieked from beneath its wing.

"GET DOWN!"

But before it hit, a sharp, white-hot trail blazed skyward from the east. An air-defense system had been hidden in the shadows of the stadium. The interceptor struck the missile mid-air. The warhead split—veering off-course in a fiery tailspin. The shockwave knocked windows out for blocks. The jet banked hard and fled.

Raines raised his head from the pavement just in time to see the rocket veer so far off-course that it crashed down somewhere in College Town. A massive smoke plume emerged in the distance. The explosion had showered the street with twisted metal, sparks, and pieces of the city's past.

"These stray jets keep breaking through! That's twice now!" a soldier shouted.

"Knock it off! Everybody up!" Raines shouted as he stood, brushing off his shoulders.

At this point, nothing was surprising. Two fighter jets firing towards the same target meant only one thing: they suspected something, perhaps their target, was in the building.

By evening, the brigade had dug in along College Avenue. The front lines were shifting once again. The Battle of Tallahassee was nowhere near finished—but at that moment, holding what they had, it felt like they just might have endured.

And somewhere beneath the concrete and fire, a prayer was whispered from the lips of a weary medic:

"We're still here, God. If that counts for anything."

* * *

Field Log – 1930 hours

Location: FSU Stadium perimeter, South Tallahassee

Unit: 3rd Infantry Brigade

Commanding Officer: Lt. Col. Lucas Raines

*Heavy push along Stadium and Gaines. Government forces are digging into Tom Brown Park to the northeast. Losses are rising—Spirit's low. Our medic, Dr. Daniel Parker, was hit by glass debris during the airstrike. He refused to leave, as he reported he could still perform his duties. He set up a mobile triage under the stadium bleachers. Treated fifteen men in an hour. He says it reminds him of M*A*S*H reruns. I've been ordered back to HQ for debriefing. The 6th Georgia Battalion is to relieve the 3rd within a few hours. Major Mason will be in charge of the 3rd Infantry until further notice.*

The men laugh less now. Not because they're afraid, but because they're tired of war.

* * *

The moon hung low over Tallahassee, casting a pale, indifferent glow over the broken streets. The city was barely recognizable now in the dark—shells of buildings, smoldering husks of squad cars, roads clawed by tank treads, and cratered by mortar fire. The 6th Georgia Battalion moved slowly down Stadium Drive, rifles shouldered, boots cracking over glass and rubble. A soft breeze stirred the oak trees overhead, whistling through the Spanish moss like the breath of ghosts.

Nighttime rotations were perhaps the scariest, as darkness concealed enemy movements. The 6th Georgia Battalion relieved the 3rd Infantry Brigade earlier in the evening so that they could move to another defensive zone.

Captain Jacob Walker walked point, his helmet dented, one eye still bruised from an ambush the week before. Behind him, the line snaked through the shadow of Doak Campbell Stadium—once the pride of Florida State University, now a looming red relic of a time long gone. The giant FSU logo over the archway had been scorched black by fire from earlier attacks, and the once-slick concrete walkways were riddled with ash and blood.

Private Danny Morales, the youngest in the unit, looked up at the structure.

"Hard to believe people used to party here," he muttered. "Tailgating with heavy drinking. Now it's just a damn tomb."

"Everything becomes a tomb eventually," Walker said without turning.

The radio on his shoulder cracked without warning.

[Radio Transmission]

"Command to Ash-2. We've got something on radar. Unidentified aircraft approaching from the north. Heads up."

Walker's eyes shot skyward. "Eyes up, we've got incoming!"

Like a blade slicing air, a low hum intensified into a scream. At times, the object sounded almost like a kid's toy. That was when their fear was exponentially multiplied: drones. In the darkness, it was impossible to see the drones flying overhead accurately. They were sitting ducks.

"TAKE COVER!"

The unit dove for whatever shelter they could find. The drones streaked toward them—dropping grenades all around them. All they could do was cover their ears and hope it missed them. Many in the unit weren't so lucky. Walker looked up, seeing two of his men blown to pieces. All he could do was look in horror.

The attack was far from over, as another drone emerged from the dark and struck a Humvee abandoned on the road. As far as Walker could tell, its aim appeared bad, as it completely missed their M1 Abrams tank out on patrol with them.

Minutes soon became hours as the men remained covered, waiting for backup with signal-jamming devices. This would only protect their position for a short distance, not enough for the ground they had to cover.

Relief was soon had sometime after the attack, as the sky bloomed in a violent burst of fire and smoke. But one fragment—like a shard of God's fury—kept flying. It struck the tree lines just to the side of Stadium Drive, destroying a neighborhood house.

"Everybody up!"

Those who remained stood to their feet as Walker did a head count. Four missing. Although not for long, as they quickly found their four comrades' bodies blown to pieces by the grenades.

"Jesus Christ," whispered a corporal, dusting debris off his helmet. "We won't survive the night if they attack again."

Morales stared at their bodies. "Us? What about them?"

They stood there, a moment of silence for their fallen brothers. The weight settled in, becoming unbearable for many of them. A call soon came on Walker's radio.

[Radio Transmission]

"Command to Ash-2, how do you read?"

"Ash-2 to Command, I copy. We lost four men in the attack. We are exposed here. Requesting permission to move to checkpoint delta and hole up until dawn."

There was a long silence before the response.

[Radio Transmission]

"Command to Ash-2, permission granted. Proceed to checkpoint delta. Hold until 0500 hours. Out."

"Ash-2 to Command, roger."

Walker turned and looked at his men. They were tired and weary from the last few minutes.

"All right, mount up! we're moving to checkpoint delta!"

* * *

The squad's boots crunched under the massive debris lying upon the streets as they advanced northeast towards checkpoint delta, within the hollow streets of Tallahassee. They moved in a loose diamond formation, eyes flicking to shattered second-story windows and abandoned cars left like corpses on the roadside. Florida humidity clung to them like a second skin, dense and wet despite the season. The air reeked faintly of old smoke, mildew, and burned rubber.

As they turned onto College Avenue, time seemed to slow. They slowly approached a familiar site that had been the chatter of the CDF since they arrived—the Chi Omega house.

Even in the dark, it was unmistakable. It stood silent and monolithic, its white pillars stained by decades of rain and rot. Ivy had long since overtaken the southern wall, weaving itself like veins through the broken windows. The roof sagged, and warped wood hung loosely where shutters had once stood proud. Greek letters above the porch were still barely visible: XΩ

The men stopped walking. An invisible weight seemed to drop across the squad. Captain Walker turned, squinting through the haze. "This is it?"

"Yeah," Morales said quietly. "This is it."

They didn't need to name it. Everyone who knew anything about American horror knew this house. The place where Ted Bundy, in the dead of night, had broken in and murdered two women, attacked two more and disappeared into the night like a ghost. Brutality so vile, it haunted the nation's psyche decades later. Affecting society so much, some wondered what type of power must have been behind it, from either this world or the next.

Morales approached the gate and leaned forward. "Out of all the buildings left standing, this goddamn thing is one of them?"

No one answered because no one could know. Despite the renovations and security in the wake of the crime, no one knows why the decision was made to leave the house standing.

The house itself seemed to breathe—quiet and cold. It was a monument to a society that never really healed, a society that buried instead of cleansed, placing a band-aid on the wound instead of operating to cut out the cancer.

Walker finally broke the silence. "Should've been torn down."

Staff Sergeant Kevin Brewer, who had been silent since the previous skirmish, slowly unslung his pack and knelt in the dirt. His fingers methodically unclipped two packs of C4 explosives. He stood, his face unreadable, gaze fixed on the porch.

"We act like evil is rare," he muttered. "Like it's a glitch in the system. Yet this house... this fucking house. Proof like so many others... evil has addresses."

Without asking for permission, he approached the rotting porch steps. Each footstep creaked ominously beneath his weight. He pried open a loose plank, revealing a hollow space beneath the floorboards. He inserted the C4 into the cavity one by one, his hands steady.

He paused. Lit a cigarette with his off hand.

"Consider this an eviction notice."

He stepped back, pulled the pin on a grenade, and tossed it into the open doorway.

There was a sharp crack—then a thunderclap of light and fire as the house's lower level erupted in orange flame. The windows blew out in perfect sync, shards of glass glinting like broken stars. Black smoke surged upward like a banshee's scream, twisting into the sky.

The blast rattled the teeth in their skulls. Fire crawled up the staircase and into the rafters. Within moments, the roof began to sag. One pillar collapsed, crashing down with a thunderous roar. The flames danced higher, as if feeding off the darkness seared into the structure's bones.

The squad stared in stunned silence.

Morales looked in awe. "Damn, that's bright."

Brewer exhaled a long plume of smoke. His eyes never left the blaze.

"That's a lovely sight, that is. Years too late."

Walker walked up beside him. His jaw was tight, close to reprimanding him. “You acted without permission. That was more than just a personal vendetta. Explain.”

Brewer nodded. “I had a sister. She pledged to Chi Omega back in the 2020s. Dropped out because she said the house haunted her. Not just the stories, it haunted her spirit. I didn’t get it then. I do now.”

The fire hissed and popped. Distant explosions could be heard, either from the government forces or from some other rogue forces caught in the crossfire.

Walker finally turned back toward the road. “We’ve got twenty minutes before we’re exposed. Let’s go. On to checkpoint delta.”

Comms man Ray keyed into the radio as they moved. “Command, this is Ash-2. Be advised—performed an unsanctioned demo on a structure near College Avenue. No civvies inside. Just... ghosts.”

“*Copy that, Ash-2.*”

The Chi Omega house burned behind them as they disappeared into the shadows. No one looked back.

The sky glowed orange. And for once, all seemed right with the world.

* * *

Field Log – 0400 hours

Location: Gaines Street, Near the Florida State Capitol

Unit: [REDACTED]

They say war is just politics by other means. That may be true. But at this hour, crawling through collapsed brick and rebar with ghosts at my heels, politics feels very far away.

* * *

The early morning fog hung low over the crumbled remains of Gaines Street, just west of the FSU campus. Thick smoke from smoldering buildings clung to the air, mixing with the damp scent of blood, sulfur, and damaged plywood. The squad moved slowly, rifles up, stepping over debris where once there had been art galleries, coffee shops, and half-lit student apartments.

Major Devin Turner raised his hand, signaling a halt.

They ducked behind the shattered husk of a vintage car dealership. Tallahassee was no longer a city—it was a corpse that hadn't yet realized it was dead. Their objective was to move to relieve the 6th Georgia Battalion, but it was easier said than done.

"Radio chatter says enemy remnants are regrouping near Cascades Park," Lieutenant Pablo Reyes whispered, adjusting his scope. "Probably the 117th Airborne—regulars, not militia."

"Then we do this quietly," Turner said. "No heroics. Just recon. We're trying to push them away from our lines, nothing more. Staying alive and making sure others do, too."

Suddenly, a faint whistle—then a blast—cracked through the southern block. A fireball erupted where a boutique once stood. Debris rained down. They all dropped instinctively, hearts pounding.

"Mortars," Lieutenant Reyes said, spitting dust. "We've been spotted."

"No," Turner said, squinting up. "Not them. That was friendly. That's our artillery—long range—clearing their fallback routes."

They resumed movement.

As the sun rose, broken streetlamps cast elongated shadows of the soldiers along chipped murals and abandoned scooters. Every corner seemed to whisper memories of peace—frat banners still waving from shattered windows, a 'Spring Fling 2042' sign buried beneath rubble.

Then came the bloodcurdling noise—the voice of a young person, a child.

Turner snapped to attention, hand signaling *hold.* He moved swiftly toward the echo, navigating a collapsed diner with cracked pastel booths and coffee cups still full of dust.

Behind a mangled fridge, they found a young boy—barely eight—curled into a ball, filthy and emaciated, his skin blotched with soot. His shirt was torn, and one shoe was missing. When the fridge shifted, he flinched, expecting pain.

Turner dropped to one knee.

"It's okay," he said softly. "We're here to help."

The boy didn't respond—he just stared, his eyes wide and hollow. Turner noticed the dog tags hanging around his neck, clearly not his own. Probably his father's, Turner thought.

Reyes knelt beside them and held out a protein bar, unwrapping it slowly. "You hungry, little man?"

The boy reached out with shaking fingers, took the bar, and stuffed it in his mouth like an animal, not even chewing.

"We can't leave him here," Reyes said.

"We're not," Turner replied. "He's with us now."

A shaft of sunlight broke through from the shattered roof, highlighting the child's face. It looked almost holy—like a stained-glass window over a pile of rubble.

Turner's voice caught as he activated his radio.

"Alpha-1 to Command—civilian located. A minor, alive. Requesting immediate evac priority."

A pause. Then: "*Copy. Extraction en route.*"

Turner turned back to the boy. "You've made it through the worst. That makes you one of us."

And for the first time, the boy blinked—just once—but enough for Turner to believe he understood.

* * *

The rain had stopped, but the sky hung heavy with a gray so thick it felt like a lid sealing them in. The air smelled of cinder and damp pine needles, and everything—the pavement, the red-brick buildings, the windshields of abandoned cars—glistened under a wet sheen, as if the world had been freshly washed but couldn't be made clean.

The squad advanced cautiously along West Pensacola Street, a street once filled with so many young college kids tailgating on a Saturday afternoon. To their left, the red brick buildings, once the tallest of their kind, were reduced to rubble. In the distance, they could still see the smoke rising from the stadium. Still smoldering from the jet and drone attacks earlier in the week, it was a symbol of where things are in this war.

Corporal Jeffery Simmons stumbled on a loose stone, then righted himself. "Feels like a lifetime ago when I went to college, partying on college campuses every other week, failing exams in the other weeks."

Turner gave a dry nod. "A lifetime ago indeed."

He gripped the boy's hand tightly as he walked slowly, matching the child's pace. Turner was scanning the buildings and the horizon for possible enemy sightings. The main force had not reached the city, but several smaller units managed to find their way in.

His hand was raised, signaling the squad to halt. At that point, he saw a smoke plume. Halfway down the block, tucked behind leafless dogwoods, stood the wreckage of a former two-story colonial: The Chi Omega house.

Turner approached it slowly, weapons raised, as did the others.

"Isn't that?" Reyes asked.

"Yeah... the house that the 6th Georgia Battalion destroyed last night," Turner muttered.

"Did you know it was... this house?"

Turner did not answer. It seemed they all knew.

The stories of FSU, its history, and tragedy were the talk of the CDF when many found out they were being deployed to Tallahassee. Even in its destruction, the house continued to remind them of the evil with dead eyes and a calm voice—one that haunted a nation in the 1970s and forever changed how people thought about the world.

"Seems this is more relevant to the CDF than anyone who was here. Seems nobody gave a shit." Reyes said, his voice low and distant. "It was forgotten."

"Because memory's a marketing problem," Turner said bitterly. "You can't sell history that scares parents."

Deep down, Turner knew that was the truth. The nation's downfall and the war they were fighting were all tied back to the same fundamental problems: morality and greed.

No one said anything for a while. They just stared.

"All right, we're wasting time."

"Agreed, sir."

The boy tugged on Turner's hand. He looked surprised and confused about why the squadron stared at the ruined building. Turner smiled and just stared at him.

"You need something?"

For the first time, the boy spoke. "Thirsty."

"Oh shit, of course."

Turner got his canteen out and handed it to him. The boy took big sips, drinking like it was his first in days. He wiped his mouth, handing it back to Turner.

"Thank you, mister."

"Do you have a name, boy?"

"Jimmy."

"Jimmy? That's a great name."

"Glad you think so. I don't think mommy or daddy did."

"Why do you say that?"

"They set me down where you found me... days ago."

"They didn't say they were coming back? Or where they were going?"

"No, mister."

Turner stood there in silence, in disbelief at the words he was hearing. *What kind of parents abandon their own son in a war zone?* he thought. *Pieces of shit.*

"Well, Jimmy, you have my word; we will find you a good home where you're loved. You have my word."

Turner turned his head to the rest of the squad.

"All right, move out!"

They turned their backs to the rubble and kept marching. The house smoldered behind them, and they carried on with their mission.

Turner spotted movement in the distance, which prompted him to radio a unit further up.

"Alpha-1 to Echo-1, movement spotted in your zone of control."

There was a pause before the crackle of the radio.

"*Echo-1 to Alpha-1, copy. We will look into it. Out.*"

* * *

Field Transmission – ENCRYPTED

Unit: 3rd Recon Battalion

Location: Inner Tallahassee Sector, ~1.5 miles west of Old Capitol Complex

Unit: 3rd Recon Battalion

Commanding Officer: 1st Lieutenant Matthew Cross

Command, be advised: building collapse has blocked the Monroe corridor. We're detouring south through Gaines. Resistance is scattered but aggressive. Casualties: two KIA, one severe evac. Over.

* * *

The battle soon reached its fifth day, becoming a meat grinder of small arms combat. The central units were fighting outside the city, deciding to avoid building-to-building combat. They moved like ghosts through a dying city.

Tallahassee had become a graveyard of memories. Each minute, each hour, grinding slower than before, with the agony of constant attacks from the air and ground. First Lieutenant Matthew Cross stepped over a bent bicycle, its tires melting into the sidewalk like tar. The street signs still read familiar names—Gaines, Woodward, College—but the city's soul had been gutted. FSU banners flapped tattered in the wind like mourning shrouds, while sidewalks once walked by students in flip-flops were now smeared with blood and grit.

Cross signaled a halt with two fingers and crouched beside a blown-out sedan. His chest rose and fell in slow, measured breaths. Every creak of broken glass beneath their boots echoed louder than it should. They were too exposed out here.

Second Lieutenant Dusty Kramer dropped beside him. "Sir," he whispered, voice trembling just a bit. "Picked up comms. Government forces guarding a two-story redbrick building—old student services."

Cross turned his gaze toward the skyline, such as it was. Smoke veiled everything, but a shattered modernist sculpture poked above the haze—a twisted metallic sunburst once meant to inspire undergrads. Now, it was just a tombstone. It seemed to be a recurring theme, a graveyard city some called it.

"They are guarding intel or a comms array?"

"Possibly. Too much heat for a bluff," Dusty said. "Sniper nests. Claymore signs on the east wall."

Cross studied the squad around him with a depressing look—down to five souls now. Most had been with him since the northern push, from the swamps near Perry up through the Ocala brush. Now, they were tired. Hollow-eyed. Sergeant Ramirez's hand bled through a torn glove. Anders hadn't spoken since Carraway fell. Halley's cough was worsening.

But like good soldiers, they kept moving, kept fighting until otherwise ordered or relieved.

"We're going in," Cross said finally. "No more fucking around. We take out anyone we find. Last thing we need is them regrouping and swarming us in the dark."

"We're with you, sir!"

Ramirez cracked his knuckles. "Copy that, sir. Let's give 'em hell."

The squad mounted up, just as they always had. As they advanced, the remains of a quaint outdoor plaza gave way beneath their boots. Charred umbrellas lay collapsed beside overturned metal café tables. A sandwich board still read "Half-Off Cold Brew Fridays" in sun-bleached chalk. They passed a mural of a smiling graduate tossing his cap into a sky now replaced by smoke.

Cross paused.

He wasn't sure if it was the smoke or the weight on his chest, but he felt nauseous. War had a way of making the beautiful seem grotesque. Or maybe it was the other way around. Cross shook off the feeling and kept moving. For survival, either in battle or combat, it cared little if you were sick or dying.

He thought back on survival, witnessing people light themselves on fire to keep warm in the winter when the electricity failed and the services to help people were unavailable or destroyed.

Cross's thoughts were soon interrupted by the arrival to their destination. They had reached the eastern edge of the old student services building. The glass façade had shattered long ago, and steel supports poked out like fractured ribs. Inside, shadows moved.

Ramirez pointed out. "Sniper—west stairwell. He's shifting."

Cross whispered into his comms. "Dusty, thermal?"

A pause. "Confirmed. At least four heat sigs. Small arms. One belt-fed. No armor I can see."

Cross made the call.

"Ramirez, breach the side entrance. Dusty, with me. We're clearing the main floor. Anders and Halley, keep overwatch. No one is to flank us, got it?"

Ramirez nodded and jogged toward the rusted side door. He placed a low-noise charge on the hinges, clicked a remote—

Pop!

The door cracked inward.

"Go! Go! Go!"

They surged inside. Darkness as far as they could see. Only broken by beams of morning light slicing through cracks in the boarded windows. Cross's boots crunched on shattered trophies and discarded graduation robes. A hallway poster read: *"Welcome Class of 2043—Dare to Dream."*

He almost laughed. But he didn't, as he felt the situation called for self-control.

They moved past a reception desk covered in mold and dried blood. Filing cabinets were overturned. One of the walls was covered in what looked like government maps—and crayon drawings from someone who had likely lived here during the early months of the war. Cross reached down and picked up a child's teddy bear with a missing eye.

Dusty's whisper crackled in his ear.

"Rear stairwell—movement."

Cross's blood chilled. He dropped the bear, raising his fist. The squad stacked quietly behind cover. Then, a click.

"Contact!"

The room exploded in fire and lead. A gunner burst from the stairwell, belt-fed SAW barking flames. Cross dove behind the reception desk as rounds shattered glass and punched holes through the drywall above him. Ramirez returned fire from the side entrance, his rifle barking controlled bursts. Dusty rolled into cover, nearly slipping on a puddle of spilled hydraulic fluid—its origins unclear.

Cross barked orders into comms. "Suppressing fire, left flank! Move on the right!"

Anders and Halley rained fire from an upstairs window across the street, picking off one of the shooters on the second floor. The sniper collapsed backward over a railing, limbs twisting like a broken puppet.

"Two down," Anders whispered through gritted teeth.

Cross rose from cover just long enough to toss a flashbang through the inner doorway.

Pop!

Then came the screaming. The window was short, so they moved fast. One combatant was clawing at his face, blind from the burst. Ramirez tackled him with brutal force, slamming him into a vending machine. Another fired wildly, nicking Halley in the leg before Dusty took him down with a clean double-tap. A massive knife had found its way into the poor bastard.

Silence fell as if a blast had sucked every breath out of the building.

Breathing heavily, Cross continued to move room to room, clearing each corner. His hands shook slightly—more from adrenaline than fear. *All right, where are you? Sneaky Fuckers.* Cross was careful as he approached each room. The possibility of claymores and booby-trapped doors weighed heavily. However, with the likelihood of more hostilities, he had no choice but to clear each room. Carefully and methodically, the building was cleared. Around every desk, behind every bookcase. Clear, and clear. *Seems that they set up a rush job.*

By the time Cross was finished, he returned to new news. Dusty found a laptop near a portable transmitter, still warm. Its screen was flickering.

"Sir. I think this was a signal booster. They were transmitting something."

"Coordinates?"

Dusty nodded. "Encrypted... but I can get our tech guys on it."

Cross stood over one of the fallen. The man couldn't have been older than twenty. His sidearm had jammed. His uniform bore no insignia—just a flag patch burned halfway off.

Ramirez, who had finished bounding and gagging the man he stabbed, stood to his feet with his prisoner.

"These aren't regulars," Ramirez muttered. "Spooks, maybe. Off-grid unit."

Cross leaned against the wall and wiped blood from his cheek. "Then whatever they were doing here... It was big."

* * *

Field Journal – Entry from Lt. Matthew Cross

October 22, 2050

Today, we witnessed something... interesting. I saw a child's drawing pinned next to military schematics. Crayon and blood, side by side. A sun with a smile. A stick figure holding hands with another. Beneath it, someone wrote in sloppy print: "Daddy, don't forget me."

I don't know if it was one of ours or one of theirs. Not sure it matters. But we've reached a point where data and innocence exist on the same boards—where a child's goodbye is stapled beside death orders.

We cleared the building. We managed to capture one spook, but I doubt he speaks. Dusty found a mile marked for satellite relay. Our techs haven't decoded it yet. It might be tied to schematics for the government's campaign in Tallahassee.

Ramirez says we should burn this place. I agree. But part of me wants it to stay. Let the ghosts sit with what happens here. Let them look at what they made.

* * *

The squad soon set up a temporary camp in a parking garage across from the ruined structure. A fire flickered low in an oil drum. Halley's leg was wrapped pretty tightly. Anders leaned against a pillar, sketching in his weathered notebook—no one knew what he drew, and no one asked.

Cross stood watch alone on the rooftop. From here, he could see the flickering lights of the Capitol district, still occupied by the CDF. A long trail of smoke marked the skyline.

Behind him, Dusty approached. "Sir... about the flash drive. We managed to break the code."

"Yeah?"

"They were transmitting troop movements in the city... for artillery and drone strikes."

"Well, that's not surprising."

"There's more, sir. They received something not long ago... an order. A directive from somewhere high up in the D.C. command structure."

Cross turned, brow furrowed.

"They were given the order to withdraw, sir."

"What?"

"They received orders to move out to another hot spot. It's a big operation."

"Did they indicate where this big operation is?"

"Target Charlie Foxtrot, sir."

"Lexington?"

"That's right."

Cross looked out again at the city. He was not briefed on every battle across every state, but deep down, he knew what this meant. The war was racing to its next stage.

His radio crackled in the moment.

"*Command to Echo-1.*"

Cross turned on his radio. "This is Echo-1."

"*Echo-1, proceed with mop-up operations protocol. I repeat, begin mop-up operations.*"

Cross and Dusty looked at one another. Within silence, they realized what it meant—the day had been won.

The Continental Defense Forces were victorious at Tallahassee.

October 23, 2050 – Tallahassee, Florida – Landis Green

The smoke was still thick over the east side of Tallahassee, but now thinning as the sun rose pale and yellow above the treetops. It wasn't the color of hope—more like parchment singed at the edges. The city had been chewed down to its bones. Blackened husks of once-familiar homes sagged inward, roofs collapsed like ribs around a hollow chest. And along the cracked streets, the wounded limped, rolled, or were carried toward makeshift medical tents marked by sheets soaked in blood, not red crosses.

Staff Sergeant Brewer stood outside the smoldering shell of what used to be a library, its stone columns cracked like split knuckles. The air reeked of burnt paper and fuel. His sleeves were torn, blood flecked his beard, and his boots stuck slightly to the asphalt with every step—coated in something between ash and sin.

His squad lingered nearby, the remnants of a unit that had once numbered well over forty. They'd all seen the worst of the city, but no one talked much anymore. They just stared into the wreckage. Or at the ground. Or at nothing at all.

Behind Brewer, Dr. Daniel Parker wrapped a bandage around Morales' arm. The boy—Brewer still called him a boy, even though he'd killed more men in two weeks than some had in a lifetime—winced but didn't speak.

"Don't flex that arm, Private," Parker said. "It's a miracle your bicep didn't come off entirely."

Morales gave a tight nod. "No promises, sir."

Brewer pulled out a pack, and he soon lit a cigarette. It was the last one in his pocket. He didn't smoke before the war, yet the stress caused him to try it for the first time. It didn't seem so bad, but it slowly became the only small joy in his current situation. He stared east, past the blown-out skyline of downtown Tallahassee, toward the horizon where the Gulf lay—still out of reach. The Continental Defense Force had held the line. Barely. But they hadn't made it to D.C., not yet at least.

A jeep bounced up the road, kicking up gray dust in its wake. A runner leaned out the window with an envelope.

"Orders from MacDill," he called out. "Brewer?"

"Here," Brewer stepped forward, grabbing the envelope.

The runner didn't stop. "Better look alive, as General Rusk is coming here tomorrow."

"Oh, lovely, just what we need. To look like we're still standing after glorious battle."

"I wouldn't know anything about that."

"Course not, bus boy..."

"Something else I need to mention... You boys will be moving north soon. A new front Rusk and High Command are set on. Kentucky."

The word hit the squad like a gust of cold air.

"Kentucky?" Parker repeated, standing. "That's in the opposite damn direction."

Brewer opened the pouch and scanned the document inside. They were ink-stamped with the seal of the CDF High Command. The language was clear, clipped, and full of names: divisions, battalions, coordinates, and codewords. But one section stuck out like a blade tip:

"Following strategic success in Tallahassee, all available infantry units not critically incapacitated are to redeploy for Operation Thunder March. Victory will begin there."

Brewer folded the papers slowly. "We're going to Lexington," he said. "It seems the President's forces are digging in there. General Rusk wants us to be the ones to dig them out."

"Sounds like a trap."

"In this day and age, where every movement is seen, I wouldn't doubt it."

"Yes, but most of the government's resources have either surrendered or are decimated."

"Or so they say," Brewer replied, puffing smoke from his cigarette.

There was a long silence. Then Morales spat into the dirt. "Well, I guess we're going hunting."

* * *

Nightfall quickly fell on the city, and tensions reached new heights when the sun went down. Brewer and his squad bivouacked in a half-collapsed courthouse on the edge of town. A few managed to sleep. Some just stared at the ceiling where rain dripped through a bullet-riddled hole. Brewer sat against a wall, writing in his field journal.

October 23rd. Hooray for it being over, I guess. The city's bones are still hotter than hell itself. But somehow we're alive. We buried twelve of ours today. Found three more buried in rubble. One was still breathing.

Parker said that, based on damage to his legs, he will never walk again. His lungs still work. Small victories, I suppose.

We didn't complete our tasks here in full. But we bled 'em hard. Command says it's time to break the back of the enemy. Lexington, Kentucky. God help us. Major Mason is now in command, and Raines spoke highly of him. But one thing is for sure: we'll follow Rusk into hell if it means this ends.

A distant thunder rolled across the horizon. But it wasn't raining. Not yet. Brewer tested the air. He liked it, but it didn't like him.

October 24, 2050 – Somewhere in Tallahassee, Florida

The wind carried the last of the ash down Jefferson Street as Major Anthony Mason stood over a folding table littered with maps, comms tablets, and ration wrappers. A fresh scar ran across the concrete, a blackened trench where an air-to-ground missile had ripped into the city just days before. Engineers worked in the background to clear rubble from the State Capitol's outer corridor, where a final firefight had occurred beneath the rotunda.

A corporal approached with a fresh intel packet. "Sir. Comms from Southern Command. Top clearance."

Mason took the tablet, his gloves dusty from soot and gunpowder. The message was brief, but enough to pull the breath from his lungs.

REDEPLOYMENT ORDER

TO: ALL ACTIVE PERSONNEL, 3RD BRIGADE / 47TH FLORIDA COMBINED

SUBJECT: OPERATION THUNDER MARCH

Effective immediately, you are to redeploy to Kentucky. Rendezvous with General Rusk's main assault force outside Lexington.

Objective: Break government lines along the Versailles Road and press into the capital region.

ETA to frontline: 86 hours

Victory demands swiftness.

- General Tavares, Southern Command

Mason lowered the tablet and exhaled slowly. "Looks like Tallahassee was just a warm-up."

Behind him, Sergeant Niles sat on a cinderblock, adjusting a bandage on his leg. "Lexington? Shit. Thought we'd all have a few weeks off after this mess."

"War doesn't work on your schedule, Niles," Mason muttered. He glanced down at his men—what remained of them. From a company of 114, only 61 stood ready for the next campaign. They were exhausted, hollow-eyed, but alive. "Get some sleep. We're heading north."

Mason's mind was troubled even though he projected confidence. He thought back to when he looked at the destruction that had been left behind—so much carnage and chaos that the CDF and government forces had left behind.

Mason saw the aftermath earlier in the day at Landis Green, where wounded men still recovered in tents under temporary floodlights. Nurses and medics moved between rows of cots. Despite the pain, there was a sense of momentum building again. The tide was turning.

He walked with the unit's chaplain, an older man named Harris who'd fought in the first week of the rebellion. "Ever been to Kentucky?"

"Once," Harris said. "It's colder. Hillier. And they say the soil runs redder."

Mason grunted. "Good. Maybe we'll finally force a breakthrough."

* * *

Morning rose fast, a little too quickly for Mason's liking. The convoy began to form at Apalachee Parkway, engines rumbled, and supply crates were loaded onto flatbeds. The roads were still damaged, and the power grid was unstable, but soldiers moved like clockwork.

While it seemed premature to leave, reports came flowing in that the government forces, or what was left of them, rushed back to Atlanta during the night. All the commanders learned in the morning briefing that the Southern Command had assigned the 6th Armored Division to remain on station.

Mason stood before his men—what was left of Beta Platoon. They were bloodied, bruised, but sharper than ever.

"We didn't ask for any of this," he said, "but we've come this far. And now General Rusk is counting on us to crack the spine of what's left of the government forces. We're not marching with a vendetta. We're marching to finish this war. So, look around. This may be the last family you ever see. And it's the only one that'll get you..." Mason trailed off.

"...It's the only one that'll get you home," he finished. His voice held no bravado, just a weary, grounded truth that settled into the bones of every soldier there.

A moment of silence followed—no cheering, no cries of "hoorah"—just quiet nods and clenched jaws. They understood. Too many had buried friends to treat this like anything other than what it was: survival.

The sound of engines starting broke the stillness. One by one, trucks growled to life, headlights slicing through the pre-dawn fog as the column began its journey northward.

As Mason climbed into the lead Humvee, he looked back at the battered remnants of Tallahassee. FSU's campus was now a shell of itself, the roads scorched, the buildings pockmarked by war. And yet, beneath the destruction, the land still stood. Still waiting for something new to rise from its ashes.

Beside him, A corporal adjusted the rearview mirror. "Lexington, huh?"

Mason nodded. "Time to go fight another."

The convoy moved, headlights flaring, tires crunching over broken asphalt. In their wake, only the ghosts seemed to remain in the city now.

March 1, 2051 – Somewhere in Kentucky

The hills of central Kentucky were deceptively green.

They rolled gently like sleeping giants, covered in fresh grass and clusters of yellow wildflowers that danced in the breeze—mocking, almost, in how beautiful they remained despite the slaughter that came. Trees budded with new leaves. A creek twisted through the valley floor, its surface glinting silver in the early light. Somewhere in the distance, a mourning dove cooed, unaware—or uncaring—that war had come to its corner of the earth.

Major Mason pressed his body low against the damp limestone outcrop at the edge of the tree line. Dew soaked through his knees. The binoculars trembled slightly in his hands, not from nerves, but from the deep chill that had settled in overnight and refused to leave. Below them, less than a mile away, the government line unfurled across the ridges like a serpent—pillboxes tucked into brush, drone towers rising like antennae, and rows of anti-armor trenches dug into the soft spring soil.

Four months. Four fucking months we've been here. Mason exhaled slowly, watching the thin fog coil around the distant machines of war like breath around steel.

"Looks like they reinforced the ridge," Lieutenant Ortega murmured beside him, flattening into the dirt with a scope in hand. "New concrete revetments. But look there—see how the APCs are lined up away from the trees?"

Mason followed her finger to a stretch of half-camouflaged vehicles resting too close to the forest's edge. "Their flank's wide open," he muttered. "That's either arrogance... or bait."

"Either way, we're going in."

Behind them, the platoon huddled in silence under the canopy, faces half-lit by filtered morning sun. Some scribbled prayers on scrap cloth and tucked them under their chest plates. Others tightened their helmet straps like nooses, hands trembling just a little. A private whispered the Lord's prayer with a rosary looped around his trigger finger. The only other sounds were weapons being chambered and the quiet grind of worn-out boots shifting in the loom.

Mason's radio clicked once. Major Fallon's voice rasped through.

"Air support window opens in 12 minutes. Once the clouds break, the Eagle group will commence heavy runs. You breach at first thunder. Rear armor is forming up on Route 421. Confirm readiness."

Mason clicked once to acknowledge. But he didn't speak.

Instead, he stood slowly, letting the fog roll around his boots like smoke rising from the earth. His eyes swept the treetops, then the faces behind him. All were younger than him now, all awaiting his move.

He cleared his throat. "For four months, we have fought here," he said quietly. "We came from the south and fought here all winter. This was supposed to break us... Yet we are still here."

He paused, tapping his rifle's magazine with his fingers. "This ridge? This valley? This is the breaking point. Theirs, not ours."

No one said anything. But there was a stillness to the men and women now—a focus sharpening like glass beneath pressure. The kind that only comes when there's no more time to pray, only time to act.

Ortega leaned in and muttered. "Major, you know that hill out there used to be a state park? People picnicked on that damn thing."

Mason glanced toward the distant slope, now laced with tripwire and scorched from overnight shelling. "Maybe they'll get to picnic there again someday."

Then the sky cracked—not with thunder, but with purpose. The fog instantly broke, swept up like a curtain God drew. Light poured down in molten shafts, igniting the valley in color—greens, reds, and steel grays. And then came the sound.

A low, rising growl. Louder. Louder still.

Bombers.

Three shapes cut through the clouds above—B-1B Lancers, their wings swept back, engines roaring like angry Greek gods. Air support had arrived. Dozens of smaller fighters followed behind, streaming contrails as they descended. Moments later, the air itself split apart as smart bombs fell toward the ridge with terrifying speed.

Mason didn't wait for impact.

He raised his fist. "All right... let's go! Go! Go!"

And the valley erupted. The hillside exploded.

The first wave of bombs hit the far trench line with devastating precision. A geyser of soil, smoke, and shredded steel erupted into the air, followed by a ripple of secondary detonations—ammunition stockpiles cooking off, drones falling like wounded birds, concrete bunkers bursting open like overripe fruit.

Major Mason sprinted downhill, boots sliding over loose rock and churned grass. Around him, his unit moved in tight formation, fanning out in wedges, rifles shouldered, eyes sharp. The heat from the burning tree line licked at their faces, even from this distance.

"Stay on me!" he barked into his comms. "Watch the flanks!"

They passed over the body of an enemy scout, face half-gone from shrapnel, rifle still gripped in death. Mason didn't stop. There was no time to process. No time to feel. Not yet at least.

The air was a mosaic of violence—crackling radio chatter, tracer fire, the whine of rotary cannons, and the heavy cough of artillery.

A fighter jet roared past, banking hard, releasing two missiles that screamed into a command trailer on the ridge. The explosion threw up a shockwave so strong that it staggered the entire unit.

Ortega ducked behind a downed tree, coughing, her shoulder bleeding. "This is madness," she gasped, voice trembling.

"Yes," Mason replied, crouching beside her. "This is madness's last gasp for air."

Mason helped Ortega to her feet, and they again pushed forward.

The government soldiers who remained began falling back in confusion. Their comms were jammed, their drones blinded, and their leadership obliterated in the first strikes. It wasn't just a breath—it was a collapse.

As Mason's unit crested the inner ridge, they saw the truth: dozens of conscripts, many of them barely adults, were surrendering. Others fled into the woods, leaving their rifles in the dirt. What was once a fortified line was now a graveyard of broken machines and smoldering flesh.

"Hold your fire! Hold!" Mason shouted, waving his arms. "Get them on the ground and cuffed! If any run, leave them be. Take prisoners if they drop their gear!"

Zip-tie cuffs were soon passed around, and the security soldiers began detaining them. Behind them, medics began tending to the wounded. Engineers moved in to sweep for mines. Supply runners climbed the slope with crates of ammunition and water. The battle was far from over, but this ridge—this part of the line—was theirs.

Mason dropped to one knee near a crater, letting the adrenaline drain from his bones. His hands were shaking now. Not from fear. From release.

A child's voice snapped him back.

"Sir?"

He turned. A boy, maybe sixteen, stood beside a captured transport vehicle, his hands zip-tied behind his back. His uniform didn't fit. His helmet had no rank. His cheeks were streaked with soot and tears.

"I—I was just the mechanic," the boy stammered. "I never even fired my gun."

Mason looked at him for a long moment. Then he turned to one of the MPs.

"Question and debrief this one first. If the commander thinks he's clean, cut him loose. Put him with the other non-combatants."

The boy blinked, stunned. "You won't... kill me?"

Mason stood slowly. "Not today, boy. We're not savages."

The sun had fully risen behind them. In the distance, the outer ridges of Lexington shimmered in the haze, beckoning.

* * *

Field Transmission – ENCRYPTED

[AUDIO RECORDING – MARCH 10, 2051 – 0846 HOURS, LOCAL TIME]

LT. COL. RAINES: Major, command briefed me on Operation Silent Thunder's completion. It seems our boys in the 3rd and 7th Air Wings broke through. Lexington's line has fractured. Repeat—fractured. Drone recon shows a breach east of the city. They want all available units redirected to support the push.

MAJ. MASON: Understood. We will begin immediate reorganization. Pulling the wounded back to Green Line Alpha and starting the rotation of squadrons into transport trucks. Requesting permission to leave a ghost unit to hold the ridge.

LT. COL. RAINES: Permission granted.

MAJ. MASON: Sir... you think this is it?

[Long Pause]

LT. COL. RAINES: This is the last sunrise of the old America, Major. Let's make sure the new one gets a chance to rise.

* * *

March 11, 2051 – Somewhere near Lexington, Kentucky

The convoy rolled over the Kentucky roads beneath a thunderhead sky.

The transport trucks jostled down cracked rural roads, their wheels kicking up the red dust that clung to everything. The trees were just beginning to turn color, golden edges peeking from late spring's grip. Farms and burned-out gas stations flicked past in a blur, reminders of a country in pieces. Lexington loomed ahead—a city wrapped in history and now, like so much else, tangled in war.

Major Mason sat in the back of the lead truck, helmet on his lap, arms folded over his rifle. Cool and rhythmic rain spattered through the open canvas flaps. His eyes were heavy, but sleep was impossible.

To his left, Lieutenant Ortega scrolled through the latest sat-feed on a rugged tablet. "Lexington is a three-ring fight," she said, voice low but focused. "Downtown's barricaded, the university's been converted into a command post, and the old farmhouses to the south are now artillery emplacements."

Mason nodded slowly. "And we're going in from the west?"

"Correct. Through a corridor between Versailles and Harrodsburg Road. General Rusk's air strike last week took out two armored divisions near Frankfort. There's a gap. We are to fill it."

He let that settle. His back ached from the long ride. So many of the faces in his unit had changed—some rotated out due to injuries, some went with Lt. Colonel Raines back to MacDill, and others were buried in Tallahassee's shattered clay. But the soul of the group remained.

"Anyone hear from the doc?" Mason asked suddenly.

Dr. Daniel Parker, a member of their unit, was spread among all the units in the Battle of Tallahassee, thanks in part to his vast medical knowledge.

"He's in Truck Four," Ortega replied. "Been tending to a kid with a neck infection. Haven't heard much from him since he seems to be called all over creation. You'd never know the CDF had more combat medics deployed."

Mason grunted. "You'd think."

The trucks slowed up ahead. The rain picked up as they approached the forward operating base. Built into the ruins of a high school football stadium, the base was temporary and ugly but brimming with activity. Supply convoys wove between tent clusters. Radar dishes spun on tripods. Like iron dinosaurs, artillery guns pointed east in rows along the track.

They unloaded in silence.

A young lieutenant—barely older than the rifles slung across the troops' backs—ran up to them. "Third Brigade? Major Mason?"

"That's me."

"Orders from command, sir. You will be first over the hill tomorrow morning—your unit's designated Hammer Lead. You'll push through the horse farms and hold Route 68."

Mason gave a tight nod. "Copy that."

The lieutenant hesitated. "Sir... I must warn you, it will be rough. They've got fortified artillery out there. And... they've started using chemical smoke now. Disorienting agents."

A disturbing fact every military personnel knows all too well: What began as a tactic in the First World War was continuously used in each war after. The horrors of chemical warfare were a risk, but had to be fought against, no matter what.

"Requisition us gas masks. And if they make us blind, we'll just shoot more."

"Yes, sir."

He turned to his unit.

"All right, you heard him. Make sure to pick up a mask. Unload, get rations, prep the rest of your gear. We're going into the belly of the meat grinder, so make peace with whatever you believe in."

The rain started to fall only lightly, as a low rainbow arched faintly over the trees, fractured by smoke. Mason stared at it, then walked toward the makeshift command tent where he'd be briefed. Behind him, the thunderheads loomed.

March 12, 2051 – Somewhere along Lexington's defensive line

By first light, they were already knee-deep in mud. Major Mason's boots sank into the soaked farmland as he crouched behind a rusted grain silo, watching smoke curl over the horizon. In the distance, Lexington shimmered under the gray dawn—a city caught between the past and a ruined future. The air smelled of wet hay, diesel, and distant fire.

"Contact in twenty," Ortega whispered beside him, watching through binoculars. "Spotters say they're setting up trench mortars near the old stables."

Mason pulled his mask over his face. Ready for battle. The briefing taught him about the new chemical smoke used by government troops—laced with psychoactive agents and pepper stimulants—turning the battlefield into a hallucination. Visibility dropped. Coordination broke. Some soldiers wandered for hours, screaming at shadows.

"Drop the smoke bombs when I signal," Mason ordered. "Use it against them. Push hard and fast."

Nearby, Dr. Parker tended to a jittering private, double-checking the filter seals on his mask. "Keep the band tight, breathe through your nose. Panic, and you die," he murmured. The young soldier nodded with terrified eyes.

Thunder cracked overhead. Not the weather, they realized. Artillery.

The opening barrage slammed into the left flank—shells tearing open the hills with brutal precision. One struck an old feed barn, blowing it apart in a geyser of splinters. Mason hit the ground, shouting. "Go! Go! Go!"

They surged forward through the smoke, a blur of motion and chaos.

Gunfire erupted from the tree line—staccato bursts from entrenched rifle squads. Mason's unit scattered, returning fire as they advanced. Bullets snapped past, slicing through the chemical mist.

"Left side, suppressing fire!" Ortega called out, diving behind a stone wall. "They've got an MG nest under the horse track!"

"Frag out!" shouted a corporal, lobbing a grenade.

The blast cleared the machine gun nest, but not before two men fell, one screaming and clutching his leg. Mason and the unit kept moving.

The ground was slick, churned with blood and mud. A soldier beside him tripped and disappeared into a shallow trench, his scream cut off by a mine detonation. Earth sprang skyward. By the time they reached the first ridgeline, more than a dozen were down.

Mason crouched behind a hay bale, panting. "Where's Parker?"

"Helping the wounded back at the silo," Ortega replied, smoke trailing from his shoulder where he'd taken a glancing hit.

"Radio command. Tell them we need mortars on the second line. They're dug in deep near those horse barns."

"Already on it."

Mason peeked over the ridge. The city was visible now—buildings peppered with defensive emplacements, roads mined, and drones circling like vultures. But the government troops were strained. Supplies were thin. Morale is even thinner. They didn't expect a push this hard, expecting their forces to bog them down in the south.

He reached for his radio. "Command, this is Hammer Lead. First objective secured. Prep phase two."

A pause.

Then: "*Copy, Hammer Lead. Preparing phase two of the operation. Out.*"

Behind him, one of the younger soldiers knelt in the grass, whispering a prayer. Mason looked up to the sky. Rain again. He didn't know if it was a blessing… or a baptism.

* * *

Within hours, the fighting had pushed into the city.

Lexington—once a quiet blend of old colonial charm and university sprawl—was now a brutal maze of fire-scorched buildings, upturned pavement, and mangled vehicles. Chipped and cracked statues of horsemen and abolitionists stood, like ancient relics watching a war they no longer understood.

Major Mason and what remained of his squadron moved cautiously through—flanked by shuttered bookstores and coffee shops riddled with bullet holes. Smoke curled up from a burned-out city bus lying on its side, its windows blown out like shattered teeth.

"Clear left," muttered Sergeant Brewer, his rifle raised as he swept a side alley.

Dr. Daniel Parker stayed close behind the formation, his med kit heavy on his back. The streets were crawling with the wounded. They moved from cover to cover—administering morphine, setting tourniquets, dragging soldiers from the wreckage, even as more shells whistled overhead.

The government's defensive line had collapsed on the western perimeter, and their remaining armor fell back into the city's heart. But the retreat was messy, panicked. Continental Defense Forces were pouring in through the breach, and Mason's unit had been tasked with cutting them off at a key choke point—an intersection just past the county courthouse. It did not take long to clear, and soon they moved on.

At the intersection, they found resistance. A column of government infantry was barricaded behind public works vehicles and concrete planters. A drone buzzed overhead, marking targets with a soft green pulse. The first shot rang out and shattered the silence. A corporal in Mason's unit collapsed instantly.

"Sniper in the parking garage!" Ortega shouted.

Mason dove behind a garbage bin, bullets shredding the sidewalk inches from his boots. "Parker, get your ass back here!" he yelled.

"We can't leave him behind!"

"You won't be alive long enough to help him!"

But Parker didn't listen. He sprinted across the street in a crouch, bullets snapping through the air like hornets. He reached the corporal, yanking the soldier behind a flipped mail truck, and pulled out his kit. This was a man who continued to distinguish himself in battle, a man who gave his life to save others, no matter what happened to his own. Though this was his biggest challenge yet as blood poured from the kid's neck. His position became lost in the smoke from grenades launched in the chaos. *Oh shit.*

Mason lay down suppressing fire as Brewer coordinated the flank. Grenades were launched in a blanket. A smoke cannister hissed, filling the intersection with dense fog.

"Move! Use the cover!"

The team surged forward. The explosions rocked the street as Rivera's fire team cleared the barricade. Mason followed last, rifle up, lungs burning from smoke and adrenaline. The unit had reached the mail truck, but they were left speechless. Mason arrived last.

The corporal was motionless. Dead from the looks of it. Parker was on top of him, appearing motionless. Half-covered debris, his uniform soaked red. A shard of rebar protruded from his abdomen. His eyes fluttered, lips moving quietly, shaky breaths as he was turned over onto his side.

"No," Mason whispered, dropping beside him. "No, don't you die on me motherfucker!"

Parker looked up at him. "Did... Did we take the intersection?"

"We're holding it. You did it, Doc. You're going to be fine."

A weak smile. "You think Jess would've... forgiven me... for leaving her alone?"

Mason blinked, throat tight. "She won't forgive you if you die, Dan."

"Tell her... I'm going to... be... with... Mitch."

Parker's eyes glazed over, still staring skyward. The unit could only watch. They shivered with cold, feeling as if a ghost emerged from the body and disappeared into the air.

* * *

The sky over Lexington dimmed as the smoke thickened. Mason sat in silence beside Parker's body while the street around them buzzed with triage, orders, and the chaos of the ongoing battle. He didn't hear any of it. For a moment, there was only the stillness of the man who'd once spoken of his estranged wife like she was the moon itself.

Ortega approached quietly, holding a folded poncho.

“Sir... permission to cover the body?”

Mason nodded. Together, they placed it gently over Parker’s chest, the only dignity they could afford him here.

“Tag his location,” Mason ordered. “Inform command Parker is KIA, and request an immediate transfer of another medic.”

“Yes, sir.”

A moment passed. Then Mason stood. “Tell the others we’re regrouping. We’re finishing this, come hell or high water.”

March 20, 2051 – Somewhere in Lexington, Kentucky

The CDF moved forward—inch by inch—through courthouse square. By dusk, the CDF had begun converging from all sides. Reports crackled over the comms:

"Division 14 holding firm at Limestone."

"Drones confirm enemy armor retreating south."

"We've got the old post office. Planting the flag."

One by one, the government's last strongholds in the city were falling. Mason's unit advanced through the University of Kentucky campus. Trees burned along the main quad. The bell tower had been hit by artillery and leaned at a slant like a snapped spine. They set up command just past the old library steps, using overturned tables and sandbags for cover.

A radio hissed. Command issued the call:

"All units, be advised. Mop-Up Operations begin at 0600. The target is the State Capitol Building. Intelligence reports that the remaining government leadership is evacuating. Intercept orders active. Repeat, intercept orders active."

Lieutenant Blake Ward looked over. "They're running."

Mason stared ahead at the dark skyline. "A collapse, more like it. They know it's over."

He stepped aside and keyed his field mic.

FIELD LOG –0600 hours

Location: Somewhere in Lexington

Unit: 3rd Infantry Brigade

Commanding Officer: Maj. Anthony Mason

Lexington cracked.

We're advancing from the west, linking up with the 9th Battalion and an armored detachment from Kentucky's National Guard. Enemy presence is thinning, but resistance is still a problem near the Capitol grounds.

Dr. Daniel Parker, my friend and our medic, died in battle. His heroics saved lives at Jefferson Square. I'll see to it he's honored.

I've ordered my team to push through to the east wing of the government plaza. Once secure, we'll raise the colors.

We're almost there.

Let this be the last place where we bury any of our comrades.

April 4, 2051 – Lexington Town Square

By sunrise, the Continental Defense Force flag was flying over the ruins of the Kentucky Capitol. Lexington has fallen. And with it, the backbone of the U.S. government's interior command.

Soldiers wept openly. Some prayed. Others stood silently, unsure what victory looked like after spilling so much blood. Mason didn't celebrate. He knelt beside a charred bench near the reflecting pool, staring at a photo he'd pulled from his chest pocket—a picture of his wife and daughter. It had been months since he last heard from them. Last he heard, his wife Margot and daughter Julia had gone into hiding due to his allegiance to the CDF.

Staring at the photo, he became homesick; it felt as if a tear would emerge from his eye. That changed at the sound of footsteps approaching.

General Nathaniel Rusk walked towards him, flanked by aides, making his way across the shattered marble plaza.

"Major Mason," Rusk said.

Mason stood and saluted. "Sir."

"At ease, major."

Mason stood at ease, unsure what he'd hear from the general next.

"You led your unit valiantly in this battle."

"With what I had left, sir. We lost a lot of good men, sir."

Rusk nodded solemnly. "So, I've heard. I know you lost Dr. Parker."

"You know of him, sir?"

"Yes. His ex-wife is pretty famous for her reporting on the *West Coast Alliance*. She's also been entrenched with Pennsylvania units for the last few months."

"I didn't know that, sir."

"Well, she hasn't reported much in a while. She'll probably go dark again soon."

"Has she been informed about Dr. Parker, sir?"

"Yes, we informed her. She handled it... emotionless."

"What?"

Rusk's gaze drifted to the smoke-streaked skyline.

"I think she's tired of war. As are we all."

"Yes, sir." Mason watched Rusk pace, continuing to look at the smoke.

June 16, 2052 – Somewhere in Virginia

They didn't enter Washington in triumph. They entered in silence.

Columns of the Continental Defense Force advanced through northern Virginia like shadows—crossing into the district not over bridges, but around them, taking the long route through the ravaged outskirts and skirting along the Potomac. The official orders were clear: No destruction or looting. General Rusk had made it plain—they were not conquerors, but restorers.

Major Mason rode in the rear vehicle of a light armored column as they passed through Arlington. The city's remains whispered around him—the abandoned buildings, shattered windows, and faint creak of flagpoles with nothing left to fly.

It was warm for mid May, a sign of the dog days of summer.

Mason leaned forward to the open turret hatch. "Lieutenant Ward."

"Sir?"

"You ever think we'd ever think this day would come?"

Ward gave a hollow chuckle. "Honestly, sir, I thought we'd all be dead by now."

They passed the Pentagon, now stripped of insignia and cordoned by burned-out barricades. Scavengers had picked at it for months. No resistance had come from the city—not since the collapse of Lexington. It would appear that the city had been abandoned by its inhabitants. The government's chain of command had evaporated. Intelligence suggested only a caretaker cabinet remained, waiting to negotiate surrender terms.

The convoy soon reached the National Mall by noon. *Damn, we made pretty quick time.*

Boots soon hit the pavement. Mason's unit deployed alongside dozens of others in orderly formations. Soldiers looked up at the Capitol dome—scarred by drone strikes, still standing. They took positions around the reflecting pool, the Washington Monument, and the Lincoln Memorial. Everywhere, they moved with purpose. But reverence too.

Not one shot was fired. No one raised a voice…

* * *

Once the perimeter checks were done, Mason wandered briefly from the unit. He crossed the silent grounds of the Lincoln Memorial and climbed the steps, his rifle slung low, helmet tucked under his arm.

He stood before the statue and stared up at Lincoln's gaze. A gust of wind blew through the memorial, causing Mason to shiver more than usual. He stood alone in the massive monument, taking it all in.

"I hope we didn't fail you," he whispered.

From the top of the hill, he could see across the Potomac towards Arlington Cemetery. There were so many graves, so many ghosts. Beside him, footsteps.

Lieutenant Ward emerged. "General Rusk is addressing all the troops. Command says we are to attend."

Mason gave a faint nod. "Very well. Let us bear witness then."

They walked down the steps together.

* * *

The stage had been set at the foot of the Capitol. It wasn't grand—just a temporary podium with weather-beaten flags and a sea of boots beneath it. Journalists, many recently returned from exile or silence, gathered near the front. Among them was a familiar face to Mason: Jessica Parker.

It seemed so. Her silver hair created a lot of unwanted attention among spectators. Mason was unsure how someone who was a strong brunette could have hair more silver than a coin. His desire to reach her became strong—the desire to tell her Daniel's final words stuck out in his mind. Yet she seemed distant, almost too far to reach.

It appeared she made her way to D.C. for when the CDF would roll in to occupy the city. She caught Mason's eye briefly. Recognition flickered, but there was no time to speak. General Rusk ascended the stage slowly. His face looked older now than even a year ago. The city fell into absolute stillness. Mason, like the good soldier that he was, focused his attention on his commander.

"Brothers and sisters," Rusk began, voice low but firm, "we stand not as the victors of war... but as its survivors."

March 31, 2054 – Washington, D.C. – Arlington Cemetery

Rain came softly over Washington. It wasn't the storm the forecast had threatened, but something quieter—steadier. A drizzle that slicked the pavement, settled in the cracks, and washed the soot from statues too tired to stand proud anymore.

Major Anthony Mason stood at the far edge of the cemetery, observing the military funeral being held in the rain. After years of battling bureaucracies for the right for a comrade, a husband, and a soldier to be buried in Arlington, Dr. Daniel Parker was given military honors and a proper burial at Arlington as an American soldier. It seemed that negotiations with the fallen government were fought over petty issues, such as CDF soldiers being given the right to be buried in Arlington as soldiers of the U.S. Military. It was agony for many CDF soldiers knowing that their comrades were sitting in freezers, awaiting the chance to be given an honorable burial.

Mason wanted to be with Jessica in her hour of need, yet he couldn't. Survivor's guilt. Something that Mason had never imagined he would have. He missed his friend and couldn't stand the thought of not being there to wish him goodbye.

I'm sorry, Jessica.

Mason stood by a tree, watching from afar. In the distance, he watched a figure move against the gray horizon—a woman in a long coat, silver streaks in her hair catching the dim light. Jessica Parker.

He watched the officer hand her the American flag, saluting her as he gave it. Jessica was emotionless, standing there just listening to the sounds around her.

The funeral carried on, and the people made their exit. Mason stood, continuing to watch. She stood with the flag folded in her arms. The old stars and stripes were heavy with rain. Then, slowly and deliberately, she let it slip from her hands. It drifted in the wind, caught once on a cracked marble column, and tumbled into the mud below.

The air didn't move. No one shouted. No one stopped her. Major Mason watched with narrow eyes. Years ago, he thought many would have considered her action disrespectful or even treasonous. Now, it felt more like a closure. It didn't matter anymore, simply because the times they lived in no longer cared about such things. He tilted his face toward the sky as a raindrop slid down his cheek. It felt like absolution. Maybe even grace.

I fought for my country, my men. Yet how did I end up like a fucking coward?

April 4, 2054 – Washington, D.C. – U.S. Capitol

The sky had cleared by the time General Rusk stepped up to the weathered podium. Cherry blossoms, against all odds, bloomed from broken branches beside the Capitol. Pink petals caught the wind and danced in the air like ash.

Rusk's uniform bore no medals, only the patch of the new flag: thirteen stars, newly aligned. His shoulders slumped under the invisible weight of the dead.

"I won't ask you to cheer," he said, looking out over the crowd of soldiers, medics, engineers, and foreign dignitaries in patched uniforms. "There is no joy in this."

Silence.

"We did not seek to destroy. We sought to correct. The old world turned its back on law, life, and liberty. When they dropped fire on our cities, we had a choice—lay down... or rise."

The soldiers stood straighter.

"We rose. And we bled for every inch of ground. For Tallahassee. For Lexington. For the coastlines and the plains and the broken farms in Georgia. We did not ask God to give us victory. We asked Him to give us strength to survive. He answered. You are the answer."

A murmur moved through the crowd. Recording from the front row, Jessica Parker didn't look away once.

"And now," Rusk continued, "we return the sword to its sheath. There will be no purges. No vengeance. We rebuild. We atone. We move forward—not as conquerors, but as caretakers. If you come here for parades and parties, then you're dismissed. But if you came to serve, your work is just beginning."

He stepped back as the breeze picked up.

Then: *"God Bless This New Republic."*

* * *

Later, in a quiet café four blocks from the Capitol, Mason sat alone with a warm mug of black coffee. The crowds were gone now. The tanks, too. Soldiers had dispersed back to their quarters. Civilians trickled into the streets again—cautiously, like waking from a long nightmare.

Many had come to support Rusk, but many were still unsure of the type of reception they would receive with the new army now occupying the streets of Washington.

Jessica's segment aired again on a nearby screen—her monologue overlaying images of the war's final days. Mason could still not get over the title Rusk had chosen to hold. *Lord Protector. Such a bizarre choice for the General. I suppose he lives up to the reputation that precedes him.*

Mason stirred his coffee and looked at the woman behind the counter. "Would it be possible if you could turn off the TV?"

"Of course, sir. I am very sorry."

"Oh no, it's quite all right. I think, all things considered, we've had enough of that for a day."

"A day? Try a decade."

"No arguments from me there."

He took a sip and watched the petals still falling from the trees. *Spring. Daniel would have probably liked to have seen the blossoms.*

Mason groaned from stiffness. He rushed to finish his coffee, rising to stretch his sore limbs. He exhaled a long breath, as if it were his first one in years. He looked down at his notepad, the pen alongside, waiting. He took a deep breath, sat back down, and picked it up. He began writing, almost holding his breath as he does so...

Dear Jessica,

Seems he wasn't such a coward after all he thought. *Well, maybe a little.* In his mind, Jessica was still owed the right to know her husband's words, he thought. All he could think about at that moment was closure.

The war was over.

But not the memory of it...

V.

Oathbreaker

June 9, 2046 – Washington, D.C. – The White House

Eli Marshall moved briskly through the dimly lit corridors of the West Wing, his mind swirling with information, intelligence reports, and the gnawing weight of the decisions that loomed ahead. At just 26 years old, he was the youngest person to be Special Counsel to the President of the United States. But on tonight of all nights, that title felt like a cruel joke to him. The gravity of what lied ahead pressed down on him like a boulder, making every step heavier than the last.

His thoughts were interrupted at the sound of his phone buzzing in his pocket. A message from Mia, his girlfriend, appeared: *"You want to pick up dinner tonight? Perhaps some comfort food?"*

He gave a weary smile, replying, *"I don't know. We have an emergency meeting in the situation room, which could take a while. But I can pick us up a late dinner."*

Eli didn't elaborate further. How could he? The nature of the meeting was on a topic that no normal person could stomach.

When he arrived outside the White House Situation Room, Eli took deep breaths, steadying himself before pushing open the heavy door. Inside, the room had a tense buzz, thick with unsaid words, fear overpowering. All the main military figureheads filled the room—generals and admirals, their faces molded with years of experience, shadowed by a rare, palpable dread.

The table glowed with an overhead holographic map of the American West Coast, with red zones marking rebel-controlled territory and flickering icons representing naval and air forces. Everyone in the room stood at attention as President William Blackwell entered. His expression was grave, and his shoulders squared as if carrying the weight of the nation on his back alone.

"Thank you all for coming. Please be seated," Blackwell announced. The room returned coldly to its seats, awaiting his next words.

"We are on the verge of a national collapse," he announced, voice steady yet cold. "The *West Coast Alliance* is no longer a distant threat. They have now aligned themselves with a foreign power—The Republic of China—which has given them the means to continue their quest against us. Including weapons, advisors, and now, a soon-to-be naval presence. Our blockade has effectively failed."

General Benjamin Whitman of the Army leaned forward, his voice weathered but clear. "Mr. President, my staff has worked to find other solutions for months now, yet we reach the same conclusion. Any further ground assaults would be highly costly. The rebels have successfully fortified key ports. If we continue with urban warfare, it will mean even higher casualties—both militarily and with civilians. Honestly, Mr. President, years of fighting overseas have royally bit us in the ass."

His words stung like hornets. The consequences of overextending the country overseas have come back to haunt the Joint Chiefs. What had begun in Europe, one war that would lead into another—first as "limited military operations," then "humanitarian interventions"—continued until the placement of troops was no longer measured in simple deployments but within generations of Americans. As they had since the end of World War II, the country poured trillions of dollars into conflicts against resurgent coalitions of the eastern powers, once again fighting in streets no American could pronounce if they tried. But domination with equipment soon ran its course. Aircraft carriers were sunk for the first time since the 1940s. Air wing battlegroups shot down and destroyed. Whole divisions and platoons came home to half-strength. Their equipment was sold to their allies to fight their people. By the time the wars reached their conclusions, the treasury was gutted. Congress, starved for power with constituents having enough, slashed the budgets, unaware of what would come. Riots, food shortages, and unemployment ran rampant in many states. The simple, bitter truth was clear to everyone in the Blackwell administration—Washington had bankrupted the country. No defaults were coming to the rescue. Wall Street wasn't a potential savior either, as they abandoned hope of future investments within the United States or Europe.

Admiral Alexander Granger of the Navy added, "A confrontation with the Chinese Navy could escalate beyond just shooting spitballs. We risk a nuclear shooting match. The political fallout alone would be catastrophic."

Secretary of Defense Jameison Tillman spoke sharply and urgently when it became his turn to speak. "We've been cornered. Our delay in action creates the risk of the rebellion gaining traction, emboldening other states on the fence to break away. But if we strike, we risk having not just the states turning against us... but the entire world."

The room became eerily silent. The suffocating tension felt like a physical force on Eli's chest. It felt as if invisible hands were strangling him. No good options were presenting themselves.

Blackwell sighed, his voice dropping to a rasp. "Gentlemen... Our options are bleak. Everything we have tried to do has failed. Sanctions and negotiations have all been ignored. They grow bolder every day. If we don't act now, we lose not just the territory but our authority as a governing body. Our union, gentlemen."

Vice President Dick Mallory, sitting stiffly, interjected softly, "We must consider the human cost. A nuclear holocaust will kill millions. I am not speaking hyperbolically when I say that. It will poison our people for generations. Are we prepared to carry out such an act?"

All Eli could do was watch and listen in silence as the most powerful men in the world attempted to decide the fate of the *West Coast Alliance*. President Blackwell turned and looked at Eli, almost as if waiting for him to chime in. He trusted his opinion and service, and he would have taken the words to heart. But Eli signaled to him that he couldn't speak of it. He could not bring himself to weigh in on such a decision. *I can't, Mr. President. I'm sorry.*

Everyone looked to each other, awaiting the next person's turn to speak. That came from Blackwell's Chief of Staff, Adam Langston, who gazed at the room with sharp eyes. "Mr. President, alternatives exist—but time is a luxury we no longer have. NSA Intel shows that Beijing has already dispersed several naval vessels. Warships. This strike might forestall a broader war, perhaps deterring a power that wants to come to our shores. But if we do this... it will ignite a fire within our borders."

Eli's throat tightened. This meeting, this war was no longer about the right or wrong of the sides. It was a debate between ruin and catastrophe.

A sudden vibration in his pocket broke the stillness of the room. He had set his phone to silent mode, yet someone was persistently trying to reach him. He pulled out his phone and looked at it. Jessica Parker's name appeared on the screen. An old friend from inner political circles. His trusted confidante. One of the few people entrenched with the people on the ground, who knew how fragile the nation was. He found himself speechless as her timing came at the most desperate hour.

He hesitated, his thumb hovering over the screen, before shutting off the screen. There was no comfort to be found in the text he received. Eli's focus was caught off guard as Blackwell made the decision that would traumatize Eli for the rest of his life.

"Alert all armed forces: We are going DEFCON-1," Blackwell announced. It was done. Nuclear had become the answer. When the President finally gave the order, the room exhaled like it had been released from years-long breath.

"Prepare the nuclear assets. Inform all commanders."

Once Blackwell stood, everyone followed. All the generals and admirals rushed out of the room, preparing for the blackest day of the country.

Eli stood slowly, taking it all in. He gathered all the papers he had delivered, his hands shaking slightly. The coldness of the order's finality still lingered in the room, stinging like a pair of hot pliers to the skin.

By now, the room was empty. Eli's phone buzzed again; this time, it was Mia. Eli swiped and answered. "Hey Mia... Yeah, the meeting is over. Let's order fried chicken," he said quietly. "It's warm, complex, and comforting. Like the last meal before a long night."

She laughed softly. "I'll get some of the hot and spicy wings."

He gave a weary smile. Outside the room, the corridors seemed darker, heavier, even a little sinister. The corridors of power are now pathways to irrevocable war.

Eli began walking when he remembered Jessica's text. He stopped in his tracks and texted her a reply.

"Keep your phone close tomorrow. It's happening."

Eli clicked off the screen. No more than a minute passed when it buzzed again. A quick reply.

"What do you mean, Eli?"

This time, he didn't answer. Instead, he continued walking. *I can't tell her.*

June 10, 2046 – Washington, D.C. – White House Underground Bunker

The sun rose like blood on the viewing screens over Sacramento, California.

Even before the shockwave arrived, Eli knew what it meant. The security briefings showed what the flicker in the sky looked like. Standing in the bunker, Eli held a coffee he had gotten before arriving at the White House. The bunker was always too cold. Not the brisk, bracing chill of autumn, but the sterile, bone-deep kind one only felt in places built to survive the end of times. The walls were matte, lifeless with its grays. The overhead fluorescents buzzed faintly, casting hard light over the long conference table at the center of the Situation Room's subterranean twin.

Eli had been in this room before—twice during crises that never made the evening news—but this time, it was more haunting. This time, the smells felt different. There was a faint, acrid tang of burnt electrical wires and a whiff from the electronics bank where the comm technicians were patching in the live satellite feeds. Beneath the smells of the electronics, a more human smell took over the senses—the smells of stale coffee, perspiration, and fear of the future.

The screens were turned on, but ran silently; no one needed the sounds to understand. The camera from the geosynchronous reconnaissance satellite stared down at California's State Capitol in Sacramento, or what was left of it. The detonation of the nuclear warhead had left a white-hot crater at the heart of the city, the shockwave rippling outward in a perfect circle of decimation. Freeways were like ribbons, and the surrounding buildings were reduced to dust before the smoke swallowed them all.

Eli had worked for President William Blackwell for almost six years—from his time as a senator to his presidential election. He'd been there on the campaign plane so many times, sitting in the jump seat as Blackwell honed his speeches on those ugly yellow legal pads. He was there when Blackwell won the election in a decisive fashion over his opponent. A moment he never forgot as the older man put his hand on his shoulder and told him that night, *"You're going far with me, son. We'll right this ship."*

But now, as Eli watched the mushroom cloud reflected in the glass of the conference table, he felt sick with disgust and felt an unwelcome rise in his throat. He had already finished the bottle of stomach medicine he had in his office and was constantly looking around the room, hoping to find another bottle.

Blackwell stood in the center of the room, precisely where the sightlines converged, arms folded. His eyes didn't dart like the others, as they didn't seem to blink often. He looked like a man observing a chessboard, calculating his next four to five moves while everyone was focused on the opponent's last move.

Someone in the back of the room whispered. "My God... Look at the glow."

Blackwell didn't acknowledge the comment.

The Director of Homeland Security, Nick Anderson, muttered something about many foreign ministers on the phone demanding to speak to the President. Still, Blackwell cut him off without raising his voice. "No, I am not taking any calls now. Inform them this is a domestic incident."

What? He's going to lie about this?! Eli blinked, forcing himself to look up. "Sir... domestic? There's nothing—no evidence—"

"That's the point, Marshall," Blackwell replied, finally turning. The light monitors painted a part of his face in cold blue, the other in shadow. "We create the evidence. Give the country and the world an enemy to blame. A reason to rally and unite."

Eli involuntarily took a step back in shock, the heel of his shoe catching the lip of the floor mat. "With all due respect, sir... no group in the country is capable of—"

"There will be," Blackwell declared, almost gently. "We have reports of many... let's just call it... gatherings of insurrectionists, secessionists, and disloyal soldiers within the southern states. They've masked their movements very well but are active in the communities. They think they can fracture the union. We're going to light the fire, and essentially burn them with it."

Eli's stomach grabbed him again. His vision tunneled within those moments, forcing him to plant a hand against the cold steel wall to steady himself. He found himself in disbelief at what he was hearing. The President of the United States had weaponized the government not just against the *West Coast Alliance*, but now against those who had yet to lift a finger in rebellion. The excuse needed to wipe out all those who defied Blackwell.

All Eli could think about was what visionary Blackwell was to him. At the same time, on the campaign trail, telling veterans their service meant something more, telling Americans that the age of war and weaponization against the world was over. Eli believed in him then, faith within the weathered voice of conviction of wanting to change the destructive course of the world.

All that vision disappeared within the ghostly glow of nuclear fire. It was as if Eli wore rose-colored glasses, which suddenly shattered at that moment. Blackwell wasn't about defending the country to begin with. He was remaking the country in his image, one manufactured crisis at a time.

The President looked down and adjusted his cufflinks, as though it was time for the next event. He looked at the press secretary and nodded, "Have my speech prepared and on my desk within the hour. Time to show the iron fist."

The taste of copper filled Eli's mouth. He bent down slowly to retrieve a pen he had not realized he had dropped in the conversation. He bent down to the floor to pick it up, but his hands lingered on the floor longer than he needed to be there. He found himself unwilling to stand up again. Eli became so disgusted that he wanted no part of what came next.

On the largest screen in the bunker, the cloud was still rising over what had been Sacramento, a billowing, searing monument to the moment. Within those moments, Eli Marshall realized that there was no going back. The man he always revered was capable of anything and everything—and that the war to come wouldn't be anything about saving America... at all.

June 18, 2046 – Washington, D.C. – Local Café

Eli sat alone, coffee on the table next to his laptop. The coffee shop was two blocks from Union Station. He chose it for the noisy, forgettable, everyday business it received—the kind of place where political staffers and the press blended into the fog of bureaucracy. His contact was running late—*as usual*, he thought. Yet still, he waited patiently. Relief was felt when his contact emerged at the front door.

Jessica Parker knew she was late, but made her way to his table. Her camera slung across her chest, hair pulled back in a way that reminded him of most war correspondents, not ordinary Sunday columnists for *The Washington Post*.

"When did you get into D.C.?" He asked.

"Today. I rushed to get here after I got your email." Jessica replied. She set her stuff down on the table, sliding into the seat across from him. "I wasn't sure I would hear from you again."

Eli kept his hands wrapped around his coffee, knuckles turning pale. "I was lost for a while. Unsure how to even process what in the fuck just happened over these last two years."

Jessica tilted her head. "What do you mean, Eli?"

"You've been on the ground. You saw the nuclear bomb land right on Americans fucking heads. This wasn't just to ward off warships. This was Blackwell... consolidating power. Taking out anyone who might stand against him."

Jessica said nothing, listening intently, but her eyes narrowed. "Are you sure he's going after the southern states next?"

"Yes. He's already trying to mobilize the bases south. But it seems to be failing. Several bases aren't responding."

Jessica pulled out her small audio recorder. "May I?"

He looked her dead in the eye. "No, not yet, Jess. What I'm about to tell you cannot be used in a story—at least not yet. I need you to listen carefully."

For the next hour, Eli told Jessica everything he had: internal memos, the war powers resolution Blackwell bypassed, black sites in Nevada, and the sudden pivot to the southern states.

"There is one militia that already has serious weight to it. It's gathered almost twenty thousand men, and they have already moved against MacDill. Find out more about this man: General Nathaniel Rusk."

"Any intel as to how they rose so quickly?"

"As far as I can gather from briefings, Rusk is a central religious figure who won over the loyalty of many soldiers in the military, hailed as a Patton-lite figure of our time. It seems that since the conflict with the *West Coast Alliance*, he has been having backroom conversations with active-duty members to turn."

"How is he doing it without equipment?"

"It seems the shipments initially going to the *West Coast Alliance* have been going to his army. Leadership felt they were in an unwinnable war, so they contacted him and made a deal six months ago."

"Holy shit."

"It doesn't end there: many of the southern states were already preparing to secede, so they funded him along with what he was getting. They now go by the name: *Continental Defense Force.*"

"Does his army have any actual teeth?"

"Off the record: We lost contact with MacDill and Jacksonville two days ago. We assess that they have been taken."

"It seems another opponent has emerged in this game of Risk being played here."

"They have been in the game for a while, since about late 2045. Blackwell had the Pentagon create plans to wipe them out via airstrikes masked as drills, but they never came to fruition."

Jessica and Eli sat silently, thinking about what had been said. Eli sipped his coffee while she stared off into the distance, pondering. She took no notes; she just listened.

"Why are you telling me all of this if I can't write a story about it? " She asked finally.

"You still have a moral compass. And what I will ask next, I would trust with no one else."

She scoffed. "You just didn't want to get caught."

He gave no argument. "I can't stand behind Blackwell anymore. He has done something you don't come back from. What I do next will be for the country... not for him."

Jessica leaned in. "Do you realize what you are saying?"

"Yes, Jessica, I do. I intend to betray the President of the United States. And you're going to help me make sure this regime falls."

* * *

Evening fell on Washington. Eli decided to work late, as everyone else went home or remained in the war room. Eli's time of betrayal began as soon as he left Jessica behind in the café. His first steps? Start leaking operational files to Jessica to pass on to the CDF. It took Jessica some convincing to do it, but she finally agreed after hours of persuasion. She took the possibility of treason and being executed as a spy fairly seriously, because it could still happen if the war shifted in the government's favor. Based on his standing and position in D.C., Eli had no connections or means to reach the army, so he decided to use other means.

To start, he copied operational files onto a decrypted flash drive hidden inside his watch. The next step was to provide the drive to Jessica in secret. A plan had already been devised for it to be passed, but the right moment had to wait. *Man, does it pay to have a top-secret security clearance.*

Eli knew the secret was top-notch in the White House, especially since the U.S. government had its own Artificial Intelligence programs operating. Eli, though, had an ace up his sleeve. Before going into politics, he worked with and designed cell phone apps for pocket change while he studied at Stanford University. AI had become a regular part of life when he was growing up, and his robots were up to the task.

Damn, I'm glad I learned hobbies in college.

By the time the downloads were finished, Eli had left the White House for another coffee shop. Using an encrypted laptop, he contacted Jessica in a secure chat.

ENCRYPTED SECURE LINE 00010001000

Red Guardian: *Blackbird, this is Red Guardian. Do you read me?*

...

Blackbird: *Red Guardian, I am receiving you. Setting up this secure computer proved to be a pain in the ass.*

...

Red Guardian: *If you need help, we can schedule a time.*

...

Blackbird: *I'll let you know. Do you have the files for me?*

...

Red Guardian: *Stand by.*

...

...

[SECURE1.FILE UPLOAD]

...

...

Red Guardian: *File upload complete.*

...

Blackbird: *I got them. I am reaching out to some sources embedded in the southern states. I will be heading to Louisiana tonight. May go dark until I have something.*

...

Red Guardian: *Understood. Contact as soon as possible.*

...

Blackbird: *Will do. Good luck.*

Eli closed the program and returned his computer to the normal screen. He sipped his coffee, thinking about what he was doing, what he would do, and what he had done. *Jess has the information now. God forgive me.*

September 17, 2047 – Washington, D.C.

A year has passed since the sky over California lit up like hell on earth. A year since Sacramento vanished in nuclear fire and blackened wind. A year since Eli Marshall—Special Counsel to the President of the United States—leaked military operation memos to Jessica Parker and crossed the invisible line between patriot and traitor.

He expected some movement or fallout, headlines, perhaps some leaks, and whispers in D.C. or on the airwaves.

But there was only silence. Almost like a calm before the storm. It made Eli nervous for many reasons, mainly because of one thing.

Jessica Parker had disappeared. She didn't run her regular news columns, and her social media accounts showed no movement or trace of her online presence. Her official line rang unanswered. It seemed that the world was continuing to spin on, numbly, blindly—TV analysts spent most days arguing if Sacramento was a false flag, if the government had really confirmed anything, if the footage from ground zero was doctored. But the message was business as usual for them: "Do not speculate," the networks warned. "Stay calm."

Eli didn't sleep most days. He barely ate, and it didn't go unnoticed. Many aides commented on how much weight he was losing. Each day, he moved through the corridors of the West Wing like a shadow among ghosts. His hands shook regularly when he typed. His ties always felt tight, like a hangman's noose around his neck. He felt sick most days, knowing the country was poised on the edge of something final. When he wasn't distracted by the prospects of being arrested for treason, he would stare at his teeth, wondering if they were rotting. *Must be that stomach medicine... rotting my damn teeth.*

Today was finally different, as a memo emerged.

It was left on his desk at approximately 7:49 a.m., buried inside a stamped manila folder titled "NSA INTEL—EYES ONLY." The courier who dropped it off said nothing, only saluted and left. Eli recognized it as the seal of the National Reconnaissance Office—deep black ops projects, inner-circle briefings. Only the top brass saw memos like this one.

The header burned through his veins.

OPERATION CLEARVIEW: PHASE II

INITIATED: 0500 HOURS

PRIMARY OBJECTIVE: DISRUPT SUPPLY LINES TO SOUTHEAST REBEL STRONGHOLDS

TARGET SITES: ATLANTA, JACKSONVILLE, PENSACOLA

SECONDARY OBJECTIVE: CREATE DISTRACTION AWAY FROM UPCOMING PITTSBURGH CAMPAIGN

MISSION STATUS: GREEN

Eli's mouth went dry. This wasn't a police action. It wasn't specific targets. These were civilian zones—southern port cities feeding the breakaway military zones. They were trying to starve out the rebel forces. Shut them down and cripple them from the coast inward.

He always figured this day would come, but it still made his chest feel like it was splitting. With steady fingers, he copied the data to a secure flash drive embedded in his wristwatch, and a redundant copy was encrypted in Morse onto a burner phone under a loose tile in his apartment floor. He had reached the point in his spy story that he could not trust anyone.

He straightened his tie using the camera on his phone, rehearsing the face of a calm man. He left the office as if he were on his way to pick up a coffee. At each checkpoint in the White House, he nodded, smiling like nothing was wrong. He flashed his badge at each checkpoint, saying nothing each time.

* * *

At 9:00 a.m. sharp, he entered the Roosevelt Room for the National Security Council briefing. The air inside felt like the still moment before a stroke of lightning struck—tight, quiet, and grim.

President Blackwell stood at the head of the table, arms crossed, staring down at a digital map of the United States. He looked different from the way he had even a few months ago. His eyes were colder. His jaw never unclenched. The nuclear strike had hardened something inside him—replaced whatever inside him that was human, some with calculation and fury.

"We move forward," he said, his voice smooth and sharp like a hot knife through butter. "The South has aligned into a functional military bloc. Florida, Georgia, Alabama, Louisiana, Texas, and now—our intelligence confirms—Missouri and Mississippi."

He clicked a remote. Red markers blinked across the map: Atlanta, Jacksonville, Tampa, Tallahassee, and Pensacola. They were all circled, and now they were all targets.

"We can't take back the states unless we crush their Gulf supply line. Operation Clearview neutralizes this axis of logistics. Naval blockades will tighten around the Atlantic, and airstrikes will begin by Friday. Phase III will be executed at Pittsburgh if all goes according to plan."

General Whitman raised his hand. "What about the International optics, sir?"

"We control the narrative," the president replied. "They will fire first, and we will respond in kind. That's the line."

Eli swallowed hard. And then—he could not help himself in that moment—he spoke up.

"What about the civilians still inhabiting those cities, sir? Many haven't been issued evacuation orders. Families, sir."

Every head turned in the room. The air crackled in silence. President Blackwell looked up from the map, with no readable expression.

"Collateral," he replied. One word, that's all he said to a crucial question. He then turned back to the map, acting as if Eli was not even in the room, or had asked the question. *Dick.*

The meeting continued for a while longer, covering logistics in other areas. Eli didn't speak for the remainder of the meeting in the Situation Room. He watched, eyes sharpened beneath a composed mask, as satellite feeds displayed a patchwork of craters and flame across the southern states. Within the digital map, hidden between static and a steady, sterile green glow, were the remains of several farms in rural areas like Alabama and Georgia.

Eli's hand trembled slightly as he adjusted his cufflink.

"Sir... We have reclassified Tallahassee as a provisional hot zone," Secretary Tillman announced. "We have several strategists wargaming out scenarios for a possible offensive in the city. We have also authorized kinetic strikes in the surrounding areas to suppress ongoing regional communication hubs."

President Blackwell gave a slight nod. "Be surgical. No martyrs here."

No martyrs? You must be joking.

"Thank you, gentlemen. That will be all."

The meeting adjourned, but Eli didn't rush out. He stood and waited by the edge of the Roosevelt Room, near the bronze bust of former President Franklin D. Roosevelt—ironic now, given how much the republic was being dismantled by his administration, in secret.

President Blackwell also lingered, staring out one of the tall windows. The American flag outside stood limp on a windless day.

"You haven't spoken your opinion much lately, Marshall," the President said without turning. His voice was deceptively calm, like a blade being sharpened behind the back.

"Just taking it all in, sir."

"You know I've read some of your assessments. Something about how logistics win battles, but moral clarity wins wars." He turned slightly. "Do you still believe that?"

Eli's pulse ticked. "Moral clarity's only useful if someone's left standing to speak it."

The President smiled, a faint twitch at the edge of his mouth. "That's what I liked about you. You always hedged your bets, but never backed down. That's why I kept you close."

Eli forced a thin smile. "I'm honored, sir."

"You should be. This is a historic occasion." He turned fully now, stepping closer. "We'll end this war. Soon. Then we're going to build a new world—in our image. One chapter at a time. But I need to know you're on my side."

Their eyes met, locked in like electricity. Eli's stomach twisted into a pretzel, but he gave a sharp nod. "Of course, Mr. President."

Fuck. You.

"Good," the president replied, almost a sense of relief in his voice. "Then let's keep moving."

* * *

Night soon fell, and Eli had never felt so happy to be in his place of sanctuary... his apartment. Eli came in late, kissing his girlfriend Mia tensely as he entered. They stayed up and talked awhile, but Mia went to bed early because of work. This left Eli once again alone, sitting at his desk, a single lamp casting a soft glow in the darkness.

When he arrived, the package was there, as Mia had told him it had arrived earlier in the day. It was plain brown paper, with no return address. Inside was a photograph of Jessica Parker interviewing a gentleman with a Colonel ranking. He turned the photo around to see the name.

"Colonel Isaiah Brand, Crimson Reapers Battalion, Continental Defense Force".

He turned and looked at the photo again. A makeshift flag fluttered in the background. Not the old Stars and Stripes, but something that had been stitched by hand—thirteen stars in a new shape. He found a small piece of paper in the envelope. On it, a note written in looping pen:

"Still standing. Digging for answers."

A lump rose in Eli's throat. He hadn't spoken to Parker in several months. Her last published article was on four Apache helicopters that had defected and attacked Naval Air Station Pensacola in July of 2046.

He booted up the encrypted terminal on his computer. Each keystroke felt heavier than the last. With nervous fingers, he attached a fresh data dump for Jessica, who in turn passed it on to the CDF.

ENCRYPTED SECURE LINE 00010001000

Red Guardian: *Blackbird, this is Red Guardian. The latest file dump is attached for you to pass on to the necessary people.*

* * *

[SECURE16.FILE UPLOAD]

* * *

Eli waited but received no answers. It seemed Jessica had opened past files, but was not online. He began typing again. Strange.

Red Guardian: *Blackbird, be advised—massive troop movements for an offensive towards Florida. The file contains radar information needed regarding the Gulf blockade. Resources are being moved from Philadelphia to Kentucky. Unknown as to where.*

He stopped again. Debating as to whether he should upload a file he recently obtained.

Presidential Memo #16-38 – Operation Citadel

This wasn't just a random bad policy. It was a blueprint for a future American purge—civil detainment camps under the guise of "population stabilization." An unspoken war against the dissenters, the press, and any outliers. Stealing plays out of the playbooks of past dictators: Hitler, Stalin, and Mussolini.

He hesitated. Then he remembered the faces in the photographs from the news articles: the farmers, their families, the children. He thought about the pictures taken near ground zero in Sacramento. *For God. For country.*

Eli typed again.

Red Guardian: *One last upload.*

* * *

[SECURE16.PRESMEMO1638.FILE UPLOAD]

* * *

July 17, 2049 – Somewhere in Washington, D.C.

Eli sat in the back pew of the oldest chapel in Washington, D.C.; a quiet colonial relic tucked between monuments to power. Sunlight filtered through the high stained-glass windows, refracting blood-red and heaven-gold streaks across the floor. He wasn't supposed to be there, not during a regular workday, especially during such an intense time.

Yet, here he was, inside the church, watching an elderly black pastor recite a prayer before a handful of seated people.

"The Lord is my light and my salvation; whom shall I fear? The Lord is the strength of my life; of whom shall I be afraid?"

Eli closed his eyes. He didn't dare bow his head—not out of pride, but because it might, in his mind, shatter the carefully built mask he had built for himself. One that he wore every waking hour and displayed very carefully. He hadn't said any prayer since the nuclear fallout. He hadn't entered this church until he started feeding secrets to Parker, who, in turn, leaked them to the Continental Defense Force.

The war was no distant fight that never reached him. It was now a deeper war, the battlefield being within his skull.

The service ended, and he lingered as the others filtered out. He stood slowly, staring at the cross above the pulpit.

"Looking for peace, son?" the paster asked gently, pausing beside him.

"Not sure. Peace... maybe forgiveness." Eli replied, his voice tightening.

"Well now," the pastor said, rubbing his chin, "that's harder to earn."

Eli couldn't help but let out a faint laugh. "I've done things that I believe are right. Yet I find myself lying to people who trust me to do what is right."

The pastor looked him over without judgment. "Then perhaps the question isn't about who you betray… but about who you're still trying to protect."

Eli stared up at the cross again, then nodded faintly. "Thank you."

He exited without another word. Outside, the wind had picked up. The summer heat scuttled across the Capitol's stone steps, and the White House loomed in the near distance—bathed in security and suspicion. He could feel the weight of every surveillance camera, every biometric scan that tracked him day and night.

* * *

When Eli returned to the White House, the President was already seated in the Situation Room with the top brass. The conversation was sharp, and there was an overwhelming sense of urgency.

"Lexington is not an isolated incident," Secretary Tillman was saying. "The Continental Defense Forces have begun staging in southern Kentucky. Their logistics are improving, thanks partly to getting reinforced from Tennessee and Georgia."

CIA Director Vincent Amar shook his head. "Satellite imagery's been inconsistent. Somebody's jamming our drone signals again—same pattern we see over Florida."

President Blackwell's eyes narrowed, scanning the room before settling on Eli.

Eli stood straight, his hands locked behind his back. "We're preparing counterintelligence. But whoever's behind their comm security…

knows what they're doing. Almost as if it's a coach on our sidelines feeding them the plays."

"They didn't learn it," Blackwell snapped. "They've been taught."

The accusation hung in the air like a falling blade. Eli didn't flinch, blinking only once.

"Clean house," Blackwell ordered. "Start an internal audit of communications staff. I want all data access logs pulled. Especially anything cross-referencing troop movement patterns."

Eli's throat dried. "Yes, sir."

Shit... I have to move fast.

* * *

Eli's encrypted signal went live at around 3:02 AM. He sat in his living room, the light from his laptop filling the room.

ENCRYPTED SECURE LINE 00010001000

Red Guardian: *Blackbird, this is Red Guardian. Be advised—leak suspected by WH. Cutting contact and destroying line.*

* * *

He waited for a reply, even though he knew it wouldn't come. *You're not very good at this whole spy thing, Jess.* He sat motionless, staring at the blinking cursor.

Below, Washington shimmered in artificial light. The monuments were polished. The people on the floor below lived as if the world wasn't collapsing—playing music and partying like it was the last night of 1999. But Eli knew better. He watched the brain rot of society happen all around him. He witnesses trendy social media dances as artillery guns fire at positions. However, he recognized that with his betrayal, he was a de facto parasite now. Draining blood from what was once the leader of the country.

But like all parasites, Eli recognized that he may eventually die with the host. And that knowledge—more than anything—kept him up most nights.

Mia was the love of his life, yet she would hang with him if ever discovered. She accepted the risk, declaring her love in doing so. *"I love you, Eli. You are doing what's right. Let them stretch my neck if it means I die with you."*

How noble it seemed to hear those words, yet Eli found himself terrified at the thought of his girlfriend dying for something he was responsible for.

She doesn't deserve to die for what I do.

October 13, 2050 – Washington, D.C. – Homeland Security Office, Internal Audit Division

Within weeks, Eli was summoned to an unexpected meeting. A woman in a gray suit met him outside the building. "Welcome, Mr. Marshall. You'll be joining us in Sublevel 2. Internal inquiry. Just standard procedure."

He nodded and followed without any protests.

They led him down into one of the lesser-known warrens—sublevel 2 of the building was part fallout shelter and part data vault. The hallways were sterile, stripped of ornament, and silent. Inside a narrow room, a screen flickered on with classified data logs.

A man from DHS Intelligence gave a brief nod. "We've seen spikes in off-hours server access. Someone with high-level clearance—internal—has been probing communications logs, drone telemetry, and logistics reports."

Eli remained still. "What department?"

"Yours, sir." The man said bluntly.

"Have you traced which computers were used?"

"No, sir. Whoever is doing this is using some computer encryption to mask logins."

"I see."

Holy. Fucking. Shit.

"We're not accusing you or anyone in your office, Mr. Marshall," the woman said evenly. "But if there's a breach... and it turns out to be someone from you or your office. You understand that it is high treason."

"I understand. You're sure it's not someone exploiting my information or those on our staff?"

"We're looking into all avenues, sir. We should know hopefully soon."

Eli nodded slowly. "Very well. Then whoever is responsible had best be found soon."

"Yes, sir."

He shook their hands and made his way out. One thing he knew for sure, despite it not being said: he was now officially being hunted.

* * *

Darkness was an ally for many. Most were in for the night, and the streets were lit for those who had trouble dealing with the day's stresses. For Eli, this was the perfect time to meet with those concealed from the day. On this night, he was meeting a newfound contact—codenamed Striker—a field operative who, like him, was also deep and had significant ties to the CDF's cause.

Jessica put him in contact with Striker when he informed her through a normal channel that he needed to leave D.C. for family reasons. He had never even heard of other potential spies within D.C. for the CDF until recently. When the war broke out, much of the information normally leaked in D.C. circles was blacked out. It was as if the government disbursed duct tape and told the politicians to each take a piece and stick it on their mouths. *Fat chance.*

Eli sat lost in thought on a park bench, the night air filling his nostrils. *I wonder why Jessica asked me to watch Tenet before my meeting.*

A strange request indeed. Released in 2020, *Tenet* was Christopher Nolan's most bizarre film. It was a plot about reverse time-traveling soldiers trying to destroy the world using inverted methods. Eli watched it twice, unable to even remotely comprehend the story. *I doubt the story was the point, though.*

"Well, this is a surprise," a voice echoed from the side of the bench. "Wasn't expecting to see you, Marshall."

Secretary of Defense Tillman appeared, walking his big white Alaskan Husky. Eli was caught off guard by his sudden appearance. He couldn't help but stare at the dog, its white hair shimmering. *That's a big son of a bitch.*

"Good to see you, sir," Eli responded.

"Well, no matter. These are strange times... feels like we're living in a twilight kind of world."

That isn't a coincidence.

There was silence. Tillman stared intently, almost as if he was studying him.

"Feels like a twilight kind of world..."

Holy shit. It's code. He's waiting.

Eli finally replied. "Indeed, sir. And dusk doesn't leave room for friends."

Tillman sighed and sat on the bench, checking his dog's paws. He looked carefully at each leg, ensuring no stones or pebbles were caught in his dog's foot.

“Is your phone bugged, Marshall?”

“As far as I can tell, no, sir. I’m being watched to an extent, but they won't find anything.”

“Very good. Some... third parties have informed me that you may need to make haste out of D.C.”

Eli stood up and began pacing, on edge.

“Homeland knows the leak came from the White House. It's only a matter of time...”

“I see... I’ll make some calls. We can get you and your girlfriend out of D.C. as early as the end of the week.”

“Thank you, sir.”

Eli sat back down again, as if he was relieved and could rest.

“May I ask a question, sir?”

“Go for it.”

“What was your reason... for splitting, sir?”

Tillman sat in silence for a moment, finishing looking over his dog’s paws.

“Rusk and I have history. He reached out through some back channels a while back. I had no intention of helping any rebellion until...”

“Until what?”

“When the decision was made to go nuclear. All those people... our people. Don’t get me wrong, I don’t have love for a lot of these fuckers out west... but what he did... unforgivable.”

“I see...”

“I assume your reason was also because...”

"Yes, sir. It was. Blackwell has lost his mind."

"You're not the only one who says that."

Tillman pulled out a cigar and put it in his mouth. Eli did not like the smell but had no reason to argue. *I'm amazed people actually like that shit.*

"Many in D.C. are preparing to turn, or have already, on the bastard. Some are holding out until the CDF gets control of Lexington."

"Do you know how many?"

"Hard to say... I know that many have reached out to Rusk, and that's why the CDF has essentially made a ton of progress."

"You... the reason for its massive progress?"

"No more than usual. Rusk knew the ins and outs of this system already. I'm merely giving him the means of what's happening behind closed doors. As you have also..."

Eli sat in silence after the statement. It was hard to believe how much distrust and disdain Blackwell had among supporters.

"He's leading in the polls, though, despite it all... he has support."

"Bullshit, Marshall. He's having us fake the data and threatening the states that remain with invasion if any of them don't show his unanimous win."

"You're sure about this?"

"I'm the one making the calls to the state officials."

Tillman stood up, preparing to leave. He put out his half-lit cigar, turning to Eli.

"Keep your phone handy, Marshall. Be ready to leave when I call you."

"Yes, sir."

October 19, 2050 – Washington, D.C. – West Wing

The White House bustled like a wounded hive. Aides rushed through the corridors, clenching data slates and muttering under their breath. Military liaisons were summoned and dismissed in fifteen-minute windows. The President hadn't slept during these times. No one in the White House had in recent months.

Eli Marshall, however, was surprisingly calm about it all now. Maybe because Eli decided to make peace with his situation; it took him a while, but that was all about to change.

He walked the marbled halls like a ghost, memorizing every corner—each camera angle, each door with biometric locks, every security shift. He had just spent the last three years building trust. Now he was walking through the most fortified building in the world as the most dangerous man inside it.

From the Situation Room came muffled shouting. One room shook from vibrations coming from there.

"Satellite footage confirms that the troops have withdrawn from the battle zone—Tallahassee is back in the hands of the CDF. Out-fucking-standing job, everyone!"

The President's voice thundered through reinforced walls. Pretty clear to everyone within shouting distance that he was displeased.

Eli didn't flinch. He walked past, waving to the two interns and stepping into his office. He locked the door behind him.

He opened the daily briefing on his computer. He read it carefully, grinning as he did. The government forces suffered a massive defeat at the hands of the Continental Defense Force in Tallahassee. Blackwell's plans to break the panhandle wall had failed.

According to the report: "*With the panhandle safely back in their hands, the CDF continues pushing government forces out of Georgia and moving to take back Atlanta.*"

Take that, you bastard.

His joy became short-lived as just then, the intercom buzzed. A tense voice filled his office: "Mr. Marshall, the President wants to see you. Now."

"Very well."

* * *

The air inside the Oval Office felt ten degrees colder as he walked in. President Blackwell sat behind the Resolute Desk, his sleeves rolled up, his eyes burning from fatigue and anger, his fingers tapping away at a folder on the desk.

Eli stood in front of the desk, waiting.

"Sit down, Marshall." The President said.

Eli obeyed, taking a seat in front of the desk.

"It seems we have some trouble... treason," the President began, bluntly stating. "Someone has betrayed us... feeding intelligence to the rebels. Someone with high clearance, working internally. We've narrowed it down to about five people. Three have been arrested, one shot himself."

Blackwell slowly slid the file across the desk. The old Eli would have looked confused and offended at the prospect of betrayal. But the times had changed, and he gave no reaction to the words. He was a true product of D.C. now. Eli took the file, opening it. His name stared back at him within the contents of the file. He didn't respond with emotion, as he did not care anymore.

The President's voice pierced through the silence like a blade.

"You understand what this means, don't you?"

"I do..."

The President leaned in. "If you've been set up: Give me a name—someone to blame, and I will make this disappear."

Eli didn't blink. "There is no one to give you, sir."

The President sighed as he stood up, walking over to the window.

"You've always been noble, Marshall. It's why I've kept you on... Never imagined this day would come," he said quietly. "That you would stab me in the back."

"You did that to yourself, sir."

He turned, eyes burning like fire coming out of them. "You have been with me through it all. You held my daughter at her baptism. Now, you've delivered my enemies to my doorstep."

Eli stood, composed but pale. "You pompous ass. It seems you've grown tone deaf to your own voice."

"We are at war, Marshall. Everything that's been done... Sacramento... was for country."

"Keep telling yourself that, you piece of shit."

The deafening silence after the statement filled the room, creating an iron wall between the two men. Blackwell reached for his phone.

"Security."

Eli moved before the call went through. He grabbed the phone from Blackwell, slamming the receiver down and backing away, breathing hard.

"I'm not here to die," he said. "Not yet."

"You won't make it out of the building."

Eli met his gaze. "Then kill me, William. Just like you did the rest."

Eli turned and never looked back. All Blackwell could do was stare in amazement. Eli made haste and started to dash.

No more than a couple of minutes passed before sirens wailed like dying beasts in the belly of the White House. The lights had gone from sterile white to pulsing crimson, casting long shadows that stretched like claws across the floor. Emergency bulkheads thudded into place one after another with a grim finality. A traitor was in the midst.

Eli Marshall didn't need a guide—he was the guide. Every hallway, every service panel, every blind corner—he knew them all by heart. Years in the President's inner circle had granted him access most could never dream of. Now, those same keys might save his life.

He ran with calculated panic—fast, but not careless. His footsteps echoed on the polished floor, joined by the distant thunder of pursuing boots. He could hear the shouts of agents behind him, code phrases barked into radios, orders to seal exits and deploy lethal force. His time was minutes—maybe less.

Down a corridor choked with old portraits of past First Ladies, he veered left and reached an inconspicuous wall panel behind a bust of Jacqueline Kennedy. His fingers, slick with sweat, punched in a six-digit code.

Beep-boop-beep-beep-boop-beep. Click.

The wall hissed open into a narrow crawlspace—once used during renovations, now long forgotten. It smelled of dust, mold, and cold steel. He squeezed inside just as a trio of guards rounded the corner.

“Stop right there, Marshall!”

Bullets ripped into the wall where he’d just stood, one slicing just next to his head. The crawlspace was suffocating as the pipes rattled above his head. Every foot forward scraped his knees. Each breath was a prayer: *Not yet. Not here. Don’t let me die here*. He followed faint markings in the concrete—his chalk symbols, left in preparation for this potential scenario. Behind him, boots echoed louder.

But ahead of him, he saw light—a dim one. A vertical shaft opened into an old service lift. He dove in, slamming the hatch shut. He frantically keyed in the override code. The doors shuddered shut. The elevator dropped.

I made it. He was alone. But he was alive, for now.

* * *

The rain fell in soft, miserable sheets. Fog coiling around the cherry trees, their blossoms sagging with moisture. Eli stood beneath a stone monument, face pale and hollow. His hoodie was soaked through. A cut across his eyebrow bled profusely. In one hand, he gripped a tattered leather bag holding his laptop and files—inside the files: the last physical records of his betrayal.

A black van pulled across the path, wipers slashing side to side.

The passenger door opened. Tillman stepped out—tall, wiry, unremarkable in every way except for the stillness in his eyes. Blackwell’s Secretary of Defense, now serving as a bridge to the Continental Defense Force.

“You cut it close,” Tillman said flatly.

Eli didn’t answer, standing silently as he awaited what was next.

Tillman tossed him a towel and a burner phone. “Your ID’s been erased. Digital and otherwise. About another hour or so before Homeland locks down the bridges. It seems things have been taken up a notch.”

Eli looked over his shoulder toward the glowing dome of the Capitol across the water. That building had once stirred pride in him, but now it was just a tomb.

“I want to talk with Rusk.”

Tillman didn’t blink. “You sure?”

Eli’s voice was firm. “Yes. It's only fair that I talk with the man.”

There was a pause.

“I’ll see what I can do,” Tillman said. “But once you get deeper, there’s no going back. No flag will claim you.”

Eli pulled his ball cap lower. “I’m already in deep. Might as well reach the bottom.”

October 29, 2050 – Somewhere in Richmond, Virginia

The room was bare except for a folding table, three chairs, and a single ugly lamp. The windows were boarded, and the air was very stale. It was the place used for when you needed privacy… or deniability.

Eli and Mia had been safely moved out of D.C., but were forced to lie low because Blackwell decided to make it his mission to blame the government's failures on the battlefield on him and his leaking. The media ripped him to shreds. *Eli Marshall: Confidant to the Commander-in-Chief, turned traitor for the so-called rebellion.*

"You okay, Eli?" Mia asked worryingly.

He placed his hand on hers, smiling faintly. "I'm fine."

They turned and looked as the door to their cabin opened. General Nathaniel Rusk entered wearing civilian clothing—boots, jeans, and a canvas jacket that still faintly smelled of ash and field mud. His silver-streaked beard looked heavier in person. He took one long look at Eli.

"You wanted to see me, Mr. Marshall?" Rusk asked plainly.

Eli stood. "Yes, General Rusk. I figured if either Mia or I are about to die, we'd better see who for."

"Well, I suppose that's a good reason. You are a wealth of knowledge, so it didn't hurt to visit you."

Eli's voice tightened. "I have some left, but not much else. They were onto me."

He opened the leather bag and placed the manila folder on the table. Inside it was whatever he could copy before discovery—maps, troop movements, briefings, nuclear bunker access logs—all damning materials of Blackwell's treachery.

Rusk walked slowly to the table, yet did not open the folder. Instead, he pulled out a cigar and lit the Cuban-flavored stick, staring at Eli intently as he did so.

"You've got a good head on your shoulders. You've done a great service to the CDF. Your intel was massive in Tallahassee this last week," Rusk said. "And now it will help us in Lexington. You have put your whole life at risk for us."

Eli leaned forward. "He bombed Sacramento, threatening the existence of so many innocent people with chemical drones. I helped him... against the *West Coast Alliance*..."

"And now?"

Eli's hands trembled. "Now? I'm burning the forest down, and him along with it."

Rusk walked over to Mia, studying her.

"What's your name, miss?"

"Mia Carter, General."

"A pleasure, Ms. Carter. I imagine that these last few years have not been pleasant."

"No, sir. Just agony, praying it will end."

Rusk turned and again studied Eli for a long moment, then nodded. "I will get you and Ms. Carter out—a clean exit, with new identities. However, I am disappointed to say that your work will remain sealed. No medals, no statues."

Eli's voice dropped to a whisper. "When the war is won, all I ask of you, sir, is this... build something better here."

Rusk's answer was quiet. "That's the idea, if we somehow make it to the finish line alive."

They shook hands—two men once on opposing sides, on different ends of a broken oath.

Outside, rain streaked the windows. The storm had yet to pass, but something had shifted. It felt as if Eli Marshall had crossed the Rubicon.

* * *

The rain had turned the old airfield into a swamp. Puddles filled the craters in the tarmac, and the hangar's rusted metal creaked with every gust of wind. It reeked of oil, salt, and mold—like a graveyard of forgotten wars.

Eli tightened the straps of his military-issued duffel, the patches torn off, and the insignia burned away. Mia leaned against the wing of the Cessna, arms crossed, her cheeks raw from wind and exhaustion. She hadn't slept in nearly 24 hours. Neither had Eli.

"You don't have to come," he said softly, for what felt like the hundredth time.

She didn't look at him when she replied. "This isn't *Casablanca*, Eli. I don't care if they hang us. I love you, and will follow you wherever you go."

Eli swallowed hard. He had never felt so loved—It hurt. He went over to where she stood and hugged her as tight as he could. For too long, he never had anyone loyal to him as she was to him. Now, he had the strongest feelings he had ever had before. For all his training, for all the weight of the secrets he carried, those words undid him.

"Eyes on the skies," Tillman barked. *The former Air Force Colonel turned Secretary of Defense was sharp as always*, Eli thought. His civilian clothes were wet, his sidearm strapped over a windbreaker. He watched a radar on a weatherproof tablet, the signal bouncing from a blacked-out satellite link van parked nearby.

"They scrambled from Andrews," Tillman said. "You've got about a fifteen-minute window. Fly south towards CDF-controlled airspace. You breach the airspace over Bermuda, you're dead."

"And if we fly north?" Eli asked, pulling on his gloves.

Tillman looked at him grimly. "You die. And probably take her with you."

Eli glanced at Mia. She was still silent, her eyes never leaving the horizon.

"How's the fuel?"

"Topped off. Auxiliary tanks are hot. Avionics are dirty, but flight-worthy. If the weather holds, you'll make it."

Thank God Daddy taught me how to fly.

Eli nodded, more to himself than Tillman. He climbed into the pilot's seat, adjusting the headset. The cabin was small, used for covert transports or crop dusting—now their lifeline to freedom. *Not as big as the ones I've flown, but it'll do.* Eli learned to fly, thanks in part to his father, who was at one point in his life a pilot, or at least for the pleasure of it.

Mia climbed in beside him and gently touched the cross dangling from the dashboard. "Figure he'll get under the wings?"

Eli adjusted the dial. "I don't know, maybe."

She didn't press any further, knowing these next steps held their lives in the balance. But her fingers lingered on the cross.

Outside, Tillman signaled the ground crew. They rolled the old plane out under a retractable hangar screen, trying to shield it from thermal scans. The wind was picking up, and rain was now coming in sheets.

The radio in the cockpit crackled.

"This is Command. Alert: Two bogeys inbound from Joint Base Andrews. Intercept protocol active. Estimated time: ten minutes."

Tillman's face turned gray. He turned and waved his arms.

"GO! GO NOW!"

The Cessna's engines roared to life, sputtering once before catching full. Eli gritted his teeth and yanked the throttle. The tiny aircraft lurched forward, bouncing hard against uneven pavement, tires kicking up water and loose gravel.

From the tower ruins came a flash—Tillman's team had detonated an old fuel tank to create thermal interference. The radar jam would give them about ninety seconds of invisibility. Behind them, the rain blurred the outline of two F-22 Raptors now slicing toward them from the east.

Eli pushed the stick forward. "Come on, sweetheart," he muttered. "Don't quit on me now."

Mia's knuckles gripped the side of her seat as the wheels lifted from the ground. The plane wobbled, but then caught an updraft. They cleared the fence by about thirty feet.

The coastline appeared ahead, the ocean a rolling field of silver and slate.

Inside the plane, the couple didn't speak for several minutes. The storm lit up the sky with streaks of lightning, and wind buffeted them in short bursts. Eli adjusted the trim and kept one eye on the altimeter, the other on the black sea below.

"Where are we going?" Mia asked, finally.

Eli didn't answer immediately. Tensions from the air caused him to grip the controls tighter. A few minutes passed before he relaxed his grip as the air eased up.

"Hopefully somewhere out of here," he said. "Perhaps out of the country for a while. A place where no questions are asked."

She nodded faintly. "You know they questioned me. A while back, it seemed they were suspecting something. Had I stayed... I don't think I would have survived."

His eyes flickered toward her, surprised.

"They were trying to get me to flip on you," she added, almost smirking. "Guess they figured I was a pretty face who'd do anything at the first sign of trouble."

"It's good that you are here with me then and not some black site prison."

"I agree. I don't think orange would look good on me."

"You make anything you wear look good, Mia."

"Hold off on the buttering, Eli. I'm still in the toaster."

They couldn't help but laugh at the flirts they passed. But then they fell silent again, the drone of the engines drowning the world around them. The sounds of the jets faded as they appeared to have veered off, heading west. They had managed to slip away.

April 7, 2051 – Somewhere in the Caribbean

The waves rolled lazily to share as wind teased the palm fronds. A modest villa sat nestled between the dunes and a line of old stone pines. Inside, the scent of salt and cigars lingered in the air. Eli stood barefoot in a white shirt, sleeves rolled up, staring at the fire pit.

In his hands was a weathered leather-bound book—*Through Hell: A Memoir of Crisis and Faith*—authored by President William Blackwell himself. The same one he had once given Eli so many years ago with the inscription: *"To my most trusted advisor and friend—may you always remember that this is what we fight for."*

Eli held the book for a long moment, the words staring back at him. Its weight was heavier than the leather binding. He ran his fingers along the signature, once so revered but now tainted with the blood of betrayal.

Slowly and deliberately, he walked to the fireplace set into a coral stone pit near an outdoor sitting area in the villa. The flames inside the pit cracked lazily, welcoming the offer. He stared into the hearth—seeing not fire but the country's burning cities. He could see Seattle, Sacramento, Atlanta, and Tampa within the flames. The flash, the ash, the silence of the screams in the distance. His stomach turned into knots again at the sight of the faces in the flames, the horrors of war, because one man decided to control the lives of so many.

Eli set the memoir down onto the iron grate. The flames caught the edge of the pages almost immediately—the cover blistered and curled; the gold lettering darkened into unreadable streaks. The fire crackled, as if it were in delight at the kindling it received. The words had vanished one by one, devoured by the heat and stroke of the fire.

The smoke and ash filled his eyes and nostrils, yet he didn't blink. Not once.

Mia entered the room barefoot, the soft white hem of her dress brushing the floor. She leaned against the chair for a moment, watching him in silence.

"You finally did it," she said.

Eli nodded. "Some things just aren't meant to be read. It weighed too heavily."

Mia approached, wrapping her arms gently around his waist. "Do you think he's going to look for us?"

Eli's eyes narrowed at the fire. "He'll sure as shit try, but the war will distract him. He may be on the run himself."

"He still has the intelligence agencies at his disposal. Won't they still try to find us?"

"They'll try," he said. "But we are ghosts in a world full of them now."

They stood next to each other in a cuddle, watching as the last embers consumed the memoir's spine. By now, the inscription had melted into ash. Outside the villa, waves rolled in steady rhythm under a darkening sky. Somewhere across the ocean, the war neared its final breath.

And the man who helped end it was about to be forgotten—by design.

June 9, 2052 – Washington, D.C.

The White House had become a defensive fortress. Sandbags lined the interior hallways. Secret Service patrols were augmented by elite Special Warfare units flown in from Pennsylvania and West Virginia. Anti-air batteries dotted the National Mall. Outside, entire blocks had been cleared to provide a kill zone against advancing forces. The people had long since fled or had been ordered out via evacuation orders. D.C. was no longer a city with a governing body—it was the last piece standing on the chessboard.

Artillery strikes had begun barraging the streets of Washington just a few days earlier, like the Russians hammering Berlin in the final days of the Second World War. Lexington was defeated, and Pittsburgh was overrun due to defectors who believed the war was lost.

President William Blackwell stood alone in the Oval Office, staring through thick security glass toward the North Lawn. Smoke plumes were emerging all over the city, and Air-Defense rockets were firing up into the sky at the emerging missiles. *This is the end... the end.*

Secretary of State Edward Wallace, loyal to Blackwell until the bitter end, emerged in the Oval Office. Dressed in plain gray slacks and a rolled shirt, he no longer wore his tie—somewhere along the road, the formalities had collapsed. His face was filled with dread, dazed, and in a panic.

"You're late," Blackwell said without warning.

"I'm sorry, Mr. President. I was tied up with emergency protocols being implemented over at State. We are burning and destroying everything we have."

"Excellent, Ed. What else?"

"I confirmed the last transmission from NORAD: The Continental Defense Forces have successfully captured Norfolk and have D.C. surrounded."

Blackwell didn't answer immediately; instead, he watched the window silently.

"It seems... that the war is lost, my friend."

Wallace looked down, as if ashamed. He set a tablet on the President's desk, alongside a crumpled old memo—a weathered piece of paper signed by William Blackwell in 2048: the order to construct *Blackout Protocol*, the plan for the nuclear strikes that would tear the country apart.

"Yes, Mr. President. I'm sorry..."

Blackwell finally turned to face him. There was no fire in his eyes—just emptiness. A cold, dense, immovable feeling.

"You... think we should declare D.C. undefended and surrender?"

Wallace sighed and took a moment to think. He pulled his glasses off, wiping his eyes.

"They already broke the nuclear codes... making sure we can't use them. Most of the generals at the Pentagon have surrendered... You don't have any good options left."

Blackwell sighed, as if a sadness mixed with relief fell over him.

"I guess I don't," he said. "I will have a decision soon. As for you... decide what you think is best."

"Are you sure... sir?"

"I've had just about everyone turn against me in this war... I don't think it would hurt if one more joined the party."

"I've served you faithfully, sir..."

"I know, Ed. But this is Washington, you do what you have to."

Ed stood to leave but became off guard when he felt something moist... a tear emerging from his eye.

"It has been an honor to serve you, sir."

"The honor's been mine."

Ed reached out his hand, and Blackwell smiled and put his out. They shook hands—perhaps for the final time. Despite the unbearable weight of emotion, Wallace held his head high and left the man he served faithfully alone.

As the door shut behind him, the room was dead still for a moment. Blackwell sat behind the Resolute Desk and folded his hands. For some time, the President sat motionless, hands trembling ever so slightly.

On the tablet Wallace left, there was one final entry—an unsigned intelligence dispatch that had reached the CDF High Command at MacDill AFB. It was a strike map, time-stamped and completely accurate.

At the bottom, handwritten in careful, even script:

"Line is open to discuss the terms of surrender."

December 5, 2052 – Somewhere in the Alps, Switzerland

Snow blanketed the distant Alps. The ice and sleet whispered against the chalet windows with a soft and constant flow, like the world outside was trying to hush itself. Eli Marshall sat at the oak dining table with a mug of coffee, warming his hands. Across from him, Mia was curled into a heavy wool blanket, legs tucked under her, reading a battered paperback she'd picked up from the Zurich station kiosk. Her hair caught the firelight, making her look warmer than the room ever could be.

For a moment, Eli let himself believe the war was far away—that the memories of the horrors faded into memories. If only that were true. Eli stood in a remote valley estate with whitewashed walls, iron gates, and silence. It was a gift from General Rusk, brokered through a third-party foundation.

Inside, Mia became bored with her book and emerged from her blanket. She arranged books on a shelf, attempting to find something to read. He watched with longing eyes, relieved that their life was at peace.

Though to his annoyance, that peace was disturbed as his phone buzzed wildly on the table. It was his burner, a secure-line phone he had received before his escape. He looked over, glancing at the display: *UNKNOWN.*

"Sorry," he murmured to Mia, walking to the doors. She was too distracted by the bookshelf to notice his words.

Eli stepped onto the balcony, the cold biting instantly into his lips. The Alps stretched in jagged white lines across the horizon, pristine and utterly indifferent to the issues of humanity. With hesitation, he thumbed the answer key.

"Fallon."

"Marshall," The voice came low and clipped. Major Fallon was a key part of General Rusk's Army, so this call meant something big was brewing.

Eli gripped the railing, watching the vapor of his breath twist in the wind. "I take it this call is not for pleasure."

"You would be correct. Blackwell is dead. He was... tried via Military Tribunal. It was unanimous. I don't think I need to tell you why." Fallon's tone carried no triumph or satisfaction—only the flat weight of finality.

Just like that. Dead. Dying with a more dignified death than those who were killed by the war machine or the nuclear blasts that came before. Eli took a moment to process the overwhelming anxiety. A man he served, a man he betrayed, was gone.

Eli exhaled slowly, eyes narrowing at the snow-swept peaks. "I see. What about D.C.?"

"That's... the problem, Marshall," Fallon replied. "The mop-up operations have gone... poorly. Pockets of resistance in Arlington and on the Hill turned into block-by-block fights. We're close, but it's caused delays."

"Well... Shit."

"It doesn't end there. Civilian government buildings were either blown up or heavily damaged. Worse than we wanted. Many factions are fractured. Many of the networks are running out of Philadelphia."

Eli silently listened, many thoughts running through his mind. None of this was new, however, as he spent many sleepless nights in the Situation Room.

"Sounds like a lot of problems... What of Congress?"

Fallon let out a short, humorless laugh. "That's another problem. Negotiations are stuck. Half of them want to comply with an unconditional surrender fully. The other half thinks they can stall until the U.N. gets involved. Rusk has run out of patience."

Eli's voice sharpened. "What is he going to do?"

There was a long pause—the kind of pause where someone looks over their shoulder before answering. "Rusk has decided to disband the entire government—the House, the Senate, and every federal department that runs. It's too rotten to salvage."

Eli straightened, feeling the cold sink deeper into his bones. "And then what?"

"Then," Fallon said, "he intends to start entirely over—a new Congress, selected under Continental authority. Until the details are worked out, Rusk decided to take a temporary role once negotiations are complete—Lord Protector of the United States of America."

Eli stared at the snow, the jagged peaks cutting into the horizon like knife blades. "You do realize, Major Fallon, that Cromwell ruled England without a Parliament for several years."

Fallon's voice didn't waver. "Yes. I paid attention in history class, Marshall. But he kept England from tearing itself apart again—for a while at least."

Eli didn't respond immediately. His mind instead raced of horrifying images: The Capitol dome gutted and blackened, the desks of the Senate chamber covered in ash, the smell of smoke clinging to the marble halls. And now in its place, a government was rebuilt at the tip of a knife, with Rusk and the CDF holding the weapon.

"So, what do you want, Fallon?" Eli asked at last.

"We want you to come back to the country...to consult," Fallon replied. "You know the Hill better than anyone left. You can help the CDF make it stick and make it look better to a country still on edge, believing this is a coup. You know better than I do—if we botch the politics now, all of this was for nothing."

Eli's grip on the railing tightened even harder, to the point where his hand turned red from pain. He thought about all that he saw: the mushroom cloud over Sacramento, the day he realized Blackwell was willing to kill his own people for power. He thought of how much worse it could be if Rusk's new government started down the same road.

"I will help via phone and video calls... But I won't come back to D.C.," he declared.

"Good enough. Rusk prefers you were here, but at this point... We'll take what we can get."

Eli was silent again momentarily, listening to the faint hiss of wind through the phone's mic. Finally, he said: "Tell him I'll do what I can. He can call me, and I'll hear him out. But don't mistake my help as loyalty. If he even thinks of turning his position into a crown, he's in for a fight—whether it's from the states or from me."

Fallon chuckled once, dry and short. "That's what I told him you'd say. We'll call you again soon."

The line clicked dead after that. Eli stayed on the balcony, the bitter cold biting through his jacket. Inside, Mia turned a page in her book, oblivious to the conversation that had just occurred—a call that had just drawn him back into the center of the conflict.

"What was that about?" she asked, speaking the words through the glass. He opened the door and walked over to her.

"Just politics," he said, sitting back beside her. But in his mind, the Alps were already fading into the fog, replaced by the cracked marble steps of the Capitol and the shadow of a man who wanted to rule America like Cromwell did in England.

April 5, 2054 – Somewhere in Northern Italy

The hills of Lake Como rolled gently in the late afternoon sun, a palette of olive green and golden yellow as the wind whispered through cypress trees and swayed the grapevines in their spring bloom. Terracotta roofs dotted the slopes, and the air smelled of wild herbs, sun-warmed stone, and woodsmoke. Far above the chaos of nations, the world moved at a pace unlike the others—slow, human, and ancient in its ways.

On a stone veranda, nestled in a house built a century before either of the world wars, Eli sat with a pen in hand and a leather-bound journal in his lap. His linen shirt fluttered lightly in the breeze. The lines on his face had softened, not from age, but from stillness. He had not run as a fugitive from justice. He wasn't running anywhere at all. He did not seek the glory of politicians or generals. And yet he had found something close to peace. His heart still bled for his friends, mainly Jessica Parker. He had found out just a day ago that her husband, Dr. Daniel Parker, tragically lost his life in the Battle of Lexington.

He texted her, *"I'm so sorry about Daniel, Jess. I wish I could be there for you, but I'm sure you understand why I can't."*

Deep down, they both knew that the world was changing and evolving faster than they wanted to. The combat reached its conclusion, but would it stay that way?

She replied, *"Thank you for your kind words, Eli. I know that you can't be here. The Cherry Blossoms are beautiful here... Daniel would have loved them... Take care of yourself."*

Those words stung his heart, almost as if his heart was being bled out. It troubled him not being there for his funeral, as he knew the hell it took just to get him a soldier's burial in Arlington Cemetery.

Eli soon found his focus again as he realized he had forgotten about his journal writing.

Across the journal page, he scribbled the date:

April 5, 2054

Lake Como, Italy

But the entry beneath it remained blank.

Inside, the faint clatter of cooking could be heard. His beautiful Mia—now his wife bearing the name Marshall—was singing in low hums as she prepared their dinner. The smell of tomatoes, basil, and garlic simmering in a cast-iron pan filled the air. Her ring shimmered in the soft light coming through the shutters, the same hand that had once held his trembling fingers under the shell-shocked skies of D.C.

He smiled faintly and glanced over at the table beside him. A folded newspaper rested near a cup, delivered from a world he now only half belonged to.

LORD PROTECTOR RUSK DELIVERS ADDRESS UNDER CHERRY BLOSSOMS DC, ANNOUNCES "PEACE MISSION" ACROSS RECONCILED STATES

MacDill AFB to host Global Democracy Summit

A photo showed the aging general—stoic as ever—shaking hands with foreign leaders, cherry blossoms in the background. The caption read below: *"No victory without cost. No peace without burden."*

Eli folded the newspaper and set it down in an old wooden box beneath the table. Inside were a few sacred relics belonging to Eli: a scorched

White House ID, a field medal from an unknown battle, a love letter written in invisible ink, and a dog tag belonging to a man buried beneath the trees in Georgia.

He closed the box with care. Relics with so much pain attached, yet these were the remains of a life once lived in the shadows. Mia stepped out carrying two steaming mugs of espresso. She set one down next to him, kissing the crown of his head.

"Dinner will be ready in a few," she said gently. He nodded with a smile, happy. She looked down at him, motioning to the open journal. "You ever going to write the last entry?"

He looked down at the empty page and the view beyond their vineyard. Light danced across the lake's surface, blinding and beautiful.

"Not yet," he said after a long silence. "Some stories... take time. I guess I still need a moment."

She smiled. "Well... if you aren't planning to finish it today, perhaps close the book?"

He realized she was right, closing the leather-bound book. As it shut, a breeze tugged at the petals of a nearby cherry tree they had planted months prior. It had bloomed on-time this season.

Like healing, Eli thought.

* * *

The sun fell behind the hills, casting fire across the sky. Down near the water's edge, Eli walked hand in hand with Mia. The evening breeze stirred the trees. In the distance, church bells chimed over a dozen times.

On their walk, it was peaceful. They passed no soldiers, no parades, no banners. It was still. Very quiet. They paused for a moment, watching the lake ripple. Mia stood beside him, fingers laced in his. She held it tightly. They soon returned to the house, with no words being spoken in all that time. Above them, the stars filled the sky—clear, defiant, and eternal.

June 26, 2064 – Washington, D.C.

The museum was quiet, save for the soft murmurs of schoolchildren and foreign tourists. A docent's voice echoed from the next room, explaining how the Battle of Tallahassee became a pivotal point in the entire Southern Theater. Holograms of drone strikes and troop movements played on nearby displays. Walls bore the names of civilians and soldiers alike.

An elderly man with a cane stood before a sign at the entrance:

The National Museum of the Second American Civil War

Slowly but surely, the elderly man made his way through the exhibits. Observing and studying each one very carefully.

He walked past a newspaper article, damaged as if it had been pulled out of a furnace. It was about the *West Coast Alliance*, written by a familiar name: Jessica Parker.

Another exhibit held a plow, an old, rusty piece of farm equipment. It bore no name, except a small inscription: "*Upon the soil, farmers toiled for country.*" He found it interesting, but boring. It is not very interesting to someone who spends most of their time in the city.

Still, he kept walking. Scanning every piece of writing on the walls. He came upon a glass box exhibit. One that stood out to him was a particular case:

"UNKNOWN PATRIOTS: The Spy Who Saved the Union"

A set of artifacts lay inside: a plain tie pin, a diplomatic security badge with the name redacted, a burned letter addressed from the President, and a piece of debris from a fallen Capitol drone—marked by the coordinates of Lexington.

Beside them was a quote etched in steel.

"Some men carry rifles. Others carry burdens no one will ever know. Both bleed for the same reasons: freedom."

— Lord Protector. Nathaniel Rusk, Inauguration Address

A young girl, following along with the elderly man, hand in hand with him, tugged at the man's coat. "Grandpa, was he real?"

He looked down at her—eyes glistening—and whispered, "Yes, sweetheart. But the best ones never ask to be remembered."

She was confused, but that was ok. Someday, when she was older, she would understand.

"Grandpa."

"Yes, sweetheart?"

"Could we get ice cream later?"

He smiled softly at her.

"Sure, sweetheart."

They moved on to the rest of the exhibits. The case stood in silence as the next group came to observe it.

VI.

Epilogue: Remember

One day, all of this will be over.

The battle lines will fade. The flags will be folded. The names will be written in stone—or perhaps not at all. The fire will go out, the cities will be built again, and the war that tore this nation apart will become lines in a textbook no one will ever finish reading.

Fields will bloom again. And new generations will ask what it was all for.

But by then, we'll be gone. All of us—the farmers who stood their ground, the soldiers who carried the wounded, the reporters who risked the truth, the generals who bore the burden, and the spies who chose people over tyranny.

But maybe—you won't forget us.

If history remembers even one in a thousand of us, let them tell our stories.

Let them remember that we did not run in the face of extinction, in the face of collapse.

We did not break.

We did not surrender.

We stood tall.

We believed in something bigger than ourselves.

Not in perfection—but in perseverance.

Not in vengeance—but in mercy.

Not in power—but in people.

When history is written and the monuments are carved,

Let them say: We lived, we dared, because freedom demanded it.

When the last shot is fired, and peace is had, when spring blooms again, when the nation buries its dead and raises its flag—

They will remember us.

www.ingramcontent.com/pod-product-compliance
Lightning Source LLC
LaVergne TN
LVHW040214110826
845146LV00005B/1286

* 9 7 9 8 9 9 3 7 8 4 1 1 3 *